# A GENTLEMAN IN CHALLENGING CIRCUMSTANCES

THE LORD JULIAN MYSTERIES—BOOK THREE

## GRACE BURROWES

GRACE BURROWES PUBLISHING

# DEDICATION

Dedicated to all the gentlemen and ladies in challenging
circumstances

# CHAPTER ONE

My task was simple, though far from easy: to ascertain whether the little fellow grubbing about in Mrs. Danforth's herbaceous borders could be the salvation of the Waltham dukedom.

The lad himself shed little light on the question. I'd put his age at about five. He was enjoying that halcyon interval between breeching in his third year and going into men's hands sometime after he turned seven. For now, all would be toy soldiers, imaginary dragons, and bedtime fables with him.

His nurse, a youngish woman in serviceable gray twill and spotless mobcap, sat on a nearby bench, handkerchief at the ready, her expression one of patient amusement.

Like the boy, I had done my earliest exploring in the wilds of a walled garden. I'd graduated to fields, forests, and eventually, when I'd joined Wellington's army, foreign territory. I was happy to be back in England and had learned to keep my hands mostly clean somewhere along the way.

"Is he quiet by nature?" I asked, searching for some visual clue that this child could be my nephew. Caldicotts tended to be tall and lean, but we had no Habsburg chin, no unusual eye color, to otherwise distinguish us.

Mrs. Danforth was a spare woman who might once have been called handsome, but her looks had been blighted by time and the hardships of military life. The boy bore no obvious resemblance to her, which was a relief.

She frowned at the busy child. "I don't know how to answer that, Lord Julian. I met Leander about a month ago, when his mother washed up on my doorstep, very ill and begging for sanctuary. Our husbands served together, and you know how the old regimental ties do bind. Does any child say much when his mother is dying?"

"You have no offspring of your own?"

"We were not so blessed. Nurse says some children chatter, some children climb trees, some turn the pages of books by the hour, and they all grow into adulthood. She would know better than I if Leander is simply reticent or if recent events have made him withdrawn. He's certainly *industrious*."

Not a compliment to young Leander. "What can you tell me of his late mother?"

Mrs. Danforth sat at her shaded garden table and sipped her tea. She was doubtless sorting through the vestiges of those regimental ties, the desire to be free of Leander, and the deference due me as a duke's son and heir.

"I honestly can't tell you much at all," she said. "Ten years ago, Martha Waites was the darling of the regiment, her husband a junior officer who'd beggared himself buying his colors. Like most of his ilk, he lived above his means and expected life abroad would magically fill his coffers. The fevers got him. Martha became widowed at a young age and without worldly security, an all too common tale for officers' wives. We scraped together passage home for her lest she fall prey to the exigencies of life at an obscure fort. She was pretty and popular. That can end badly."

Another sip of tea, while Leander came upon that most versatile of toys, the stout stick.

"I received a note of thanks months after Martha left for home," Mrs. Danforth went on more quietly. "I was relieved that she'd survived the journey. Then I heard nothing from her until we bumped into one another outside some shop or other in the spring. She turned up weeks later, seeking refuge. Unless the boy is very, very small for his age, and quite slow, he was not the product of Martha's first marriage."

The stick had become a mighty broadsword, and Leander was laying about, intent on subduing Mrs. Danforth's perfectly mani-cured lavender. I waited for the inevitable scold—Mrs. Danforth's expression had become thunderously composed—when the nurse took up a stick of her own and began to battle the fierce warrior.

"Surrender!" she cried with mock severity. "We will have no truck with barbarians in Londontown."

"I conquer in the name of Good King George," the boy yelled back. "I will never surrender."

The nurse rapped his stick lightly with her own. "Not even if we feed our captives pudding?"

He delivered a stout rebeat. "It's too early for pudding, and you didn't say *pret, allez, en-garde.*"

The nurse pretended to look chagrined and lowered her sword. "I am sorry. I thought you were being a Visigoth. Are you an officer in the 95th Rifles, perchance?"

"I'm a light dragoon!" He cantered around, waving his stick in the air. "I'll show old Boney!"

The light dragoons had, alas, become infamous for showing their impulsiveness and lack of discipline, as had the heavy dragoons.

"He speaks," I murmured, though who had taught him that bit of French fencing protocol?

"And he yells," Mrs. Danforth observed repressively. "Nurse says children should exercise their lungs. She is insistent that he have regular fresh air and exercise, despite the noise. Junior officers benefit from the same regimen, in my experience."

Having been a child myself, and a boy child at that, I agreed with Nurse. "She appears devoted to him."

Master Leander was now engaged in a postmortem examination of the fallen lavender sprigs. The nurse crushed one and held it to his nose. He pulled buds from the stems and enthusiastically ground them in his grubby palms.

"She's overly patient, if you ask me," Mrs. Danforth replied. "While I... Mine is a widow's household, my lord. I haven't a proper schoolroom, and even a devoted nurse expects some remuneration."

That remuneration was clearly not in Mrs. Danforth's budget, and the lady had a point. Children grew hungry with predictable regularity. They needed shoes, which they promptly outgrew. They required clothing, which they tore and stained upon first wearing. They deserved an education, which meant governesses and tutors or, in families of more modest station, buying an apprenticeship in a respectable trade.

"I will send along a bank draft to assist with the boy's upkeep for the nonce," I said, "but he might well be no relation of mine. Mrs. Waites told you that my brother is the boy's father?"

"She implied as much. I was hoping the child bore sufficient resemblance to the late Lord Harry that you'd see fit to take him in."

I considered Leander, who was still absorbed with dissecting flowers.

He was a sturdy little lad, no longer given to the roundness of toddlerhood, but neither was he what I would call lanky. His hair was reddish and would probably fade to brown as he aged and spent less time out of doors. Harry's hair had been brown.

"What color was Mrs. Waites's hair?"

"Brown, my lord. Medium brown."

"Her eyes?"

"Blue."

As Harry's had been. "The boy's appearance doesn't tell me much, and you say Mrs. Waites only implied that Lord Harry could be the father. Can you be more specific?"

Mrs. Danforth's gaze narrowed on the child playing in the dirt. "She told me Leander had Lord Harry's laugh and his chin. Why say that if Lord Harry is no relation to him?"

I retreated into polite silence. The late Lord Harry, sought-after bachelor and hero of various battles, had also been the ducal heir at the time of his passing. The obvious motivation for attributing paternity to him was money, closely followed by social standing. Aristocratic by-blows were not typically apprenticed to tailors or coopers.

"If Harry sired this child," I asked, "why didn't Mrs. Waites come to the Caldicotts when she realized her health was failing?"

Why not come to us when the child was born? When conception had become evident? But then, perhaps she'd gone to Harry, and he'd settled a sum on her or rebuffed her claims.

"I cannot answer for the choices Martha Waites made, my lord, but neither can I be expected to raise the child. If my aunt hadn't left me this house..."

The threat was clear. Leander would be put on the parish—assuming somebody could sort out which parish he belonged to—or, failing that, left with his favorite toy soldiers at some busy tavern, there to be claimed by the nearest chimney sweep in need of a climbing boy.

Or worse.

Mrs. Danforth wouldn't abandon him personally. Officer's widow that she was, she'd delegate that task to her scullery maid or groom and maybe even put tuppence in the boy's pocket for a meat pie.

"You would not agree to keep him in your household even for a sum certain?" I asked. Proving paternity of an orphaned five-year-old would require several miracles, good luck, and an outlandish coincidence or two.

Mrs. Danforth delayed her reply by pouring herself another cup of tea from the jasperware service. Twenty years ago, the pale blue cups and saucers with their classical cream relief might well have formed the most impressive article in her trousseau. Now, such

night's additional charity. She doubtless regularly attended divine services and even put an occasional penny in the poor box when the congregation's ranking beldames were watching.

"I will send along that bank draft and some coin for the nurse. I'd appreciate it if you could make notes for me regarding Mrs. Waites's particulars. I'd also like to have a look through any effects Mrs. Waites left behind."

"I gave her clothing to charity. Come by the day after tomorrow. I will document everything I know regarding the late Martha Waites, though she might have remarried."

That possibility was offered grudgingly. "Because she was pretty?"

"Pretty, charming, and ambitious. The ambitious ones tend to land on their feet. Until Wednesday, my lord." She curtseyed and left me to wander out through the garden gate. I paused to sweep the bits of lavender from the walkway with the toe of my boot and to consider the past hour's discussion.

I knew little more than I had when I'd arrived, ostensibly because Mrs. Danforth had little to tell me. I had hoped she'd lie to me, hoped she'd state unequivocally that Martha Waites had named Harry as the boy's father. Such was Mrs. Danforth's sense of military hierarchy that she would not offer outright falsehoods to a man far above her station, one who'd *served under Wellington.*

She had lied about Martha Waites's clothing, though. I had every confidence any dresses, cloaks, reticules, or bonnets had been sent to Rosemary Lane to fetch a few coins, and that was a pity. Clothing didn't necessarily maketh the man, but it might hold a few clues to the lady.

I crossed to the garden gate and resigned myself to talking directly with the boy. He might know details of his origins without realizing he was in possession of such facts. He might have memories that bore significance he could not understand.

I had hoped to be spared an introduction to him, which spoke poorly well for my sense of charity. The lad was orphaned, his prospects uncertain, and nobody was stepping forth to look after him.

Harry's passing had left me orphaned in a sense, forever parted from a certain innocence and from a once-spotless reputation. I no longer blamed myself for his death at the hands of French captors, but that left room for barge-loads of regret.

The latch on the gate was rusty, and I had to use some force to get it up. As I stepped through into the alley, I happened to look back at Mrs. Danforth's personal castle. A modest half-timbered home, separated from its neighbors by two mere yards on either side. Those two yards imbued the house with miles of social significance, giving it a gentility that attached domiciles in this neighborhood lacked.

I was wrestling the latch back into place when I noticed the nursemaid standing in a third-floor window. Her arms were crossed, her expression pensive.

I would have to talk to her, too, and find a way to do that outside the hearing of either the boy or Mrs. Danforth. I didn't want to. I wanted to saddle my horse and quit the stifling confines of London in high summer, but I'd been given my assignment by His Grace.

I would successfully complete my mission, even if that required me to play toy soldiers in the mud or impersonate a rampaging, fire-breathing dragon in the middle of Hyde Park.

~

"Would a call at Horse Guards serve any purpose?" Arthur asked when the footmen had left us to serve ourselves. "Chat up the old connections, dinner at the club with any who might have known Mrs. Waites?"

Our midday meal was served on the shady back terrace of His Grace's town house. I dwelled under the same roof as my brother for the nonce. The staff at my more modest abode had mostly taken summer leave to see family in the shires, and Arthur was soon to decamp for a tour of the Continent.

Then too, some time to better acquaint myself with His Grace seemed needful, when his upcoming travels would doubtless be extended, and I had been away at war for years.

I had returned from my Continental battles only to commence battles of a different sort at home. Like Harry, I had endured captivity at French hands. Unlike Harry, I had survived the ordeal and was regarded as a possible traitor. More than a few of my fellow officers suspected me of having given up vital information to preserve my life.

I hadn't, though I'd been reduced to such a state by my tormentors that I had doubted my own recollections for a time. My hair had turned white—the new growth was blondish, let it be said—and bad luck on the battlefield had left my eyes overly sensitive to strong sunlight.

"I am not welcome at Horse Guards," I said, taking a spoonful of cold soup in the *crème gauloise* style. Arthur's chef was determined that His Grace should eat like a duke. Arthur had John Bull's meat-and-potatoes palate. Battles on every hand.

"If you don't like the notion of visiting Horse Guards, then drop in at The Garter or its lesser incarnations," Arthur said. "Have a pint and a pie someplace the denizens of Horse Guards are likely to frequent. Nobody would begrudge you that."

"Some veterans of the Peninsula begrudge me the air I breathe, Your Grace. Why don't you drop in at The Garter?"

In addition to being the duke, Arthur was a conscientious landowner. He tended his acres with all the latest advances in agricultural science, read all the pamphlets, and could maunder on about fencing, foaling, and foot rot at tiresome length. He was a country squire at heart, one now eager to see the Continental capitals in the tradition of the old Grand Tour.

London was not his cup of tea, nor was it mine.

"Might raise a few eyebrows," Arthur said, finishing his soup. "I am not reputed to frequent London pubs. Somebody must recollect something about the woman."

"Mrs. Danforth knows more than she's telling." I helped myself to a toasted sandwich of roast beef and Stilton. "She seemed to resent Martha Waites, or perhaps to resent that Martha had a son, while Mrs. Danforth remained childless."

"Always a touchy subject," Arthur, who had neither duchess nor heirs of the body, understated the matter. "Does the boy resemble Harry?"

"Not overtly. Leander's hair is a bit reddish. Eyes are blue. He seems quick, sturdy, a bit opinionated, such as will happen when a nurse is tolerant and the tutors haven't started in yet whittling down a boy's confidence and curiosity. Mrs. Danforth has given me two weeks to find a suitable situation for him if I can't ascertain his paternity."

"That boy could solve a lot of problems, Julian."

"Or create a lot of problems when it comes time to prove that he's your legitimate heir, and I haven't one shred of documentation with which to convince Privileges."

Arthur and I were dancing around the fact that the Waltham succession was imperiled. I had recently learned that Arthur preferred men in the intimate sense, and one man in particular. Osgood Banter, scion of the Sussex Banters, was to be Arthur's traveling companion. They'd met in public school, grown closer at university, and conducted a clandestine liaison ever since.

Devotion that risked public hanging had to be sincere. Just as Arthur hadn't begrudged Harry or me our years on campaign, I wished Arthur and Banter a pleasant and happy journey. They would be safer on the Continent, where laws weren't so murderously Puritan.

Above all things, I wanted my lone remaining brother to be safe.

Arthur did not regard marriage to a lady as honorable when he was incapable of providing his duchess the primary pleasure for which a husband was responsible. As for me...

I had come home from Waterloo incapable as well, a malady I had been assured would resolve itself with time and rest. I had rested to the best of my ability for nearly a year and saw no improvement in the condition.

Little Leander, if legitimate, would be the answer to more than a few prayers, though not the sort of answer I'd had in mind.

"Healy West is in Town," Arthur said. "He served. Knows everybody. Much liked. He can tell you who else is underfoot. Send him on reconnaissance among the denizens of Horse Guards."

"He wasn't in uniform ten years ago when Mrs. Waites's husband was extant, and he did not serve in India."

Arthur started on his second sandwich. "Do you want to solve this riddle or not, Julian?"

"Both." I took a sip of an exquisite Bordeaux and considered the question. "I resent that Harry, though deceased, can solve a problem I cannot. I also hope he *has* solved it, for both our sakes. I resent that Leander might be legitimate when I am not legitimate, and yet, Leander is an orphan, while I was raised with every privilege and many kindnesses, even from the man who had the most reason to resent me."

"Papa did not resent you. To the contrary, I suspect he appreciated that with you on hand, a few of his own indiscretions might not loom so large. Your existence absolved him of having to make too many apologies to Her Grace."

Interesting perspective. "He was beyond decent to me, and there's Leander... no mother, no father, no family, unless we can find some for him."

"Or be his family. Whether he's legitimate or not, a Caldicott or not, I refuse to turn my back on the lad. Harry was connected to Mrs. Waites somehow, and that means we are connected to the boy."

No, it did not, but His Grace had spoken, and I saw no reason to argue. With his departure date looming closer, Arthur finally seemed happy. He pored over maps by the hour, read travelogues, met Banter for supper at the club, or hacked out with him first thing in the day. Banter dwelled with us, too, using the same excuse I did: Nobody wanted to unnecessarily force staff to remain in Town over the sweltering, disease-prone weeks of high summer.

My presence added credibility to the argument, and thus we muddled on, sharing the newspapers at breakfast, grabbing the wrong walking sticks, and leaving the knocker off the front door.

Why did everything strike me as a phallic symbol of late?

"There's somebody else you might chat up," Arthur said, pouring himself more wine. "I hesitate to mention the name."

"Harry's old mistresses?" He'd been notoriously fond of the ladies, and he'd maintained a liaison of appearances with Lady Clarissa Valmond.

"Them, too, legion though they are likely to be. I was thinking of St. Clair." Arthur sipped his wine with studied casualness. The duke was a good-looking devil, tall, dark, and dignified, but he had little talent for playacting. This *casual suggestion* ought to have earned him a fist to the gut.

Sebastian St. Clair occupied a place of esteem in my mind well below that of Old Scratch. The Fiend was the Fiend, after all, with a role to fulfill in the great conflict between good and evil. A dirty, sulfurous, job, but celestial tradition decreed that somebody had to do it.

St. Clair had chosen to become the most feared interrogator in the whole French Army, and Harry and I had both fallen into his snare. I had survived—barely—while Harry had not.

"How long have you been hatching this absurd notion, Your Grace?"

"Since we learned of the boy. St. Clair was the last to see Harry alive, probably the last to speak to him."

"And you think, while St. Clair was merrily torturing our brother, that Harry would have politely asked to be remembered to his only son?"

Arthur stopped playing with his wineglass. "I think St. Clair was known to use physical pain only as a last resort when inspiring his captives to yield their secrets. He might have drugged Harry, might have bargained with him. You don't know what exactly went on at that garrison, and you were there at the time."

I wanted, badly, to leave the table, leave London, and most of all, leave the memories Arthur shoved across the table at me.

"I was there in body," I said, "much of the time kept in complete darkness, in bone-chilling cold, alternately overfed or starved, given good wine or deprived of any drink at all. I was half mad when I wasn't completely parted from my reason, and now you want me to *chat up* the man responsible for my worst nightmares?"

Arthur was quiet for a time, staring at his empty plate. I could not read him, not as I'd been able to read Harry and could still read our sisters.

"They might well be his worst nightmares too, Julian. He might well be evil incarnate, but he spared me a brother when he did not have to."

By reputation, St. Clair had *spared* many British officers, provided they'd spilled their guts to him first, and thus my continued existence was proof of treason in the minds of many.

"Your surviving brother," I said, "is not entirely whole and might never be. I cannot marry. I cannot abide thunder. Problems with my memory that might have resolved by now are as bad as ever. For months, I was terrified to fall asleep..."

I had said more than I meant to.

Arthur took up another sandwich. "Every man who went to war likely endures the same problem, Julian."

"No, they do not. Those other fellows were welcomed home as heroes, with parades on the village green and drinks all around at the pub. My fellow officers see me, and most of them cross the street. They accuse me of yielding my honor, when they have no idea... no earthly, hellish idea..."

The darkness without end, the hours that might have been days or weeks or minutes, the hunger and thirst, the dreams more vivid than reality...

And the sweet, seductive thoughts of death that should have been horrifying, but eventually came to offer obscene comfort.

"Then don't talk to him," Arthur said. "I certainly cannot, for reasons of state, but the half-pay officers and drunken hotheads at Horse Guards will not allow St. Clair to draw breath indefinitely. They might let him live long enough to secure his own succession, but he's on borrowed time."

I should have found the notion that St. Clair lived under a death sentence cheering, but to my surprise, I did not. On my worse days, I believed he deserved to live with what he'd done, to live into a miserable, lonely, tormented, vilified old age. The war was over. His suffering need not be.

On my better days, I simply wanted to forget the man existed.

"I will return to Mrs. Danforth's the day after tomorrow," I said. "She will document what pertinent facts she can regarding the late Mrs. Waites, and if the opportunity presents itself, I will talk to the nursemaid as well."

A clatter of shod hoofs and the creak of carriage wheels sounded from beyond the garden wall. Arthur's countenance underwent a subtle transformation. He neither smiled nor left the table, but I could feel his spirits lightening.

"Banter returns," he said, patting his lips with his table napkin. "Spent the morning with the solicitors. He'll want wine and sympathy."

While I wanted to spare myself another meal ignoring glances and silences that spoke of matters I should not be privy to.

"I will pay a call on Healy West," I said. "He won't have known Waites, but he might know somebody who did." Any excuse to avoid billing and cooing that bothered me not because two men were involved, but rather, because I wasn't billing and cooing with anybody and might well never do so again.

# CHAPTER TWO

---

I chose to walk to the West family town house, a distance of about a dozen streets.

After my ordeal with the French, I'd been given leave to recuperate. I'd come home to Caldicott Hall barely able to shuffle from one room to the next. Upon my eventual return to the regiment, I'd been given a staff position, and even those sedentary duties had tried me sorely.

During the Hundred Days, I had managed to rise to the challenges put before me, but many a soldier overtaxed himself in anticipation of battle and realized his error only in hindsight. After Waterloo, I'd been a wreck, floating about in a sea of rumor, nightmares, and ill health.

I was clawing my way back to some semblance of fitness, grateful for every night of sound sleep, every meal that stayed down, and every hour I could spend on my own two feet or in the saddle.

Then too, I'd learned as a reconnaissance officer that walking and problem-solving were a good combination. The idle mind in an active body ranged far afield of its usual paths. I'd hatched many a useful insight while hiking the Spanish countryside, and Leander's situation left me in want of insights.

My peregrination on this occasion yielded no such bounty. I rapped on the West town house door and was shortly admitted by a butler I did not recognize. The underbutler perhaps, if his supernumerary was enjoying a half day.

He took my card, glanced at it, and something in his expression became less cordial. "I will see if Captain West is in. If you'd like to wait in the blue parlor, my lord, this way."

I had run tame in these premises as a younger fellow. The blue parlor occupied that terrain between the formal parlor, where dignitaries would be received, and the family parlor, where I would have expected to wait. Healy was only a couple years my junior, our family seats weren't much distant from each other, and I'd regarded him as a friend.

A casual friend, but a friend nonetheless.

The man who greeted me a tedious quarter hour later was not friendly at all. "My lord." He bowed first, as protocol demanded. "Good day."

"West, thank you for seeing me."

He closed the door and stood by it. "I didn't want to. You dwell under a cloud of scandal, and that's without mentioning your cavalier behavior toward my sister. Hyperia was nonetheless good enough to treat you civilly at the Makepeace house party, and you abandoned her there without a by-your-leave. She is dragooned by Lady Ophelia into visiting at Caldicott Hall, and more mischief and haring about ensue. I am not best pleased with you. State your business, and then you'll oblige me by being on your way."

I had become the next thing to a recluse rather than deal with the Healy Wests of polite society. He knew just enough about my circumstances to appoint himself the judge, jury, and executioner of my reputation, and I deserved better from him.

"I was not invited to the Makepeace house party in the first place," I said, keeping my tone pleasant, "and Lady Ophelia's dragooning powers are apparently already known to you. Had you bestirred yourself to attend—you having been invited—then you'd know exactly why I decamped when I did. As for the situation at Caldicott Hall, my reconnaissance abilities were needed to prevent scandal from befalling two families. Your sister enjoyed a pleasant visit, as far as I know. Please give her my regards."

I was pulling rank, not as a former officer, but as a ducal heir.

"None of that recitation absolves you of nearly jilting Hyperia when you mustered out. She would have had you *even then*, despite your captivity, and now..."

"She deserves a man who can give her children," I said. "I am not that man, and I might never be."

Whatever West had expected me to say, it hadn't been that. I'd surprised myself, too, though if the past had taught me anything, it was the futility of dissembling. I was not the fellow I had been—robust, confident, more than a trifle arrogant—and I was gradually coming to terms with my present incarnation.

Physically, I was unlikely to enjoy the strength and stamina of my war years ever again. Mentally, I was plagued by spectacular lapses of memory, odd fears, and strange quirks, but emotionally, I was knitting myself back into a more substantial fellow than I'd been before buying my colors.

Some days.

"You cannot...?" West stared at me, probably looking for evidence that I'd suffered injury to my breeding organs. "You aren't *capable?*"

"A problem with the humors. The lady has been made aware and does not question my decision. Besides, Hyperia and I were not engaged."

"You might as well have been." A grumbled rear-guard insult in the midst of a grudging retreat. "She suffered, you know. You came home on medical leave and didn't bother to look in on her, then after Waterloo... You have much to answer for, my lord. She had other offers and gave none of them the time of day. Now William

Ormstead is dropping around with predictable regularity, and she'll send him packing as well."

That was news to me. William Ormstead was another former officer. He was from a good family, cut a dash, and hadn't fallen afoul of any French interrogators. I daresay he could sire children, too, damn and blast him.

"I esteem Lady Hyperia greatly, and she deserves to be happy. She is aware of the particulars of my situation. Might we leave the matter there?"

"I don't want to."

I was supposed to quake in my boots while anticipating a long-overdue and terrifying challenge to my honor. West was posturing, though—Hyperia would skewer him with her knitting needles should he engage me in a duel—so I schooled myself to silence.

"Hyperia defends you," West said, finally quitting his post by the door. "You don't deserve her loyalty, but she doubtless pities you."

Another insult. I gave Healy marks for consistency and tenacity, but had to deduct a few points from his score for lack of originality.

"As it happens, I am here to discuss my late brother, Harry," I said, waiting for my host to offer me a seat, a drink, or any sort of basic hospitality.

"What has his late lordship to do with anything?"

"A woman named Martha Waites, a military widow now deceased, claimed to have given birth to Harry's son. The boy is orphaned, and I am trying to establish the truth of the mother's allegation regarding his paternity. Her husband served in India, where he expired of a fever. I am trying to locate any who might know more of the mother. Where she was born, where the marriage took place, what her plans were upon returning to England."

"Why come to me?"

"Because you know half the uniformed world, are universally liked, and do the hail-fellow-well-met in the clubs better than anybody else. Does the name Waites ring any sort of bell?"

Healy was on the tallish side, though not as tall as I, and he worshipped at the altar of Bond Street's tailors, as all fashionable young men must. In addition to those unremarkable attributes, though, he had charm.

Of necessity. The West family was old and respected, also quite solvent, but not titled. They were wealthy gentry, the backbone of the nation, and a source of well-dowered brides for the aristocracy, but they were not of the peerage.

When I'd declined to propose to Hyperia, I had dashed the dreams of her whole family. Had she been able to bag a ducal courtesy lord in the person of my handsome self, her daughters could have aspired to lesser titles and heirs thereto. Doors would have opened for Healy—as an investor, diplomat, and suitor—that remained closed to him now.

All because I couldn't... rut.

Healy took a wing chair and casually waved me toward the sofa. "Waites. First name?"

"Thomas, wife Martha. The boy is Leander. His looks might resemble Harry's generally, but not specifically."

"Age?"

"I put him at about five, though I'm hoping the nursemaid knows his natal day." The whole matter might, in fact, revolve around that fact. Harry had been home on winter leave from the first of December to the middle of February for several years. That narrowed the window of possible birth dates considerably.

The boy should have been born between early September and mid-December, if all had gone according to the usual plan, though babies showed up early or late, according to the whims of providence.

"I want to tell you that the name Waites means nothing and send you on your way, but..."

"But?"

"I cannot. It's not that common a name, and I seem to recall talk, a wisp of gossip, a bit of tattle. He served in India?"

"Would have gone out about ten years ago, didn't last long, and not from a family of any great means."

"Then somebody should see what some of the old hands at Horse Guards have to say. They all served under Wellington at Seringapatam, to hear them tell it. But what's your interest in Waites if he was dead long before the boy was conceived?"

"I am looking for Martha Waites's maiden name and for any general details of her situation and origins. She safely returned from India, and in the normal course, her husband's family would have been expected to take her in. Failing that, her own people should have offered her a welcome."

"You are looking for the proverbial needle in a haystack."

"Correct, but you are a reliable magnet, so I entrust general inquiries to you." I rose, having *stated my business.* "My regards to your family. I can be reached at Waltham's residence. I will see myself out."

In the spirit of the general rudeness West had shown me, I expected him to remain seated and leave me to make my own way to the front door.

He rose. "Very odd business for the boy to surface only now. Lord Harry—God rest his soul—was not exactly a monk. Wouldn't have pegged him for the sort to trifle with regimental widows, though."

"He might have set her up for a time, might have been courting her. I simply do not know, and Waltham has tasked me with getting to the bottom of the matter."

"The duke is in Town?" That query translated to, *Will you tattle to His Grace about my earlier poor manners?*

Of course I would not. I took perverse satisfaction from demonstrating courtesy in the face of those rude to me. "Waltham is much taken up with travel plans for this autumn. He's off to tour the Continental capitals."

West accompanied me back to the front door. "A journey in the autumn? Who will oversee the harvest at Caldicott Hall? Waltham has been perennially absent from the Little Season because he's always minding his acres." A sly implication underlay that observation: Waltham used harvest as an excuse to avoid Town.

When had Healy become such a brat? "I have promised Waltham I will bide at the Hall in his place." I was, after all, Arthur's heir presumptive, lest West forget that detail. I tended to forget it myself, whenever possible.

"I'll shortly be off for the grouse moors," Healy said. "I prefer to let the weather moderate before I go shooting. Even Scotland can be beastly hot this time of year."

Also swarming with midges and armed, drunken Englishmen. "I will bid you farewell," I said, collecting my hat and walking stick from the butler who had materialized from the porter's nook. "My thanks for any assistance you can offer."

West was shrewd, and now that he'd delivered the scolding he believed I deserved—and now that he'd realized Arthur was in Town —he changed tactics.

"You know, I might curse you to perdition for any number of reasons, but that business..." He waved a hand near his falls. "I'd not wish that on anybody, save perhaps the Corsican monster."

How comforting to know I hadn't quite reached Napoleon's equal in the ranks of demonhood. "Your solicitude is appreciated. Thank you for your time."

"My regards to His Grace," West called after me as I took my leave. "Best of luck with your inquiries."

So kind of him to alert half of Mayfair to my undertakings. I moved along the walkway at a deliberately relaxed pace, though my mood approached furious. I understood why the Healy West and his ilk felt entitled to judge me. For all they knew, I had betrayed my brother, my king, and my honor, and such lapses must be punished by all and sundry, no matter how extenuating the circumstances.

Arthur's influence had gained me tolerance in some circles. In others, where soldiers could consult their own wartime memories, I might even find understanding. West—a soldier himself—had shown me neither, until he'd learned of the dysfunction with my manly humors.

Then he'd offered me a sort of backhanded compassion, and for that, I nearly hated him.

"My lord, a moment."

A footman had waited until I'd turned the corner to catch up with me. So lost had I been in contemplation of life's injustices, I hadn't realized he'd been following me. A lapse like that could have seen me killed in Spain.

"A note, my lord, from Miss West. I will convey your reply directly to her."

The footman stood about six feet and had the blond hair and handsome features required for his post. If Hyperia had entrusted him with a note, he was also possessed of loyalty and discretion.

Hyperia's epistle was succinct. *Hype Park. Seven o'clock tomorrow, weather permitting.*

"Please inform Miss West I will be happy to oblige. She will know where to find me." By a certain tall hedge, where she and I had been meeting since the year she'd made her come out.

"Very good, sir." He trotted off, and I continued on my way, my mood greatly improved.

Healy West's behavior had left me sulking and seething, but Hyperia sought a moment of my time, and that prospect improved my spirits significantly.

~

"My lord, good day." Hyperia nodded at me from atop her mare.

The sight of Perry by the park's early morning light was unaccountably dear. To the casual observer, she was no great beauty—a touch too curvy, hair merely brown, eyes merely green, no willowy height to lend her consequence.

But those eyes were bright with intelligence, and when they snapped with righteous ire or softened with compassion, classical panegyrics would not have done them justice. She had the heart of a

"Where were you?" Clarissa asked me. "I don't recall you in Town, and Harry hadn't said anything about you being down at the Hall."

"I remained abroad." In the Spanish countryside, impersonating a tinker of French descent, an itinerant shepherd, or a deserter variously from French or British forces. I learned a lot that winter, not about French battle plans, but about how to do reconnaissance as I could do it best, not as Harry instructed me to do it.

"We missed you," Hyperia said. "Arthur stood up with me when our paths chanced to cross. I took his attentions for an offer of mutual comfort."

Very likely exactly as they'd been intended, unbeknownst to Arthur himself.

"I'm most interested in Harry's movements. Was he in company with any other ladies? Did he show attention to any particular actresses or opera dancers? Did any woman appear to take him into inexplicable dislike?"

Clarissa slanted a look at me. "Is somebody trying to blackmail you? Claiming Harry disported with her and she's prompted after all this time to spoil his memory?"

I knew Clarissa's family woes, but I was uncomfortable trusting her with the Caldicott linen. "Something like that. Allegations have surfaced regarding Harry's conduct during that winter. Anything you recall might be useful."

"Then talk to the servants at Waltham House," Clarissa said, turning her mare down a shady path. "The servants know everything."

A good suggestion. "I'm mostly concerned with Harry's socializing. When he wasn't squiring you about, with whom did he stand up?"

Clarissa brushed past a low-hanging branch of maple, which swung back to smack Hyperia gently in the shoulder. Perry rode on without comment.

"He stood up with everybody," Clarissa said. "My job was to

dance the supper waltzes with him so he'd not have to spend a meal with an ambitious young lady, or fend off the advances of the widows. I was also to be available for the carriage parade when the weather permitted, and Harry occasionally needed me for informal gatherings. He wasn't wrong to pay for my escort. Some women see a dashing fellow in uniform, and all they think of is how to get him out of it. What is all this about?"

"I need to account for Harry's whereabouts that winter and to talk to any women with whom he might have been keeping close company."

I dropped back, because we passed another pair of riders, the first of whom was known to me. William Ormstead acknowledged me with a nod, while the sight of Hyperia inspired him to a beaming smile.

"Miss West, good morning. A pleasure."

Because Ormstead drew his horse to a halt, the fellow a few yards behind him on the path—they did not appear to be hacking out together—also had to halt, and Clarissa, likely the better to eavesdrop, brought her horse to a stop as well. Short of sending my horse bounding up the bank in an awkward retreat, I was hemmed in, with no means of extricating myself from a face-to-face encounter with the rider on the path behind Ormstead.

"My lord," he said, "good morning."

My body reacted before my mind grasped the truth. That polite voice, with its hint of a hard-to-place accent, belonged to an Englishman who'd come of age in France and dwelled exclusively among the French for years. Like me, he'd probably heard both languages from the cradle. Like me, he'd joined up because that had seemed the only thing to do, though he'd joined the Grand Armée, while I'd fought under Wellington.

"St. Clair." I nodded, grateful for the blue spectacles that would hide the shock in my eyes. "Good morning." I *would not* be rude. To give this man even the cut direct would acknowledge the havoc I felt at the sound of his greeting and the sight of his face. His polite voice haunted my nightmares. Thoughts of revenging myself upon him had sustained me during the miserable, shivering weeks when I'd lived like an animal on the slopes of the Pyrenees.

"I am glad to see you enjoying good health," St. Clair said, "and good company."

No irony laced his words, and no contrition that I could hear. "You appear to be thriving." I tried for equal dispassion. St. Clair was trim but in good enough weight—he'd been spectrally gaunt when I'd fallen into his hands—and as well turned out as an English lord should be.

"I am tolerated," he said, "by some. One accepts what cannot be changed. Excuse me, Ormstead, my horse grows restless."

Was St. Clair asking me to accept the past? To let go of it? Whatever else was true, I doubted he'd succeeded with either challenge any better than I had, and the thought yielded a grim sort of consolation.

"You are biding in London?" I asked.

"Sometimes. A moving target is harder to hit, and Englishmen do so appreciate a test of their sporting skills." He nudged his horse forward, touched a gloved finger to his hat brim as he passed Hyperia, and disappeared around a bend in the path.

"Was that him?" Clarissa whispered, swinging her horse across the trail. "Was that the Traitor Lord?"

"That was Sebastian St. Clair," Hyperia said. "The Traitor Baron, or the Traitor Lord, and I've heard worse as well."

"I felt the temperature drop when he rode past me," Clarissa said. "Napoleon's prize interrogator, right here in Hyde Park. Too delicious for words. A man with his reputation should be little and hunched and sniveling."

"That man has never sniveled in his life." Hyperia was not offering a compliment.

"Tall, dark, and diabolical." Clarissa gave a mock shiver. "Who would have thought? Julian, if you are done nosing around Harry's ancient indiscretions, I must be getting home. I am famished, and I have a fitting first thing this morning. One never goes to a fitting on an empty stomach."

"Take the groom," Hyperia said. "Julian will accompany me home."

Clarissa cantered away, the groom in tow. She had seen the Traitor Lord himself, and by noon—according to her hushed recollections—she would have suffered a greeting from him. By supper, he might well have offered insult to her person with his bold gaze, or perhaps attempted to charm her with his smile.

Though as to that, I'd never seen St. Clair smile.

"Jules, are you well?" Hyperia had brought her mare alongside Atlas.

"I find I am."

"Was I right? That was St. Clair?"

Nobody had introduced him, though I had referred to him by name. "One and the same. I knew him as Girard. He looks well." Not happy, not thriving, not at peace. As if some part of him still bided in that rocky fortress rattling about in chains of suffering and secrets.

"What did he say to you?" Hyperia asked.

"We exchanged civilities." I assessed my reaction to the conversation, if one could call it that. Not relief, to have faced an old enemy with my manners intact. Not fear, certainly. St. Clair was no threat to me now.

"And?"

I urged Atlas forward at a relaxed walk. "He seemed to convey that his days are numbered, and I need not trouble myself over his continued existence much longer." Typical of the odd politesse St. Clair had wrapped about himself like a shroud.

"You would not condescend to end his days," Hyperia said, "though you are among the most entitled to bear him a grudge."

"I escaped, in theory, or St. Clair let me go because his cause was lost and he was not by reputation a murderer. A torturer, yes, but not a murderer."

"Then how do you explain Harry's death at his hands?"

We rode along in silence, while I pondered the mystery of Harry's passing. My French captors had told me only that he'd died honorably, which I'd taken to mean he'd died without yielding strategic military information. I had not seen Harry's remains, and I did not know where he'd been buried.

"I cannot explain Harry's death, unless torture ended in murder."

Which again flew in the face of St. Clair's reputation. A British officer was to prefer death over dishonor, and St. Clair's method had withheld death by design.

"But then," I went on, "I've seen men die for no apparent reason. A hard march under a hot sun wouldn't kill them, but they'd lie down on a bedroll beneath a pretty summer moon and never rise. A kick to the head from a fractious horse would leave them cursing and finishing the day with nothing more than a headache, and yet, they, too, would fall asleep after supper and be gone by morning. I simply don't know what Harry's exact fate was."

St. Clair did know. I had to face that fact now in a way I hadn't when his presence in London had been little more than rumor.

"What of Lady Clarissa?" Hyperia asked. "Was your discussion with her at all useful?"

We rounded another bend, and the Serpentine lay before us, sparkling in the morning sun. "Useful, yes. Everybody recalls the year without a Christmas, the difficult business of putting the Regency in place, the arguments over a Council of Regency and who should be on it. Arthur claims the merchants and hostesses were delighted to see Town so lively through the winter."

"While Clarissa has only generalities to impart."

"Yes, but I gave her only generalities to consider. Will she respect a confidence?" I trusted Hyperia's judgment more than my own, at least in this.

Hyperia watched as a family of ducks trooped down the bank and went honking across the water, Mama in the advance, Papa bringing up the rear. A prosaic, oddly touching sight. Everybody paddling madly beneath the surface, all the while appearing to make a placid progress across the water.

"Harry might well have a son," Hyperia said, "conceived at a time when Harry was very publicly keeping company with Clarissa. If she doesn't want rumors to start up that she's the boy's mother, she should be both more forthcoming with you and very discreet with others."

I voiced the thought Hyperia was too polite to state aloud. "And if the boy is Clarissa's, foisted off on an old school chum or convenient acquaintance in need of coin, will Clarissa find it more expedient to tell the truth or to continue lying?"

# CHAPTER THREE

"You make all these entries yourself?" I asked, closing the bound ledger book and rubbing my eyes.

"I am less likely to misconstrue my own handwriting," Arthur replied. "Mama is a firm believer that the head of a household must know where the money is spent. She kept the books at Caldicott Hall until two years ago, at which point, I stepped in."

The ledger book was green—Mama's preferred color for domestic accounting—and embossed with the family crest, Virgil's famous aphorism about love conquering all tucked beneath it where the family motto should have been.

Mama had given as good as she'd got with the old duke. Nobody crossed her lightly.

"You still allow the stewards to keep the estate books?"

"I do casual audits," Arthur replied, rising and bringing the brandy decanter to the library table. "I've found only harmless errors, but I suspect that's in part because the stewards know I'll check up on them. You'll be responsible for all the tallying that goes along with harvest."

"I did a fair amount of quartermaster's work after Napoleon's first abdication." Endless days behind a desk, burying myself in figures, trying to cipher my way past nightmares. "I'll manage."

Arthur poured two servings and resumed his seat at the head of the table. "You'll bide at the Hall the whole time I'm gone?"

His travel plans were growing more elaborate by the day. An initial stop in Brussels, then autumn in Paris, Berlin, Prague, and Vienna. Budapest if the weather allowed, otherwise, he and Banter would be in Venice before winter set in, and from thence... Greece, the splendors of Italy, and in late spring, he'd make a leisurely progress across southern France to Bordeaux.

Or he and Banter might settle in Brussels and spend a year dwelling in domestic bliss, but the plan was to go everywhere, see everything, and return home, exhausted and appreciative of all Merry Olde had to offer.

I would be very much on my own, holding the reins in Arthur's absence; but then, a reconnaissance officer was expected to be self-reliant and resourceful.

I took a sip of excellent brandy. "I will bide primarily at the Hall during your absence," I said. "Clarissa was peculiarly unforthcoming this morning. She claimed to have forgotten about the only winter in memory when Parliament didn't rise for Yuletide. She described herself as nothing more than a tailor's dummy Harry trotted out for the supper waltzes and the carriage parade."

Arthur wrinkled the ducal proboscis. "Harry claimed she was trying to interest him in marriage."

Harry had claimed that German princesses (plural) remembered him fondly in their secret dreams. "She insists nothing intimate occurred between them."

"Do you believe her, Julian?"

I considered the stacks of ledger books and what I knew of Clarissa's past. "If she and Harry were lovers, that is no business of ours. Leander is unlikely to be her son, and it's possible she just wants the whole interlude with Harry behind her. She suggested I talk to your staff, and that was good advice."

away from home in their prime years, when a fellow can have a better time making a proper adventure of the undertaking. I really do appreciate your understanding, Jules."

Perhaps Arthur had been at the brandy longer than I knew. Perhaps he was drunk on anticipated joy. Before he left the room, he squeezed my shoulder.

"Don't stay up too late. You have an appointment with a lot of toy soldiers and an imaginary dragon or two in the morning."

Another squeeze, and Arthur was gone, leaving me to the familiar companionship of the ledgers and the brandy.

I did not hold out much hope of finding Harry's old staff, but the notion held merit, and I wasn't yet ready to seek my bed. A humid breeze stirred the curtains, though the house was otherwise quiet.

The numbers, kept in Harry's hand, seduced me. He'd spent prodigiously on claret at a time when the best red wines were hard to come by. M. Beaujolais had been a frequent recipient of his coin, abbreviated simply MB in later entries.

Mme Clicquot had received some payments as well. The widow Clicquot was mistress of a notable champagne vineyard, a lady whose products ought not to have been finding their way to England at all in 1811.

*Shame on you, Harry.*

Wages had been paid weekly to a staff of nine. Housekeeper, cook, scullery maid, two chambermaids, two footmen, a boot-boy, and a combination groom/coachy, but no butler. Mrs. Millicent Marie Bleeker had served as the head domestic, and the cook's name was listed as Helvetica Ann Siegurdson—I pictured her wielding a meat cleaver to good effect—while everybody else had merited only initials and surname.

C. Cummings and L. Fielding had been the footmen, and they were more likely to have remained in service and in Town than the female staff. But then, Helvetica Siegurdson wasn't a name quickly forgotten. Surely I could find one of them, and they might recall something of Harry's guests during that winter.

I turned pages, seeing a window on my brother's life latticed in columns and rows. The enlisted men were supposed to receive their new uniforms each year at Christmas—a tradition frequently honored in the breach rather than the breeches. The officers did likewise, though they paid for their own kit, and went home to London on winter leave or sent to Bond Street to have those uniforms made up.

Harry had replenished his wardrobe in triplicate, but then, he'd had independent means, unlike many who'd bought their colors. Three pairs of riding boots—a small fortune—and an enormous bill to the mercer.

Three new pocket watches, along with three compasses, three pairs of field glasses and shaving mirrors—signal mirrors, more like— and plenty of civilian attire too. Harry would pass variously for a merchant, a landed gentleman, a horse dealer, an Italian baritone... His disguises tended to be more stylish than mine, and he liked working in the towns and cities, while I preferred the villages and countryside.

I turned another page and came across expenses incurred at one of London's more fashionable modistes. A milliner had got her fingers into Harry's pockets, as had a lady's glovemaker. Harry had made notes alongside his entries. *Sunday finery* beside one, *in anticipation of spring* beside another.

But whose Sunday finery, and who had made such a fetching picture in the spring of 1811? Or had the lady's fashionable clothing become too snug by spring?

I was on the point of closing the journal, the examination of which had become more an exercise in sentiment than an investigative foray, when I noted an entry logged as £5 *DC.*

Cryptic, given that Harry had elsewhere provided myriad details not strictly necessary in an account book. I set the ledger aside for further study and made my way to my bedroom. A light shone beneath the door of the ducal suite across from mine, and quiet voices murmured in the gloom.

And then soft, shared masculine laughter.

I had never heard Arthur laugh, not even politely, but he was laughing now, and God be thanked for that.

I tended to my ablutions and lay down atop the covers. The night was close and hot, but one did not sleep on London balconies, and the heat had been worse in Spain. I was drifting off to sleep at long last when, for no reason at all, my mind presented me with the fact that a prospective groom in search of a special license paid five pounds for that article at Doctors' Commons.

~

"My notes," Mrs. Danforth said, handing over a sheaf of papers. "If I recall anything further, I'll send it along to Waltham House. I've informed Miss Dujardin that she and the boy might well be changing abodes."

My commanding officers, when sending me on a particularly difficult mission, had adopted Mrs. Danforth's same air of let's-be-off-with-you, nothing-further-need-be-said, despite endless questions remaining unanswered and haste being a certain recipe for disaster.

"No change of abode for another two weeks at least," I countered, tucking the papers into the tail pocket of my riding jacket. "I do recall you allowing me that much grace to sort out the boy's particulars."

"Twelve more days, my lord. No more. I will not have my household become an object of talk."

Mrs. Danforth was an obscure military widow living on an obscure street in a neighborhood nobody would call fashionable. I was tempted to allude to those facts, except that I knew all too well how easily a reputation could be tarnished, never again to shine as brightly.

"Leander will not be left here any longer than necessary. The nursemaid's name is Dujardin?"

A nod. "She's devoted to the boy, I'll give her that. Spoils him, but her regard for her charge is sincere, and he's quite attached to her. He would be, of course, what with his mother gone and no father, and I hope you will take that into account when you settle him elsewhere."

I was to settle the nursemaid as well, apparently, though I would hardly leave the woman to starve. "Might I have a private word with Miss Dujardin?"

"Dispatch the boy to the kitchen for jam and bread. I'll send Dujardin to you." She rose and marched off, and while I wanted to be sympathetic to Mrs. Danforth's circumstances, her put-upon, uppish airs made that difficult.

But then, she had no children to show for her years of loyal service in the ranks of military wives, and that—as I was coming to know—had to hurt.

Miss Dujardin and Leander appeared hand in hand a few minutes later. The nursemaid wore the careful expression of a domestic facing an interrogation, while the boy's gaze was curious.

I rose. "Julian Caldicott, at your service." Honorifics struck me as unnecessary in present company, particularly in a garden little bigger than a foaling stall.

Miss Dujardin curtseyed. "Leander, make your bow."

The boy dropped her hand and complied. "Pleased to meet you, Mr. Caldicott. I am Master Leander Merton Waites, at your service."

The name, and confidence with which Leander introduced himself, gave me pause.

"Well done," Miss Dujardin said. "Your soldiers are where you left them yesterday. You can play Waterloo."

Children all over Europe likely knew the order of battle that day as well as or better than Arthur knew the royal succession.

"I'd rather we played hide-and-seek."

She folded her arms. Just that.

Leander's air of insouciance faltered. "I'd rather we played hide-and-seek, *miss*."

"Your soldiers can play hide-and-seek," I said. "Have them dodge the French patrols and then circle round to ambush them behind the rain barrel. Just don't forget where you positioned your scouts. They should be on high ground, but not too far from the action."

Leander stared hard at me. I looked for traces of Harry in his piquant little face, but found only a suggestion near the chin and in the earnestness of his gaze.

"I can use bricks to make high ground," he said, "and I can make a bog, and the Frenchies will try to cross the bog, like the Jacobites at Culloden."

"A fine plan." If a bit ghoulish. Leander scampered off to make war on the French, and I gestured to a bench. "Shall we sit?"

Miss Dujardin perched on the very edge of the bench. She was the picture of domestic propriety, in sturdy gray twill, her collar the merest dash of lace. Her hands were folded primly in her lap, and her hair was tucked beneath a pristine cap.

Where to start with such a citadel to decorum? I took a seat on the opposite end of the bench. "The boy has a lively imagination."

"Leander must often entertain himself. He hasn't had many play-mates." Somebody was being reproached with that observation, and the child was being defended.

"He has you."

She smoothed her plain gray skirts. The fabric was good quality, and the clothes fit her well. Not quite a uniform, more of a governess's ensemble, despite the capacious mobcap.

"He has me for now. I did not know who you were, my lord, or what your errand was when you called two days ago. Mrs. Danforth saw fit to inform me of the details only this morning."

Not simply decorum, then, but also affronted dignity. *Splendid.* "You were ambushed?"

She nodded. "Mrs. Danforth hasn't had children. She doesn't grasp that upheaval can be hard on the little ones. She herself cannot abide disruption, though. Leander just lost his mother. He has no memory of a father. If the chambermaid accidentally tossed out the boy's favorite stuffed horse, he would be justified in becoming hysteri-cal, and now... I am talking out of turn."

Very much so, though perhaps she spoke out of fear. "You feel genuine concern for Leander, which I commend." She was also judging her betters, but because her opinions matched my own, I could hardly castigate her for them. "He will be provided for, Miss Dujardin. Whether he is my nephew or simply the offspring of somebody my brother once esteemed, we will not allow him to come to harm."

She tucked a coppery curl under her cap. "We?"

"We Caldicotts. We are few in number, but fiercely loyal."

She remained demurely quiet, gaze on the uneven bricks of Mrs. Danforth's terrace. My mother's silences could take on the same dense, accusatory quality.

"What do you know of Leander's antecedents?" I asked.

"His mother recently went to her reward, such as it was, and his father apparently perished in the wars."

"Is Leander legitimate?"

"I don't know. Mrs. Waites retained me when the wet nurse's milk dried up. Leander would have been coming up on a year. He was taking his first steps, saying a few words. He could manage porridge and simple foods. The particulars of Mrs. Waites's relationship with Leander's father did not come under discussion."

In the usual course, infants went to live with a wet nurse. In loftier households, the wet nurse bided with the family until her charge outgrew her services. For villagers and lesser folk, the baby was fostered out. Nothing unusual there, except that one could not foster out a child if one lacked coin.

"Is it fair to say you know Leander better than his mother did?"

She watched while, down the walkway, the boy was arranging bricks and dipping water from the rain barrel into a depression in the soil. His makeshift lake would be mud by the time he arranged his soldiers, but then, bogs were supposed to be muddy.

"Mrs. Waites loved her son," Miss Dujardin said, "but her means became limited, and she had no family willing to acknowledge her. I was to say that Leander was her husband's offspring, but as far as I know, she was married only the once, and her husband died in India well before Leander was conceived."

"She never remarried?" This mattered above all else, in terms of the factual record.

That pale hand once again smoothed over drab fabric. "If she had, why continue to use her first husband's name? If a ducal heir had proposed to me, do you think I'd disdain to use his name?"

The biddable nursemaid hadn't always been in domestic service if she could challenge me with such a question. I had not admitted that Leander could be Harry's son, but Miss Dujardin had stated the assumption plainly.

"You might avoid use of that ducal heir's name," I said, "if the fellow was a brute who'd shown only enough charm to manipulate you to the altar." Harry had been many things and had had charm aplenty, but he'd never have raised his hand to a woman or a child.

"Can a ducal heir be a brute?"

"Yes, he can. Or a drunkard, or destitute and mean, though his unkindness leaves no marks."

My reply gave Miss Dujardin pause, but not for long. "Mrs. Waites spoke only rarely of Leander's father. Said the boy bore a resemblance to him about the chin and eyes, said the father was very determined on his own ends too."

A polite way to say that Harry could be selfish and pigheaded, which was true enough. "Do you happen to know Leander's date of birth?"

Leander ranged his men atop the bricks and dug a bunker behind which he positioned a lone scout. The French advanced single file down the walkway, all unsuspecting of the danger ahead. The scene was unsettling and all too realistic.

"We celebrate Leander's birthday on September 12, my lord."

Odd phrasing. "Was he born on that day?"

Perhaps watching the boy play so realistically at war upset Miss Dujardin as well, because her manner had become testy.

"I would not know that, my lord. If he wasn't born on the twelfth, he was certainly born near that date. I can think of no reason why Mrs. Waites would have dissembled."

I could think of one very specific reason. My grandfather had been born on Friday the thirteenth. His birthday had been celebrated by family tradition on the twelfth for the entirety of his life. Another ancestor, born the very same day Good Queen Bess had been gathered to her reward had similarly celebrated her natal day on March 23 rather than March 24.

A childish imitation of musket fire broke forth across the garden as Leander knocked over the French soldiers or sent them pelting beneath the lavender border. The English delivered a much more rapid volley than we'd been capable of in the field, and two Frenchmen fell to their doom in the temporary bog.

"He could well be a Caldicott," I said softly as Leander's men swarmed down from their lofty bricks and chased the cowardly French into the undergrowth.

"I beg your pardon, my lord?"

"That boy could well be a Caldicott. Arrangements must be made." Was I pleased? Relieved? Or simply... baffled, to have come this much closer to acquiring a nephew? And what of the boy? How would he feel?

I would have to consult the calendar, but every instinct told me that September 13, 1811, had fallen on a Friday.

"The Caldicott family has a tradition of moving birthday celebrations from the actual anniversary of a child's arrival if the more accurate date is ill-omened."

Miss Dujardin's expression suggested she did not care two rotten figs for Caldicott family tradition. "The boy's name is Leander Waites, my lord."

Leander marched his prisoners back to the scene of battle and arranged them in a circle around the bog.

"A name can be changed by deed poll. His putative father also had Merton as a middle name."

"You cannot change that boy's name without his baptismal lines." Miss Dujardin was forgetting her place again, and she was right.

I brought my focus back to the puzzle of Leander's legitimacy. His birthday fell within the relevant window, regardless of family traditions. The boy himself had blurted out his full name.

"Where was Mrs. Waites living when she hired you?"

The question provoked a puzzled frown. "Here, in London. Well, Chelsea, actually. She'd rented a cottage from a widow, more of a made-over carriage house, but snug enough."

"Then the boy might well have been baptized in a London church. If I search baptismal records starting with the last quarter of 1811, I will eventually find the church where he was christened. I will begin in the neighborhoods on the southwest side of Town and work my way east and north. We can get the boy properly situated, and I'll hire private inquiry agents to comb the records."

Her pretty profile acquired a hint of mulishness about the jaw. "You will upend a boy's whole life because of some tale about a family superstition?"

"How many families do you know with the same superstition?"

"Probably half of those with a child born on a Friday the thirteenth."

Fair point. "How many give their sons a middle name of Merton?"

She treated me to another reproachful silence.

"Lord Harry claimed Merton among his middle names, Miss Dujardin. He was in London during the relevant time."

"So was all of Parliament and most of polite society."

Her recollection was clearly better than Lady Clarissa's, who numbered among polite society's ranks. "I grant you, the evidence is purely circumstantial, but it is convincing evidence."

As I spoke, I realized that I had been convinced, but Arthur and any meddling authorities would want confirmation. Had Miss Dujardin simply stated the boy's natal day, without embellishment, I would not have been half so certain. Had the boy himself not told me his middle name... London *had* been full of officers on leave, MPs, peers, their families...

Leander had been conceived during the most social winter in recent history, and yet, this call had yielded details that all but proved to me that the boy was Harry's child.

Miss Dujardin—the sole potential witness in possession of the relevant facts—looked to be on the verge of recanting her recitation, though, and that would not do.

# CHAPTER FOUR

"Twelve days from now," I said, using my intimidate-the-recruits voice, "Leander will no longer be welcome under this roof. Mrs. Danforth has been very clear about the limits of her charity, and I doubt her kind offices will extend to writing you a character. Would you have me article the lad to a cobbler while I look for baptismal records that will prove his patrimony?"

Miss Dujardin's hands fisted in her skirts. "She said that? Twelve days?"

"When I first called, it was a fortnight, and she's apparently counting the very days. I don't intend to try her patience."

"Twelve *days?*"

"She wants him gone, Miss Dujardin. I asked Mrs. Danforth if she'd be willing to foster Leander. She fears a stain on her reputation and refused."

Miss Dujardin directed a contemptuous look at the house. "Has it occurred to you, my lord, that *Martha Waites* was fostering Leander and that her stories regarding his father were convenient fabrications designed to ensure Leander had some lofty connections?"

I would have wandered 'round to considering such a theory, eventually. Maybe. "Do you have evidence to support that conjecture?"

Leander was replacing the bricks in the stack from whence they'd come and washing off his unfortunate Frenchmen in the rain barrel.

"Martha was charming and imaginative by nature," Miss Dujardin said, taking out a plain handkerchief. "I can see where an officer on leave would have been taken with her, but I can also see why she'd invent fabrications to better her child's lot in life. She may not have known for certain who Leander's father was, and she simply chose the best of a randy lot, or chose a passing fellow who'd do as well as any other. Consumption took some time to kill her, and she was doubtless making what plans she could for her son."

Leander finished at the rain barrel and shook out his forces. "The Frenchies lost, miss. Good King George's men beat them to flinders."

"Was Wellington on hand?" I asked.

"Nah. He was at the duchess's ball, but we lads were a credit to our uniforms."

I had played with soldiers as a boy. Twenty years of warfare, of militias parading on village greens, units being called to active service, and casualty lists posted on the church doors, had doubtless inspired a booming business in toy soldiers and miniature artillery.

But to hear this small child so casually parrot an infantryman's words and tone unnerved me.

"May I have some chocolate now, miss? I'm thirsty."

Miss Dujardin knelt to examine the boy's dirty hands and applied her handkerchief with vigor. "Leander, the day is quite warm. Wouldn't cider or lemonade do?"

"I like chocolate." He beamed up at me. "I like chocolate with nutmeg on top."

Expensive tastes for such a small lad. "I like mine with a dash of whipped cream, but only when it's cold enough to snow."

Leander scowled at me. "That's wintertime, and it's not wintertime."

"Right you are, lad. In summer, it's cold meadow tea, cider, or lemonade for me." Or a good summer ale, brandy, or hock.

He looked from me to his nurse, who had finished with his hands. "Not chocolate?"

"Not for me," I said, assisting Miss Dujardin to rise. "Wellington wouldn't have been caught dead drinking chocolate on a summer's day. Lemonade with a bit of lavender garnish, but never hot chocolate."

Leander eyed the lavender border.

"A few sprigs," Miss Dujardin said. "If you pick three for you and three for me, how many is that?"

"What about *him*?"

"None for me. I'm about to take my leave."

"Will you come again?"

"Yes." I answered without hesitation, because I knew the child would note reluctance or prevarication. This might well be Harry's child. In the alternative, Miss Dujardin, who'd had years to speculate on the matter, might have put her finger on the truth: Harry was not the boy's father, though he'd been close enough to Martha Waites that she could pretend he was.

I wasn't sure which outcome I preferred, but on no account could I allow this child to be cast upon the charity of the parish.

Miss Dujardin folded her handkerchief and stuffed it into a pocket. "You have made an impression, my lord."

On her? On the boy? A good impression or some other kind? She had perfected the art of scolding by inference. My mother had the same ability. While I weighed her words, Leander secreted his men beneath the arching fronds of the lavender border.

"You have made an impression as well, Miss Dujardin. Leander is lucky to have you."

My sincere compliment earned me the most subtle relenting.

"Leander," she said, "when you've chosen your lavender, take it to the kitchen and wash your hands properly with soap and water." She smiled at him, and he was soon sniffing one sprig after another.

"You will come back?" she asked.

"The day after tomorrow. The questions you raise bear not only on Leander's paternity, but also on the identity of his mother. Your theory that Mrs. Waites was fostering the boy might have merit."

"You think his real mother was some Society belle passing her indiscretion off on her companion?" Said with no inflection whatsoever.

"Or an opera dancer unable to support her offspring. Or a servant, though I rather hope not. Harry had scruples."

She leveled a flat stare at me. "Servants can have scruples too, sir."

For a nursemaid, Miss Dujardin had a propensity for fierceness. I liked that about her and approved of her boldness because she exhibited it in defense of the child. She and Hyperia would understand each other without a word being spoken.

"Servants are," I said, "in my experience, generally more principled than their employers, but having scruples and having the latitude to uphold them are not always synonymous in service. If you know anything further about Leander's antecedents, I trust you will pass it along to me?"

She nodded, but her compliance was distracted by some other thought. "Twelve days, sir?"

"Less than that, if I can bestir the staff at Waltham House. The nursery hasn't been in use for decades, and the governess's quarters will want a good scrubbing and airing."

Leander was ready for an old slug of a pony, too. I mentally added a stop at Tatts to my day's itinerary.

"She'll need to be patient," Miss Dujardin said. "The governess. The whole nursery staff. He's been through so much, and Mrs. Waites told him this is his new home."

Miss Dujardin had been snappish with me, disrespectful, and difficult, all of which had saved some time and earned my respect. Leander's personal dragon now looked to be blinking back tears.

"I was rather hoping that governess would be you, miss. What I know about the care and feeding of little boys wouldn't fill a lady's dancing slipper."

She blinked at me, her scrutiny putting me in mind of the lad. Too serious to be polite. "You want me to come with him?"

"For the nonce at least. I understand that at some point, governesses give way to tutors, but surely not when a lad is only five years old?"

A sniff, another blink. A slight nod. "We can discuss those particulars at a later time. Leander should visit you before he's uprooted again."

She'd saved me having to make the suggestion. All children were reconnaissance officers at heart, and Leander would appreciate an inspection tour of the ducal quarters before moving there.

"I will come by Friday to collect you both at eleven of the clock. You can be my guests for luncheon, if that suits?"

Another nod, then she bounced a curtsey, summoned the boy and his half-dozen lavender sprigs, and disappeared into the house. The soldiers had been left to maintain surveillance from the depths of the lavender border.

I made my way in the direction of Hyde Park and Tattersalls. Miss Dujardin and her charge had given me much to think about, not least of which was the possibility that Martha Waites, regimental widow fallen on hard times, might not be the boy's mother, though she had claimed to be.

Lady Clarissa, by contrast, might have given birth to the child, but was professing to know nothing of him.

A conundrum, and a ducal title could fall into escheat if I did not find the solution.

~

"I am the last man to know anything about our brother's opera dancers," Arthur said, tilting his hat a half inch to the right, then returning it to level.

"Who would know about his liaisons and flirtations when on leave?" I took the hat off his head and replaced it, tilted a half inch to the left. "Better."

He regarded himself in the mirror over the sideboard. "Better how?"

*More dashing.* If I said that, Arthur would smite me with a scowl, and I had been scowled at enough for one day.

"Ask Banter why you should tilt left. He has more of an artistic eye than I do, but I think it might have to do with which hand carries your walking stick. We become accustomed to presenting ourselves to the world in a certain posture, and that posture becomes ingrained."

Unless, of course, in the interests of appearing harmless and trustworthy, one purposefully altered his posture to that of an old man three sheets to the wind, or a simple-minded drover happy to jaunt across the miles with his livestock.

"I like that," Osgood Banter said, coming down the steps. "Your Grace cuts a bit of a dash with your hat angled just so."

Arthur's gaze and Banter's collided in the mirror. *I would like to see you wearing only that hat.* The admission twinkled in the depths of Banter's eyes, and I wanted to hit him. Not because he was flirting with Arthur, but because I was interviewing a potential witness, and my witness, before my very eyes, had just gone witless and besotted.

"We were discussing opera dancers," Arthur said, tossing Banter his own hat, such that it spun across the foyer like a fashionable discus. Banter caught it one-handed.

"Jules," Arthur went on, "has come up with the notion that Leander might not be Harry's son, or the late Mrs. Waites might not be his mother, even if Harry is his papa. His lordship's mind has turned to opera dancers and love nests and vexing conundrums."

"All the best conundrums are vexing," Banter replied, tapping his hat onto his handsome head. He was lanky, dark-haired, likable, and more shrewd than he wanted people to know. "Waltham labors under the impression that we owe our loved ones discretion, though, so Harry's habits would have been unknown to His Grace. Perhaps

Harry confided in an old tutor or former amour? Upon whom would any soldier call when he's in London on winter leave?"

I gave Banter's excellent suggestion some thought. "Old school chums. Harry enjoyed his years at Oxford." I had come along after him, and his reputation had preceded me. I hadn't been nearly as frolicsome, to the disappointment of all and sundry. Given my memory problems, chronic inebriation had struck me as begging for trouble.

"Harry was senior wrangler in fornication and drunkenness," Arthur said. "Papa did not know whether to be proud or despairing. Mama threatened to go to the lawyers about Harry's funds, and Harry learned a little moderation."

This was news to me, but then, Arthur was not one to bear tales.

He shifted his walking stick from his right hand to left and struck a contrapposto stance before the mirror. His Grace of Waltham, the personification of dignity, was *preening*.

"Harry was great friends with the Dortmund brothers," Arthur said, switching his forward foot. "One of whom is yet extant, one of whom perished at Badajoz. He was also on famous good terms with Alexander Newton."

"Newton is in Town," Banter volunteered as Arthur tossed him his more serviceable walking stick. "Bides in Knightsbridge above the King's Helm, belongs to the Arthurian Club. Something of a scribbler these days. He wrote a comedy that was quite well received in the spring. Ready, Your Grace?"

"I have been dawdling about this foyer for the past quarter hour while *some people* dithered over their choice of cravat pin. Don't wait up for us, Jules."

I had no idea where they were off to. Supper at the club, perhaps, or strolling at Vauxhall. "I've asked the housekeeper to tidy up the nursery suite."

Arthur waved a gloved hand. "Of course, and you probably warned the stable that we'll be acquiring a pony. I trust you to have all in hand, Julian. *Adieu. Bonne nuit.* Banter, come along."

I vow the scent of roses followed them from the foyer, and yes, I was jealous. Of the abundant affection, of the sense of shared mischief, of absorption with another person so complete it precluded anything as mundane as fretting over a potential nephew—or over a brother grappling with the family's latest vexatious puzzle.

The sooner I got the pair of them off to the Low Countries, where the law had better things to do than invade a person's very bedroom, the better for all concerned.

~

Alexander Newton welcomed me into a modest pair of rooms above a venerable inn. He was two streets south of Hyde Park, meaning rents were manageable, the air less foul, and the neighborhood less fashionable. I applauded his choice, though it was likely born of necessity.

"The year without a Christmas," he said, verbally caressing the syllables as only a man with a native Scottish burr could. He sat back in a worn wing chair and crossed his bony knees. "Though, in fact, that was the year we all stayed in Town and socialized and gossiped like mad for the duration of Yuletide. I do recall Harry's visit. He looked so damned hale and hearty."

"Any detail might be helpful, though I'm particularly interested in his lordship's social activities. We have reason to believe Harry did not die without issue, but we have more questions on the matter than answers."

Newton's appearance was ascetic, pale, thin, languid, and I would have termed him effete, but for a pair of green eyes that conveyed keen intelligence. From prior acquaintance, I knew he had the writer's habit of viewing the whole world as so much material for his next magnum opus.

Reconnaissance officers had the same observant quality, though our imaginations went to tales of war rather than *belles lettres*.

As a playwright, Newton occupied Society's penumbral ranks. When his works were well received, he would be well received too. Not so when his efforts were less successful.

"I'd be surprised if Harry hadn't left you a few mementos," Newton said. "He was dedicated to his pleasures, though I understand he was an equally dedicated officer. My condolence on your loss."

Civil of him. "Thank you. If I might speak in confidence?"

"You may. A Scotsman learns to listen more than he talks when dwelling among the heathen English."

If Leander came to live at Waltham House, all of London—and half of Edinburgh and Dublin—would soon know of Harry's indiscretion. The overwhelming majority would think nothing of it. The Regent himself was said to have sired by-blows. Provided a fellow looked after his progeny, no judgment attached to him.

Judgment fastened like a set of shackles to the woman involved and to her family. The child was affected to a lesser extent, particularly if his father's family had means and standing, and acknowledged the illegitimate offspring.

"His Grace," I said, invoking Arthur's standing purposely, "received word that a Mrs. Martha Waites had expired in the home of a friend, leaving behind a child she claimed Harry had fathered. We have no documents, no witnesses to the relationship, no arrangements in Harry's will that support or refute the allegations."

"Martha Waites?" Newton rose and took down a bound volume that looked to be some sort of journal. "The name is familiar. Brings to mind..." He flipped to the middle and stared hard at the lines on the page. "*The Taming of the Shrew.* 'I see a woman be made a fool, if she hath not spirit to resist.'"

He sat with the book open in his lap. "Moreton did an adaptation of the original tale, set among polite society, a penniless belle, her military swain from Society's highest ranks... Martha found a job as a seamstress because she knew all the uniforms. She had a great eye for altering what was on hand to suit who was cast for a part. The poorer ladies can often work wonders with a needle from a young age."

His observation struck a discordant note. "Martha was from limited means?"

Newton set aside his book of plays. "She referred to herself as the parson's wayward daughter. She did not elope with Waites, but it wouldn't have made much difference if she had, because her dowry was so modest. He was to grow rich in India, but alas, he expired before making his fortune. She was cast on her wits when she returned to Town, though I think she had a sister or a cousin who helped her get back on her feet."

*Progress.* "How do you recall these details?"

He looked me up and down. "Martha would have made a fine tragic heroine, though nobody is writing many of those lately. The audiences want farce, satire, humor, song. Sheridan in as many guises as we can provide him. For our tragedies, we need only read the newspapers or look out the window. We can't afford bread, but fellows like me can obligingly turn the theaters into histrionic circuses for those too fashionable for Astley's. Martha was consumptive, and that never ends well."

Was Newton consumptive? I hadn't heard him cough, but many consumptives fared better in warmer weather.

"She was ill even then?"

"Brave with it, but what choice did she have?"

Would Harry have dallied with a consumptive seamstress? I was reminded of that five-pound expense and of the stupidity that sometimes passed for military gallantry. A man returning to war might have married a dying woman he felt sorry for, if that man believed his own days were numbered.

But the whole point of such an undertaking would have been to place Martha under the protection of the Caldicott family shield for whatever years remained to her, and that, Harry had not done.

"Did you ever see her with Harry?"

"I did, aye. They were friendly, but you know how Harry was. He could flirt with the best of them or pretend to politely discuss bonnets on the bridle paths with a woman he'd been swiving twelve hours earlier. The stage lost a talent when he bought his colors."

But had Leander lost his father, or had Martha, as Miss Dujardin had suggested, designated a plausible wellborn fellow for that honor, one now unable to refute her tale?

"Not a complete loss," I said. "Harry's work required him to play various roles in service to his country. He was good at it."

"Harry was spying? Naughty, naughty. I honestly can't tell you if he was naughty with Martha Waites. She didn't strike me as a game girl. Wayward only by the standards of a Puritan, and a woman can't help it if she's pretty, can she?"

I was more inclined of late to believe that women could not help it if men were arrogant, philandering boors.

"What did she look like?"

"Pretty, pale. Good teeth. Not much sugar served in a parsonage, I suppose. Beautiful hands. Hair shading auburn by candlelight, brownish otherwise. She knew her letters, had a bit of French, could manage well enough on the pianoforte. She hummed airs and hymns rather than drinking songs."

This man should have been a reconnaissance officer. "A lady fallen on hard times?"

"A parsonage is often the last stop before a family loses any pretensions to gentility. Yes, the vicar is a gentleman, but his means are notoriously limited, and his children are thus unlikely to make advantageous matches. They might not slide into ruin, but penury is near at hand from birth."

The cushion upon which I perched was thin, Newton hadn't offered me any refreshment, and yet, I was enjoying his company. He'd known Harry and not been taken in by Harry's charm, nor had he judged my brother for his foibles.

"What of the sister or cousin?" I asked. "Was she on the verge of penury?"

"She had a decent roof over her head, I know that, and she was gainfully employed. She'd also been raised by a parson. Martha stayed with her from time to time between productions, took meals with her sometimes. Nobody likes to rely on charity, but family is supposed to look after family."

He'd laced the last observation with a hint of a warning.

"The boy will be cared for, Newton. Whether he's Harry's progeny, Martha's indiscretion, or just some lad cast upon the world's kindness at too young an age, Waltham and I will ensure he's well fed, clothed, housed, and educated."

Newton rose to return his book to the shelf. "Even if Martha were gracing Haymarket street corners, the child is blameless. Perhaps especially if she was on the stroll, the lad's blameless. It's not my place to judge, but for the sake of Harry's memory, I hope you do right by the child."

I stood, having been given much information to consider. "You will immortalize me in a play as the arrogant lordling if I don't see to the lad?"

"I'll do as half of London has done and cast you as a traitor." Not a hint of humor laced his words. "Though, as to that, Harry always said you were too honorable for your own good. If anybody was likely to sell his soul to the devil, I'd put my money on Harry, and his lordship would get the better of the bargain too."

Was that a compliment, an insult, a test?

"I'm safe from your pen, then." I retrieved my hat from the hook on the back of the door. "You said audiences want humor, farce, and comedy, and a man betraying his honor would never be anything but tragic."

He smiled, his green eyes dancing. "Suppose it would. Good point."

I was headed back to Tatts, but I put one last question to mine host. "I don't suppose you know the name of Martha Waites's sister or cousin? The one with the roof over her head and a decent post?"

Newton stared into the middle distance. A sparrow lit on the windowsill, as if waiting for his answer. He waved a hand, and the bird flew off.

"Little shite comes around beggin'. He's early today. He does that when rain's on the way."

"You feed him." Prisoners in Newgate had the same habit. A man with crumbs to give away was still, in some regard, human.

"The cousin was Mel," Newton said. "Maybe Melisande, Melanie, Melody. Mel is the best I can do, no last name, but she wouldn't have been Waites, would she?"

A first name was something. "And Martha's home parish?"

"No idea. She hadn't an accent to speak of, more evidence of a decent upbringing. She wasn't a village girl."

The sparrow came back and commenced strutting about on the windowsill. I was keeping the local dignitary from his nooning, apparently. One of the local dignitaries.

"My thanks. I don't suppose you have another play in the works?"

"I always have a play in the works. Don't worry. Just another comedy. The last one earned some blunt, so it'll be smiles and laughter all around this autumn when the great and the good are done murdering me uncle's grouse."

He was putting on the plaid for me, and I appreciated the performance. "You've been a considerable help. Best of luck with the play."

I left him swearing affectionately at the bird, who was perched on an ink-stained finger and looking hungry and hopeful.

# CHAPTER FIVE

Despite having held an officer's rank, I had seldom ordered other people about while in the military. I'd roamed the countryside on reconnaissance or been given staff work. In battle, I'd been sent where I was needed.

I thus had little experience with keeping subordinates occupied. My domestic staff was experienced enough to execute their duties without my hovering, and my men of business knew better than to bother me over details.

Arthur had tasked me with taking charge of Leander's situation. Not only was I to learn the truth of the boy's provenance, but also to see the child comfortably settled into a new life. The particulars of that challenge eluded me, and when baffled by life or my fellow humans, I knew of only one sure tonic, that being the company of horses.

"We're off to Tatts?" my tiger asked. Atticus's age was difficult to determine. He might be as young as nine, possibly as venerable as twelve, though he had an innocent faith in life that argued for lesser years.

"Pony shopping. Not the most agreeable task, but preferable to a moment to consider what you're requesting. Nobody respects a ham-fisted coachy. Surely you've picked up that much?"

Atticus had probably sorted out *gee, haw, whoa back,* and *steady on,* but theory and practice could be miles apart.

"Not used to sitting up here," he said as I guided Beecham into the flow of traffic on the street. "Don't know as I like it."

He did, however, take to driving Beecham with an instinctive knack, both for respecting the beast's common sense and for maneuvering the vehicle smoothly. Turns could be challenging, but Atticus apparently had the sort of mind that grasped spatial questions easily.

He was no sort of rider yet, which was why I'd brought him along to try out the ponies. Bouncing about on their backs, reins held wide, no style at all... He was the perfect test of a creature's patience and kindness. I chose a pair who'd be largish for Leander, but then, the boy would be on a lead line for some time.

An hour into the exercise, Atticus was already becoming at home in the saddle, which had also been one of the outing's objectives.

I dealt with payment while Atticus scratched hairy ears and stroked muscular necks. I needed to find a calling for the lad, and the stable might serve. On the return journey, I allowed Atticus to manage the whole route, including the turn into the last alley.

He brought the curricle to a stop precisely by the mounting block.

"Well done," I said, climbing down. "In future, I will alight at the front door, and you will drive the curricle around to the mews." I conferred with the groom, alerting him to the impending arrival of the two ponies. I further suggested the ponies not be allowed to share a stall, lest they become soured on the company of any other equines.

Atticus was listening, of course. He had a fine talent for eavesdropping.

"Jameson, were you on hand five or six years ago?" I asked.

"Aye, milord. Been on the duke's staff since I come up from Sussex ten year ago. Me uncle serves at the Hall."

The smile was the same, though the uncle was a good thirty years older. "One suspected a relationship. Were you assigned Town duty the year without a Christmas?"

"That I were. His Grace said we was to have the Christmas pudding and the goose and the whole bit, but it weren't the same as being with everybody down home. Haring all about Town in the mud and sleet... I didn't care for it a'tall. We none of us did, and I daresay the duke dint neither."

"Lord Harry came home on winter leave that year."

"Aye, and we was all that glad to see him. He didn't bide with the duke, but we saw plenty of 'im."

"Lord Harry resided on Dingle Court. I don't suppose you recall who was assigned to his mews?"

Jameson took off his cap, scratched the back of his neck, and gazed down the leafy tunnel of the shaded alley.

"We took turns. Old Belcher slept over the stable, and he did the muckin' and waterin' and such, but if his lordship wanted a coachy, and the duke's man were busy, we took turns. Belcher's been gone two year or more."

Not what I'd wanted to hear. "What of the household staff? Are you in touch with any of them?"

Another squint and a scratch. "Lord Harry's cook were a fine figger of a woman. Coulda tossed me like a caber, though she wasn't stout. She were that formidable. She's on staff with the Duchess of..."

I waited while Jameson did his own version of paging through Debrett's.

"Lives over on the street with all the hydrangeas, drives matched grays, dotes on a mastiff the size of a ellie-phant."

"Her Grace of Ambrose?"

"Aye, that's the one. Her Grace loaned the cook to Lord Harry because Cook wanted to bide in Town over the winter, and the duchess wanted to spend the holidays in the country."

Progress, yet again. While I'd not been puzzling over Leander's situation for long, the matter had admitted of more questions than answers. A short chat with Helvetica Siegurdson might reverse that trend.

"You've been very helpful, Jameson. If you recall anything else about that winter, about Lord Harry's comings and goings, who called upon him, or who might have caught his appreciative masculine eye, please do let me know."

Jameson put his cap back on. "Beggin' milord's pardon, but the half of London wearin' petticoats generally had Lord Harry's eye, and maybe a few other parts of 'im too."

"He was a flirt, but my interests lie with the ladies who inspired him to more than flirt."

"I'll give it a think." Jameson touched a finger to his cap and sauntered off. He'd likely give it a think over a pint down at the corner pub, get the other lads to thinking, and who knew what intelligence their recollections might yield?

Beecham had been unhitched from the curricle, and Atticus held his reins while two grooms backed the curricle by hand into a carriage bay.

"You're doing up the nursery," Atticus said. "Chambermaids is all aflutter. Say only married fellows need nurseries."

Atticus was keenly attuned to anything that might topple him from his post. Were I to marry, a wife might take him into dislike or find fault with his manners. The duke, jaunting off to the Continent, was clearly not of a mind to take a bride.

"You heard me asking Jameson about Lord Harry's winter leave."

"I did."

"Lord Harry might have left a son behind. The boy needs a home."

A groom came to take Beecham into the stable, to remove the harness and give the horse an entirely unnecessary brushing down.

"If I was grandson to a duke," Atticus said, "wouldn't be no maybes about it. My ma would make sure of that, and a lordship would do right by me, or she'd know the reason why."

"You're saying Lord Harry would have married any woman he

got with child?" What an exalted view Atticus had of aristocratic honor.

"Not marry. Don't work like that 'zactly, but he'd have provided. But then, maybe Lord Harry's lady didn't know she had a problem until himself was halfway back to Spain. Babies take forever to get born, and there was a war on. You're bringing the lad home?"

"In less than a fortnight."

"Well, he's not allowed to be your tiger, guv. That post's taken."

A groom from Tatts appeared at the end of the alley, leading two shaggy little equines.

"Those ponies are your responsibility, Lord Tiger," I said. "Jameson will show you how to go on with them if you have questions, but for starts, get them bedded and settled, see they have hay and water, and give them a decent grooming."

"Both of 'em?"

"Ponies don't groom themselves."

Atticus positively swaggered up to the fellow from Tatts. "I'll take 'em from here."

The groom handed over lead ropes, caught the coin I tossed him, and winked. The ponies might not be in the most educated hands ever to wield a curry comb, but they would want for nothing.

I, on the other hand, had been presented with yet another question that wanted for an answer. Atticus was correct that Leander's mother might not have realized she was with child until Harry had left Town, but that possibility made it all the more puzzling that she'd not come to Arthur or the old duke for support.

Vexatious conundrums on every hand.

~

I had made it halfway across the garden when a banshee standing perhaps five feet and two inches in heeled slippers shrieked at me from the alley.

"You ain't gettin' me son, be ye milord or mister. Leander is my boy, and the likes of you isn't to have 'im." She stormed through the gate and clattered up the walkway. "You 'ear me? Doesn't nobody ignore Clothilda 'ammerschmidt or they'll be sorry they tried."

Miss Hammerschmidt had troubled over her appearance. Her paint was subdued and applied with a skillful hand. Her heeled slippers might be two sizes too large, but they matched and were reasonably clean. Her clothing fit her, and while not in the first stare—or the second or third—her attire was clean and modest.

Her hat, however... Clearly, that article had been fashioned by Miss Hammerschmidt to attract notice. Three birds—a robin, a cardinal, and a miniature facsimile of a dove—nested among silk foliage and a profusion of roses. Ribbons of green, pink, and white trailed down to curl about Miss Hammerschmidt's ample bosom, and a green, pink, and white beaded reticule in the shape of a duck completed the ensemble.

"Miss, you have the advantage of me." I kept my tone merely curious, lest Miss Hammerschmidt's pique give more volume to her declarations. Town was less crowded during summer, but by no means deserted.

"Your bruvver done took advantage of me more like. Now you want to snatch me boy, and I'm not 'avin' it."

I put her age at about five-and-twenty, hardly venerable, but no longer of tender years. Nor did I make the mistake of concluding that a lack of Oxford diction meant a lack of brains.

"Shall we sit?" I gestured to the grouping situated in the shade of the terrace. "And perhaps you won't mind if I ring for some lemonade? The heat works up a thirst."

She settled herself with regal dignity on a cushion, reticule perched in her lap. "Suit yerself."

I retreated to the house, found a footman, asked for a tray, and requested that he take up a post on the terrace near the door.

"Now, then," I said, returning to my guest. "Might I sit?"

She looked puzzled, then waved a hand.

"You claim to be Leander's mother?"

"I don't claim to be 'is mum, I *am* his mum. Lord Harry fancied me when he were home on leave. Nature took its course, and now you want my boy."

I asked the only relevant question. "Can you prove Leander is your son?"

"He's got red hair."

Miss Hammerschmidt was acquiring aitches, now that she'd been civilly received. "So did every fifth infantryman recruited from Scotland. That proves nothing." Miss Hammerschmidt's own tresses—gathered in ringlets and cascading over her right shoulder—appeared to have benefited from a liberal application of henna.

"Ask anybody," she retorted. "Lord Harry were keepin' company wiv me the whole of his leave. Took a fancy to me, like I said."

"His lordship took many fancies in his day. Did you sign a contract with him?"

"Be ye daft? I was dancing for me supper. He seen me ankles, and that were that."

"What about baptismal lines for the boy? Did you keep them?"

"I give Leander to the wet nurse, and she saw to the baptizing. I sold the baubles Lord Harry give me to pay for that. I had to get back to work, didn't I?"

The tray arrived, which was fortunate, because Miss Dujardin's theory—that Martha Waites had been fostering Leander—had just acquired a few supporting possibilities. Not facts, but not complete fancies either.

I offered my guest a tall glass of cool libation garnished with sprigs of lavender. Miss Hammerschmidt watched me set the lavender on a saucer before she did the same with her own. I offered her the sandwiches—she took one—and I took two, while her gaze went longingly to the plate of biscuits and orange slices.

"Are you telling me," I asked, "that between Harry's gifts of appreciation and your own enterprise, you've been supporting the boy since birth?"

"I took up me needle and make decent money at it. I know the

"Please do finish the biscuits. The footmen will just gobble them up otherwise."

She took the last two.

"If Leander is Harry's son, and you are Leander's mother, what objection do you have to Harry's family looking after the boy?"

"No objection a'tall, but if you're so all-fired determined to finally take a hand in the lad's upbringing, then it'll cost ya. The sweeps will pay good money for a healthy little boy. I might have nothin' to prove he's mine, but you got nothin' to prove he's yours. I have friends in the penny press, and I got friends—*good* friends—in polite society."

She let the threat of scandal hang in the humid air while she polished off the last biscuit. The problem was not that Harry had had a by-blow, but that Harry and his family had made no provision for the boy for *five years.*

Though her threat was flawed: Where had this outrage on Leander's neglected behalf been as Martha Waites had been dying of consumption? Where had it been when Harry had been lauded as a fallen war hero? Miss Dujardin's version of events certainly varied from Miss Hammerschmidt's, but then, Miss Dujardin had been late to the party, arriving only after Leander had been weaned.

As for Miss Hammerschmidt... If her protectors in polite society were fellows of such impeccable lineages and fond devotion, why were her shoes two sizes too large?

I set those questions aside and considered what else I knew of Harry's circumstances. Harry might well have disported with both Martha and Clothilda, and though Clothilda had borne the child, Martha might have somehow got wind of Harry's arrangements to support the boy.

Martha might perhaps have assured Harry that she—parson's daughter, lady fallen upon hard times, respectable-ish widow—would see the money used for the child rather than for Clothilda's bonnets. Clothilda, relieved to be free of Leander, might have handed over the boy along with the occasional coin, and...

That was all just a little too farfetched to merit much consideration, particularly given that Clothilda had had several years to come forward on Leander's behalf. Arthur was frequently in Town on parliamentary business, and while His Grace was formidable, Clothilda, in her way, was equally impressive.

"You understand that before I can make any offers, I must confer with the duke?"

Her shoulders relaxed, her chin came up. "That one. He weren't the duke when Harry was on leave, but Harry didn't have much time for him. Said the heir has one job, and his older brother wasn't seeing to it. Harry never wanted to be the duke. He did the pretty, but he liked his freedom."

The implication being that Harry had preferred the joy to be found in Clothilda's arms to all the wealth and privilege in the world.

And that was likely true—also irrelevant. "You are correct that we have no record of Leander's birth or baptism, but was the child given a baptismal name?"

She set the table napkin beside her cup and saucer. "A middle name? Harry, o' course. You nobs like that, putting the same name on every generation. It's a wonder you ain't all called Moses and Adam. I figured a wee lad ought to have some reminder of his old pa, and Harry's a fine name."

"And the name of the wet nurse?"

The briefest of hesitations, then Miss Hammerschmidt popped to her feet. "Mary Smith. She left Town when Leander were two. I have no idea where she got off to. Probably back to Ireland."

I rose, intent on escorting my guest to the door, so to speak. "And where can I find you, Miss Hammerschmidt, should we need to chat again?"

She scrutinized me, and a seamstress could deliver a minute visual inspection. She either concluded I was sincere in my inquiry, or she decided I wasn't worth flirting with.

"Drury Lane. You lot go to the country and the seaside in summer. We're in rehearsals, painting sets, sewing eighteen hours at a stretch, and sweating like plow horses. Costumes don't make themselves."

"You'll be hearing from me shortly."

"You got one week, and then I'm makin' some noise. Depend upon it."

I walked with her to the gate. "Tell me, how did you learn that I was inquiring into Leander's circumstances?" Newton might have sent word to her, but that would have been fast work, even for London theater gossip. Then too, she'd nimbly dodged this question when I put it to her earlier.

"Martha said I could have her dresses, and I told her the same. When you ply the needle for your living, you won't never be rich, but you'll dress better than some. The house is dark today, so I dropped by that la-di-da widow's place to get what's mine, but the dresses has already been given to charity."

"Sold on Rosemary Lane?"

"Bet your fancy boots they was. That Danforth woman got no respect for the dead, and them dresses brought a pretty penny too. Housekeeper told me you'd been coming to call, asking questions about the boy."

I bowed Miss Hammerschmidt on her way, assured her that she would hear more from me within the week, and watched her clatter down the alley's cobbles.

Atticus did likewise from the stable door.

"Follow her," I said. "Discreetly."

Atticus winked, tossed me the curry comb, and sauntered along in Miss Hammerschmidt's wake.

With Arthur and his *dear friend* getting ready to decamp on extended travel, I could not countenance scandal for the convenience of a scheming seamstress. She'd spun a fine yarn, one that was likely half true.

But she'd also lied. The boy knew his name, while Clothilda Hammerschmidt, his putative devoted mother, clearly did not.

# CHAPTER SIX

I'd planned to call upon Helvetica Siegurdson before Miss Hammerschmidt had so enlivened—and further complicated—my afternoon. The delay meant I risked interrupting dinner preparations, though a chat with Her Grace of Ambrose might prove every bit as illuminating as any conversation I'd manage belowstairs.

Heat took a greater toll on horses than humans, so I strolled the few streets to Her Grace's residence. The day had reached the stultifying depths of misery, when the air held dead still and warmth oppressed the spirit like a guilty conscience.

Rain on the way, which might provide temporary relief from the dust, but would make the plague of insects and humidity worse.

Her Grace received me in her garden, an enormous mastiff panting at her feet. The breed had become fashionable in the last century, the preferred canine ornament for young men. Dowagers like Her Grace of Ambrose were supposed to favor lapdogs.

"Have a seat, my boy," she said, rising and offering me her cheek. "What is Waltham thinking, dragging you up to Town at this time of year? Though, I must say, you do look a bit more the thing."

My mother knew everybody. Her Grace knew everybody.

Duchesses of a feather might not flock together, but they were cordial allies against society's foolishness and ill-bred behavior. The patronesses at Almack's were one sort of social institution, while dowagers of the peerage served another, less frivolous role.

"I wasn't sure you'd receive me." I took my seat, wondering where in the hell that admission had come from.

"Don't be a clodpate. I knew you when you went scampering around Caldicott Hall, wearing only a nappy that drooped to your chubby knees. How is your mother?"

What a mortifying—and comforting—image. Her Grace served hot, strong tea, lest the summer weather get airs above its station. I offered my recitation as my hostess poured out.

Mama and my sisters were thriving, Mama having retired to the seaside for the nonce. Waltham was preparing for extended travel with all the glee of a former schoolboy readying for his first term at the university bacchanal.

Her Grace listened, exuding that blend of materteral goodwill and cordial dignity that had always characterized her. Her looks had not changed in all the years I'd known her, but for more blond threaded through darker locks.

"While I am pleased to have the report," she said when I'd duly answered the predictable questions, "you called on me out of more than gentlemanly duty. Waltham will be fine, by the way. Banter is the sensible sort, and they aren't striplings kicking their heels away from Headmaster's watchful eye. They will actually see some art and architecture when they aren't sleeping until noon and enjoying foreign vintages."

I sipped my tea, an excellent blend. "Am I that obvious?"

"Perhaps not to yourself. You've been home less than a year, and off His Grace goes, possibly for more than a year. You had a terrible war, not that one can have a good war, and at your age, the body often recovers more quickly than the mind. I notice you are still wearing those blue spectacles."

She'd seen me coming up the walkway, then, because I'd pocketed my tinted eyeglasses as soon as the butler had shown me to the back terrace.

"My eyes object to strong sunlight. Other than that..."

She skewered me with a glance over her tea cup. "Other than that, you are merely skinny rather than emaciated. Your hair is paler than a Viking's tresses when you used to sport chestnut locks. You probably jump at loud noises and dread thunder, but you are no longer subsisting on tea, brandy, and toast. You've given up any notion of returning to the man you were, not that Society would ever allow you to. And yet, the idea of managing the dukedom in Waltham's absence daunts you, as well it should."

Maybe I had come for this parade inspection of my most private concerns rather than any chat with the cook. "Society trying to tell me who I am annoys me the most. I served loyally and well. I lost a brother. I took so many risks, on my own, behind enemy lines, and never once..."

I fell silent, surprised and not a little impressed by the wrath and hurt in my words.

"Good," the duchess said, patting my hand. "Be angry and sin not. Society can be a devil. A lot of waltzing ninnyhammers pretending to consequence that exists only in their own minds. You owe them nothing, Julian, though if you don't have at least a biscuit, I will have to refrain myself, and these are quite good. Cook has the lightest hand with the butter."

I took a biscuit, the better to recover from Her Grace's broadside. Why was it my battles these days were fought over tea trays on terraces?

Though Her Grace was not my enemy. Far from it. "I've come to speak to your cook, actually."

The duchess took a sweet as well. Cinnamon with a hint of other warm spices that put me in mind of Spain and Portugal, and Leander's odd preference for nutmeg on his chocolate.

"Do tell," she said, "and spare no detail."

I explained, about a boy who might be the next duke, or who

might be an ambitious seamstress's scheme to perpetually annoy funds out of the present titleholder.

"And you are wondering about Lady Clarissa, too, I'll warrant. One does. She and Harry seemed devoted, but then, appearances are deceptive, and Harry was half chameleon."

I'd have put him closer to three-quarters, a rare asset in time of war. "The boy's paternity does not appear to be in doubt. Mrs. Danforth, the late Mrs. Waites, the present Miss Dujardin, Lady Clarissa, and even this Miss Hammerschmidt are all happy to accept that Harry left a son behind, but the matter is either of no importance to them, or they benefit from the boy having a ducal connection."

"So you seek to discuss Harry's months of leave with Siegurdson, a neutral observer. She will likely tell you exactly how much salt he preferred on his eggs, but little beyond that. The kitchen is a passion with her, not merely a place to earn a wage. What does Miss West make of this matter?"

"Miss West?"

Her Grace smiled like a cat greeting the unsuspecting resident of a mousehole. "You rode out with her, Julian. You were nearly engaged to her. At the Makepeace house party, you were observed to be quite cordial with dear Hyperia. She and Lady Ophelia came up to Town for Lord Reardon's art exhibition with you and Waltham. I've commissioned a portrait from Reardon, by the way, and I do not expect the young genius to work in silence."

Before the paint had dried, Her Grace would know at what age Reardon had cut his first tooth, if any young lady had caught his fancy, and a good deal of the territory in between.

"Miss West," I said, "is concerned that a little boy has lost both his father and the woman presenting herself as his mother. She cautions me to focus on that fact when matters of coin and social repercussions threaten to distract me."

Her Grace motioned with her hand, and a footman appeared as if from thin air. The dog, who'd been panting, chin on paws, for the duration of the discussion, looked up.

"William, you will please ask Cook to present herself in the library," Her Grace said. "She will be appalled to have supper preparations interrupted, offended to be expected abovestairs with no notice, and fretting over some sauce on the boil. Tell her a guest would like to compliment her on her biscuits. We won't keep her long."

The footman—a strapping Adonis in summer livery—bowed. He apparently knew better than to wink or offer a cheeky riposte when I was on hand, but I had no doubt Her Grace enjoyed the sincere affection of her staff.

Did I enjoy that same affection? Arthur did, though they were mindful of his station and his insistence on a degree of privacy, but their loyalty was to him, not simply to his coin.

"You would do well to heed Miss West's advice," Her Grace said when William had departed on his errand. "Consider how badly a small boy needs to know the truth about who his antecedents are and what fates they met."

That was, if not a warning shot, something close to it. I did not know my father's identity, and my mother hadn't seen fit to tell me—if she knew. Lady Emily Cowper was said to dwell under a cloud of uncertainty similar to my own, and the mystery merely added to her cachet.

"A child can adjust to what can't be changed," I said, feeling a bit resentful. What sort of ally made allowances for my horrible war, but threw my dubious paternity in my face?

"Dear boy, you know not what became of your brother. You have some notion, some suspicions, and a few theories, but Harry disappeared like a thief in the night, as I hear it, and you have no idea why he went so willingly to his death. Leander is just a lad, and all he knows is that his parents are gone. He won't make sense of that either easily or quickly."

Another salvo, and I could not exactly return fire.

She rose. "Come along, pup."

For an instant, I thought she was addressing me, but the mastiff

tell me about Lord Harry's leave that year. A small boy has been presented to me as Harry's son, conceived while his lordship was in London, but details are few and contradictory about both of his parents."

She considered the portrait holding pride of place above the empty hearth. A mastiff very like Her Grace's current pet sat at the late Duke of Ambrose's booted feet, man and dog both exuding a sort of dignified pugnacity.

"I learned to cook good English beef that winter," Miss Siegurdson said. "Really cook it—sauces, presentation, wines... A roast is no great feat, but I had to range well past that. Lord Harry said if he never ate another rabbit, partridge, or goat, he'd die happy."

I doubt Harry had died happy, and diet hadn't figured in the matter. "He wanted beef?"

"Beef, beef, and more beef. I know the officer's messes were supposed to feature regular servings of beef, and Wellington would not allow foraging, so his lordship's choice intrigued me."

Wellington had not allowed *pillaging*, and yet, particularly after broken sieges, pillaging and worse had occurred to the resounding disgrace of the whole military.

"Lord Harry's duties often took him out of camp," I said, which Miss Siegurdson had apparently deduced from his menu preferences. "What else can you recall?"

"He was out a lot while on leave too. London was very social that winter, thanks to the Regency Bill. I thought his lordship would go home to Sussex for Christmas—what soldier doesn't want to be home for Christmas?—but his older brother remained in Town, and so Lord Harry bided here as well."

Her question, about a soldier being within a day's journey of home and not even peeking in at his birthplace, struck me as her most perceptive observation thus far.

Which was saying something. "Did his lordship favor any particular company?"

Miss Siegurdson looked around the library, a room she likely hadn't been in but once or twice before.

"Lord Harry had me send some stollen to Lady Clarissa Valmond on two occasions. Said she liked it, and he owed her an apology over some social misstep. He went to the opera from time to time, though I gather that was more of an excuse to sit with his fellow officers and drink. He went to services about every other week. On Boxing Day, he made the rounds of those also on leave. He met with his solicitors and complained about them loudly."

All of this sounded like vintage Harry. "He sat in your kitchen and aired his woes?" Had he sat on her bed and aired his woes?

The first hint of a smile drifted from Miss Siegurdson's eyes to her lips, and ye gods... beauty and benevolence beaming from one female countenance. Five years ago, she would have been barely an adult, by polite society's standards, and in her kitchen, Harry would have found warmth, good food, sympathy, hot tea on frigid afternoons...

"He aired his woes in my kitchen, in the library, in the mews. But the grousing was supposed to be good-natured. Mrs. Bleeker saw that at once. His lordship was setting us at our ease, pretending he was chafing to get back to Spain, pretending he was making merry for want of more interesting pastimes in uniform."

"Mrs. Bleeker was...?" I should know. I'd come across the name previously, but no bells were ringing.

"The housekeeper. Very conscientious and capable." High praise, from Helvetica Siegurdson. "His lordship hacked out with his friends, played cards, did the Christmas open houses, but Mrs. Bleeker said what he truly wanted was slippers warmed by the hearth, good brandy for a nightcap, the fires kept going in his bedroom. He wanted peace, quiet, and creature comforts. She made sure he had them in abundance, and I made sure he had beef three times a day, if that was his wish."

I could not ask, *Did he have you as well?* But I saw a possible resemblance to Leander about the eyes.

"Did any particular ladies provide him the kind of creature comfort officers on leave are notorious for craving?"

She dropped her figurative portcullis, raised the drawbridge, and shuttered the castle windows. "Do not be impertinent, my lord. I am a cook, and a good one. I remain belowstairs because I like it there."

She'd rapped my knuckles with her figurative wooden spoon, hard enough to bruise.

"I am not questioning your morals, Miss Siegurdson. If Harry had a son, that son has—or had—a mother. One of the candidates for that honor recently expired of consumption and would have been somewhat ill when Harry was on leave. I cannot see him... Well, suffice it to say, her claim is unsubstantiated."

Miss Siegurdson was at least listening to me.

"Another candidate," I went on, "had five years to thrust a hand into the ducal coffers on behalf of her son and is only coming forward now, thus rendering her claim suspect as well. Lady Clarissa is a possibility, albeit a remote one, and she would never admit to having had a child out of wedlock, any more than she'd hide being the mother of the legitimate ducal heir. Need I go on?"

"Isn't three possibilities enough?"

"No, unless one of the three is truly the boy's mother. If Harry kept a *chère amie* here in Town, I've yet to discover her particulars. I'm hoping that you, a footman, the coachy, somebody will recall Harry's movements closely enough to shed light on the matter."

Then too, I planned to spend the evening communing again with Harry's account book, and I had yet to pay a call on the clerks at Doctors' Commons.

"I'm sorry I cannot be of more assistance, my lord. Your brother was an unhappy fellow. The footmen might recall more than I do, but only Charlie Cummings is still in service, and he's gone to the country with his employers."

"How do you know that?"

"Because I ran into him at market last month, and he was buying provisions for the travel hampers. Off to Derbyshire, I believe."

She could probably tell me what he'd purchased, in what quantity, and how much he'd paid for the food, but nothing of my brother's intimate companions over the relevant winter. I hadn't held out much hope to the contrary, but apparently I'd held out some.

"Then thank you for your time, Miss Siegurdson, and if you recall anything else that might be remotely pertinent, please send for me at Waltham House. We are prepared to deal very generously with both the boy and his mother."

She curtseyed and headed for the door.

"One other question," I said.

She turned slowly. From a less self-possessed woman, I would have called her posture wary.

"What of the housekeeper? Mrs. Bleeker. Where might I find her?"

"She took a new post when Town grew more crowded in spring and Lord Harry returned to Spain. I don't believe she was engaged as a housekeeper. Perhaps as a lady's companion in a lesser household. I haven't seen her in years."

Another curtsey, and then I was left alone in the library with the disapproving duke and his disapproving dog. I followed Miss Siegurdson from the room just as a rumble of thunder sounded in the distance.

The reverberations, so like cannon fire, no longer entirely unnerved me. I made a forced march back to Waltham House nonetheless, and dashed through the door just as the first fat drops of rain speckled the dusty flagstones.

# CHAPTER SEVEN

Harry's account book was like the Spanish countryside, hiding salient facts amid miles of seemingly monotonous terrain. A region might be mostly given over to sheep farming, but one fellow's riding horse was in a better trim than anybody else's.

Was he the local informant, and if so, to how many sides of the conflict did he peddle his wares? Was he prospering because his information was reliable, or were all his lies about to catch up with him? Or perhaps he'd simply happened onto a thrifty equine specimen who kept well in sparse pasture.

Had a barn recently burned to the ground because of an unlucky lightning strike, or had the owner run afoul of Bonapartists, Spanish monarchists, or guerrillas loyal only to their brethren and their bellies? Who had been warning whom with the conflagration, and what had been lost in the blaze?

For years, I'd spent most of my waking hours on such puzzles, and now, as evening rain pattered gently on the garden beyond Waltham's library, I pondered Harry's expenditures. His most vexing entry—£5 DC—had not been repeated, which might mean he'd paid a gambling debt, donated to a *debtors'* charity, or made a discreet loan to a friend.

Harry had been the sort to do all three.

A soft rap on the library door was followed by the butler's appearance. "A caller, my lord. Miss Hyperia—"

Hyperia tacked around him as nimbly as a naval cutter heading for home port. "I realize this is a ducal household, Cheadle, but you've known me since I was in leading strings. We won't need a tray, and I won't be staying long."

Cheadle sent me the look of a man trying to singlehandedly uphold the dignity of an august household and having a provoking time of it.

"I haven't enjoyed supper yet, as it happens," I said. "Two trays, Cheadle, if that won't instigate a rebellion in the kitchen."

"No trouble a'tall, my lord." He withdrew, sparing Hyperia a glance of veiled exasperation.

"The heat wears on Cheadle," I said. "Excuse his testiness."

Hyperia peered at the ledger on the desk. "Cheadle is wroth with me because I'm calling at such an hour and without a chaperone. I didn't want to bother recruiting Lady Ophelia for guard duty, my companion has been overtaxed by the heat, and what I have to say didn't lend itself to a note."

"Propriety's loss is my gain." To vastly understate the matter.

She looked more closely at Harry's journal, but I hoped the genuine compliment pleased her. Her presence certainly pleased me.

"This is Harry's handwriting."

"You see before you his account book from the year without a Christmas. He paid his tithe to Bond Street and the other shops, tended to the household wages, stocked a generous larder and cellar, and otherwise kept the books, but I don't see any indication he was keeping regular company with a specific woman."

"And thus, not with Martha Waites?"

"No sign of her at all."

Hyperia turned a page. "What of the payments to Clarissa? She

'conniving' has likely been applied to them. Do small boys like raspberry fool?"

Hyperia rose and returned to the desk. "In the general case, yes. Just as large boys do." She resumed her seat and pulled Harry's ledger closer. "He had such a tidy hand. Your writing has more personality. Your J's would rule the world if you weren't such a gentleman."

That was precisely the sort of odd, insightful remark I could expect of only Perry. I abandoned the table and took a seat before the desk.

"I looked for patterns, for any disbursement that might have been to a lady in anticipation of an interesting event, particularly as Harry prepared to sail back to Spain. Now that you point out a lack of remuneration to Clarissa, I'm wondering if he truly purchased three sets of uniforms and so forth, or if two sufficed, and the rest of the money was only disguised as tailor's expenses."

"And by the way he crossed a t, or capitalized a word, Harry would have left himself a coded record very different from the one we think we're seeing?"

"That would have been like him. Harry was inclined to complicate life and then enjoy grumbling about the challenge of coping with the tangles."

She ran her finger down a column of figures, while I appreciated the garnet highlights in her hair and the silky curve of her cheek. My thoughts were not exactly sexual, but they were sensual. Perry was lovely, as a work of art was lovely and as a loyal, courageous, kind human heart was lovely.

Part of me was missing her—missing a future with her—even as she sat four feet away, scowling at an old account book. Bedamned to Ormstead and his polite social calls.

"Harry was a generous employer," she said, turning a page. "Very generous."

"I suppose temporary duty should pay more, especially when nobody wanted to be in Town that winter."

She looked up. "Everybody wanted to be in Town that winter. The merchants were delighted, the hostesses, the coalmen ... You were smart to stay out of it."

*Did you miss me?* "I had work to do elsewhere. I'm hosting Leander and Miss Dujardin for lunch tomorrow. Part of me would rather be back in the Sierra de Gredos, setting snares for rabbits, instead of sifting through my brother's past."

"So you were hiding in Spain?"

"I bided where I was useful."

She studied me, candlelight finding every pretty plane and hollow of her face. The ceromancy branch of the divination arts dealt with studying candles—their flames, the patterns of the wax, the behavior of the smoke—but I could read little in Hyperia's expression.

"Were you hiding from me, Jules?"

"From French patrols, Spanish rebels, local Bonapartists, the elements. Harry sometimes. My own commanding officers if they were bent on sending me back out on a cork-brained assignment. Not from you. Never that."

"Good." She went back to her scowling perusal.

"Will you join us for lunch tomorrow?"

"Yes. Remind me to take up keeping house for officers on leave. Harry paid this Bleeker woman a small fortune."

"Miss Siegurdson was complimentary toward her, said she tended to everything from stocking the decanters to keeping Harry's bedroom fires..."

"Yes?"

*Saint George and all his dragons.* "His bedroom fires *lit*."

"That's a footman's job, Jules. At the direction of the butler."

I mentally reviewed my discussion with Miss Happy Belowstairs Siegurdson. "Harry hired no butler."

"Why not? The holidays are a social time, and most male staff prefer to answer to a male superior."

"More significantly, any footman would have enjoyed even a

brevet promotion to the butler's job." The ducal household, between Sussex and Town, employed at least two dozen footmen. They often eyed the underbutler's and butler's posts covetously, assisted with polishing the silver, vied for turns escorting guests...

Why no butler? Why the lavish wages to Mrs. Bleeker? "Damnation. I don't suppose you've come across a Mrs. Bleeker in your London travels?"

"I can ask at the employment agencies. You believe her to be another of Leander's possible mothers?"

"Mrs. Bleeker's wages were suspiciously generous, she warmed Harry's slippers by the hearth, served him the occasional nightcap, and kept his bedroom toasty *at all hours*. She was either the most attentive housekeeper in the history of the post, or she was warming Harry's sheets with her very person."

"She might have simply hoped for a promotion to the ducal ranks when Harry decamped. Harry was one to allow himself to be cosseted."

Oh right, or she might have been smitten with Harry—so many had been—and making overtures to which he was unreceptive, because he was already swiving half of London. And yet, the details of Mrs. Bleeker's situation promoted her to the ranks of women who merited closer scrutiny.

"She had intimate access to him, she was on hand at the relevant time, she appears to have been paid for services beyond beating carpets and blacking andirons, and she was genteel enough to become a companion when she left Dingle Court."

A weight of frustration bore down on me. The situation was growing more complicated, not less, and I had little more than a week to see Leander ensconced under the ducal roof, if that's where he should be.

I did not doubt that Mrs. Danforth would put him on the parish, or Miss Hammerschmidt would go to the penny press if I failed to deal with the situation in a timely and appropriate fashion.

"We have a few days," Hyperia said, getting up and coming

around the desk to take the other guest chair. "Not long, but you can work wonders in a few days. After lunch tomorrow, we'll call on Clarissa. Send a note to Lady Ophelia tonight with the pertinent facts and see what she can turn up. She hears all the gossip and knows more than she tells."

"True enough." My godmother was also the inspiration for many juicy on-dits, though her talent for causing tattle had waned in recent years.

"It was like this with the Makepeace house party, Jules, and like this with that business in Sussex," Hyperia said. "Matters grow increasingly muddled until you sort them out. We will get to the bottom of Leander's situation."

"You use the plural. Good of you." *Eat your heart out, Ormstead.*

She rose. "You didn't plan to ask me to lunch tomorrow, did you?"

I was on my feet as well, and weary feet they were too. I was not the tireless soldier I'd been a few short years ago. "I didn't want to impose."

She patted my chest. "Next time, impose. I'm off to collect my footman from the kitchen."

"Then collect him, or send Cheadle to break up the card game, but I'd like to walk you home. Consider it an imposition if you must, but I am asking."

She studied me as if I'd called some great philosophical tenet into question, and I was inordinately concerned that she'd reject my offer. Whatever shortcomings I might have—and they were legion—I could be a conscientious and attentive escort, and for her, I wanted to be.

"Very well, then. See me home."

We traveled arm in arm down the quiet streets, two footmen trailing us. I tried to simply enjoy Hyperia at my side on a damp, gusty summer evening, but I was too preoccupied with Leander's growing legion of putative mothers to properly appreciate even that boon.

∼

"Have you come to take the boy?" Mrs. Danforth posed the question before I could even introduce Hyperia.

"I have come to fetch him and Miss Dujardin for a luncheon outing," I replied. "We will likely go for an ice thereafter, and then I will return them here. Allow me to introduce Miss Hyperia West. Miss West, Mrs. Danforth, who has graciously provided a refuge for Leander in his bereavement."

"How generous of you," Hyperia said with every appearance of sincerity. "How kind. In these times, so many would have turned their backs on a small child's sorrow. You restore my faith in humanity, Mrs. Danforth."

Mrs. Danforth would clearly rather have restored the tranquility of her household, but she nodded grudgingly.

"One does one's Christian duty. Nonetheless, the child deserves to have his situation settled, *one way or the other*." She directed a housekeeper to send a maid for the boy and his nurse and kept us waiting in the foyer.

Hyperia engaged her on the riveting topic of how much to water hydrangeas, given the abundance of both heat and rain lately, while I noted a shadow of rising damp making inroads above the foyer's flagstones.

Bad news, that. The umbrella stand had been positioned to hide another patch, and a potted fern obscured a third.

Leander came down the steps, holding the hand of a maid perhaps three times his age. "Good day, my lord," he said, grinning at me. "I still like nutmeg on my chocolate."

"Master Leander." I bowed, though the boy really ought not to have addressed me until I'd acknowledged him. "Miss West and I are here to take you and Miss Dujardin to lunch."

The maid dropped his hand, bobbed a curtsey, and withdrew into the house's lower reaches.

"Can we go to Gunter's?" he asked. "I had an ice there once. Miss had lemon, and I had chocolate."

Mrs. Danforth scowled down at him. "Where is your nursemaid, young man?"

He peered up at her, and clearly the boy lacked guile, because his annoyance with Mrs. Danforth was evident on his face.

"She's out. Today is her half day, and she went out. She said Pansy would look in on me, and Pansy just now came to fetch me."

This recitation of facts sat ill with my hostess. "Out where? She's keeping Lord Julian waiting."

Leander's chin acquired a stubborn angle. "Out. That's all I know."

"Leander," Hyperia said, "perhaps you'd show me your room? I can read you a story while we wait for Miss Dujardin to come back."

A fine notion. I wanted a look at the particulars of the Christian charity Mrs. Danforth was extending to the boy, and I also found it very odd that a nursemaid would take her half day in the morning and without informing Mrs. Danforth.

To that lady's credit, Leander's quarters were tidy, if cramped, and blessed with two windows. Miss Dujardin's room across the corridor wasn't any larger, and she had no window at all.

"This is my pony," Leander said, taking from his pillow a ragged creature of a brownish hue with four legs and a recognizable tail. "His name is Dasher."

Harry's first pony had been Dasher, but then, the ranks of ponies were probably as rife with Dashers and Dancers as they were with Thunderbolts, Lightnings, and Crumpets.

"He's very handsome," Hyperia said, taking a seat on the cot. "Do you ever braid his tail for parade inspections?"

Leander plopped down beside her with no self-consciousness whatsoever. "I don't know how to make a braid."

"I'll show you, and perhaps Lord Julian can find us a story to read while we wait for word of Miss Dujardin's whereabouts."

Mrs. Danforth was having inquiries on that topic made below-stairs and had waved us up the steps with no mention of a tea tray, lemonade, or other gestures of hospitality.

"Miss has my books," Leander says. "She doesn't want anything to happen to them."

Meaning she did not want them to disappear to the used booksellers' stalls in Bloomsbury.

*Ye gods.* "I'll have a look in Miss Dujardin's room," I said as Hyperia carefully separated Dasher's tail into three skeins.

I hadn't intended to pry, but the opportunity to inspect Miss Dujardin's personal quarters was too intriguing to pass up. Her room was orderly in the extreme, her narrow bed neatly made up, her four dresses hanging in a wardrobe missing one of its doors.

Two gray dresses for every day. One older frock in faded lavender with a wisp of lace about the collar, and a dress in light blue velvet with lace at both collar and cuffs. A Sunday item, or perhaps for occasions even more special than divine services. Miss Dujardin had a spare pair of house slippers, and she was apparently wearing her boots, wherever she was.

A workbasket, painfully neat, held a pair of dingy cotton stockings already mended once about the toes.

The wardrobe smelled pleasantly of lavender, despite the missing door, and lavender sachets hung from a sconce near the door. Nothing under the bed, where I half expected to find a battered valise, save for a plain porcelain chamber pot. A cloak too heavy for summer hung opposite the dresses, and a shawl had been folded on the vanity stool. The vanity itself was a rickety little relic, its mirror speckled and cracked.

Hairbrush, comb, and hand mirror likely dating from the last century. The washstand stood in a corner—no privacy screen for the nursemaid—and lacked even a cracked mirror. On the shelf below the basin, I found a tin of soap redolent of lemons and lanolin. A bottle of hair tonic, also bearing the scent of lemons, sat beside the soap.

No salve for the lips, no lotion for the hands. Nothing to darken the eyebrows or otherwise enhance a lady's appearance.

I set the bottles back precisely where I'd found them.

The minuscule fireplace was swept clean, and the absence of

both andirons and a coal bucket suggested that even on a chilly, rainy night, the nursemaid was denied a fire.

A spy had quarters such as these. On first appearance, Miss Dujardin kept the sort of Spartan chamber any domestic would maintain. Plain, tidy, sweltering in summer, frigid in winter, but treasured for the privacy it afforded—or would afford, had the door sported a lock rather than just a latch.

Except that nothing made these quarters unique to Miss Dujardin. No sketch of a cousin lost at Waterloo. No framed sampler from Proverbs. No bonnet halfway through a retrimming. The sole artifact of a personal nature was a *Book of Common Prayer* on the bedside table.

I opened it and read an inscription in a spidery hand: *To my darling girl, on the occasion of her first communion. Love, Mama.* The initials in the upper right corner were hard to decipher, MF or MP, possibly a faded MB. Certainly no D for Dujardin.

A prop, then, bought used and intended to assure anybody prying that here dwelt a good, trustworthy Anglican soul. I moved to the lone shelf of books, hoping for any clue to the truth of that person. I found only a picture book about a bear cub who ran away from home, *Aesop's Fables*, a book of recipes for removing stains, and another book of medicinal remedies for female complaints. No inscriptions.

No lurid French novels either, not even a worn copy of one of Mrs. Radcliffe's tales. Miss Dujardin had been in residence for more than a month, but her quarters stated clearly that she hadn't expected to stay even that long.

I took Aesop with me back to Leander's room, a sense of foreboding accompanying me across the corridor.

"I like the tale about Androcles and the lion," I said, brandishing the book. "Perhaps Miss West will read that one?"

"I want a pet lion." Leander bounced off the cot. "He would be very fierce and roar a lot and eat Mrs. Danforth up." The boy made loud smacking noises and snapped his teeth together several times.

"She might give him indigestion," I said. "Starch, lace, and hair-pins probably don't go down that easily."

Hyperia tended to her braiding.

"He'd spit them out," Leander said, making *p-p-p-p* noises as if spitting pips onto the carpet. "And Dasher would stomp on them." *Stomp, stomp, stomp.*

There being no other place to sit in the room, I settled on the thin mattress two feet from Hyperia and patted the place between us. The situation was growing awkward. We weren't precisely guests, but we were callers and Mrs. Danforth's social superiors.

She was either without the first inkling of proper hospitality, or she was desperate to ensure we felt unwelcome.

"Your lion is an angry fellow." I opened the book to a random page. "I wonder what has put him so out of sorts."

"Maybe Mrs. Danforth hit him."

Hyperia's hands went still on Dasher's tail of yarn. "I beg your pardon? Did Mrs. Danforth raise her hand to you?"

Leander turned away, but not before I'd seen that stubborn little chin quiver. "She said I was a disgrace to a Christian household, and I wasn't to leave my room without Miss or Pansy, but Miss went out, and I had to use the necessary, and that's in the garden. Pansy took my pisspot for washing, else I'd have used that. Mrs. Danforth oughtn't to have smacked me."

As a small boy, I'd earned regular swats on my little bum. Imper-tinence had been the usual charge. Climbing doorjambs in the formal parlor was impertinent. Tracking mud across Mama's marble foyer twenty minutes before guests were due was impertinent. Farting in church was impertinent—and had won me some memorable bets with Harry.

I'd taken my punishments in stride, knowing they hadn't been intended to harm me. A minor hazard of doing business, as it were, and proof that adults as a class had little notion how to motivate me to good behavior.

The effective torments had been Papa's brooding silences and Mama's cuts direct. If I was ever so fortunate as to become a father...

No point in pursuing that thought.

Coming downstairs to use the necessary—or more likely to search for an errant nursemaid—was not impertinent. Not even close when that nursemaid was Leander's sole ally, in this household and in the entire world.

"Did leaving your room without permission get you a spanking?" I asked, idly flipping a page.

"She slapped me," Leander said, miming a stout backhand followed by a forehand blow. "Both cheeks. Hard. I told her she oughtn't to have done that and ran up the stairs. I thought she'd chase me, but Pansy came out and said the tea was ready, so I got away."

"But you didn't get to use the necessary," Hyperia said. "Shall we tend to that now?"

I rose. "There's a chamber pot in Miss Dujardin's room. Nip across the corridor, and then we'll be on our way. The hour is advancing, and you, my lad, are expected for lunch at Waltham House."

"What house?"

"Where I'm living for the nonce. Miss West will join us, and I was hoping Miss Dujardin would as well. Is Friday always her half day?"

Leander watched while Hyperia finished her braid and used a lone strand of tail yarn to secure her work.

"Today is Miss's half day. She said. She hasn't taken a half day since forever."

"Since your mother died?"

He looked decidedly uncomfortable at that question. "Since we came here. I don't like it here."

*Neither do I.* "I heed nature's call, and then we're leaving. Lunch followed by an ice, if we're spared afternoon thunderstorms. Miss West, let's be on our way."

She replaced Dasher on the pillow and rose.

Leander snatched up the horse. "Dasher comes with me so nothing happens to him."

Hyperia sent me a look: *You have to get him out of here.*

I had to get me out of there, too, and before I took to lecturing Mrs. Danforth about the stupidity of smacking worried little boys who did regularly have to pee.

We were soon in the foyer, waiting for the estimable Pansy to find us Leander's hat, when Miss Dujardin emerged from the lower reaches of the house. She wore a straw bonnet, cream cotton gloves, and a plain brown cloak—no parasol—and carried a burgundy velvet reticule. Suitable attire if she'd been interviewing for a new post.

"My lord, good day. I see you are punctual."

"We were a few minutes early, as it happens, and I was dismayed to think you might not be joining us." Leander had been dismayed. I had felt the battle in him between the desire to leave the house and his dread of going anywhere without Miss Dujardin.

"As it happens," Miss Dujardin said, "I have finished my errands on schedule and am prepared to accompany Leander on his outing."

She'd cast herself firmly in the role of the child's nursemaid rather than my guest, but I was too interested in quitting the premises to spar with her.

"My coach awaits in the alley." I'd chosen the alley for its shade and because watering the horses was easier there than if I'd kept them waiting on the street.

When we'd crossed the garden, we found Atticus at his post, holding the onside gelding by the bridle, not that a sensible equine would be inclined to go anywhere faster than a shuffle in the heat, and not that John Coachman would permit naughty equine behavior in any weather.

"You have a carriage." Leander gaped at the lesser of Waltham's two barouches, an open vehicle with a bench before and two seats vis-à-vis. A commodious conveyance for seeing and being seen rather than for extended travel or protection from the elements.

"That belongs to my brother. I'll hand the ladies up, and if you like, you can ride on the bench with John Coachman. My tiger is Atticus. He'll ride up there with you because he's learning to handle the ribbons."

Whether or not I was Leander's uncle, I could see that I'd just become the most exalted of men in his eyes. I handed the ladies onto the forward facing bench and climbed in after them. Atticus and Leander bookended John Coachman, who was peppered with questions from his new best admirers, and off we trundled.

I was on the rear-facing seat, and thus I had a clear view into the stable that served Mrs. Danforth's household. Inside the open barn door an old valise sat off to the side, bound with a single bright red strap.

An article I'd expected to find under a nursemaid's temporary bed, rather than sitting in the shadows of a stable. Perhaps Leander had been right to fret over his nursemaid's whereabouts, and now I was curious as well.

# CHAPTER EIGHT

I could not interrogate Miss Dujardin while Leander was present, so I tried casting lures before the boy.

I had served in Spain under Wellington.

I had once known a real pony named Dasher.

I'd known another fellow with a middle name of Merton.

Nothing I said or hinted at inspired Leander to mention his father. He'd either been taught not to broach the topic, or having had no experience of a father in life, it didn't occur to him to embark on such discussions.

By the time we were enjoying our ices beneath Berkeley Square's maples, I had given up my reconnaissance efforts.

"Let's have a constitutional," Hyperia said, rising and smoothing her skirts. "If I'm to walk anywhere in this weather, I'd prefer to walk in the shade." She extended a hand to Leander, who popped off his bench and toddled off at her side.

"Miss Dujardin?" I rose, and before I could offer assistance, she was on her feet. Not to be outflanked, I winged my elbow. "You've been notably quiet."

She accepted the courtesy, which I found a trifle disappointing.

Miss Dujardin on her mettle was impressive, but she was apparently choosing her battles today.

"Leander has been notably voluble. He has so few people to talk to. Mrs. Danforth ascribes to the theory that children should be neither seen nor heard, and that doesn't leave much room for a small boy to be himself."

"A Miss Clothilda Hammerschmidt paid a call on me yesterday," I said, purposely opening the topic without preamble. "She claims to be Leander's mother."

Miss Dujardin's gaze was on Leander, who had stopped to inspect a bug, or a rock, or clover growing from a crack in the walkway. At his age, the world should be full of wonders.

"Did this Miss Hammerschmidt offer any proof of her claim, my lord?"

"She offered threats. I'm to see a generous sum settled on her, or she will interfere with my attempts to improve Leander's situation."

A hint of displeasure crossed Miss Dujardin's damnably serene features. "She cannot threaten a ducal household and hope to gain by it. Besides, she's not his mother."

"Right, his mother was the late Mrs. Waites, who would have been consumptive at the time of his conception. Then too, I can find nobody who places Harry consistently at Mrs. Waites's side during the relevant winter. The path through which they became acquainted—backstage at the theater—serves more credibly for Miss Hammerschmidt's purposes. I can place Harry at the opera that winter, and I do know he was popular with ladies of a certain ilk."

"Lord Harry was the son of a duke. Of course he was popular with the ladies."

"I am the son of a duke, and yet, I cannot make the same claim."

She stopped on the walkway. "Nobody disputes that Lord Harry is that boy's father."

"Nobody can prove it either. Mrs. Danforth struck Leander today, hard. Forehand and backhand to the face, and all he could do was run away. She clearly has no respect for the boy's paternal antecedents, or perhaps she knows they are lowly rather than aristocratic."

Bad of me to ambush Leander's nursemaid, but Miss Dujardin had been lying to me from our first encounter. She sank onto the nearest bench.

"She *struck* him?"

"He came downstairs on his own, ostensibly to make a short trip to the garden, probably in search of you. She caught him outside of his room without supervision and chastised him. His room was devoid of a chamber pot at the time."

I did not want to loom over Miss Dujardin, so I shared her bench.

"That woman... Martha said Mrs. Danforth wasn't so bitter, so contrary, in India. Time can change people."

Time had certainly changed me. "Here is my challenge, Miss Dujardin: If Leander is illegitimate, then his mother is his legal custodian. At any point, she can disrupt his life, whisk him from whatever security I can provide, and threaten scandal and mayhem. I need to know who his mother is even more than I need to know his father's identity. Leander's current situation is untenable, and if you know anything—anything at all—that would illuminate the truth of his antecedents, you owe it to the boy to share that information with me."

She swiped at her cheek with a worn handkerchief. Somebody had taken the time to embroider a border of violets and greenery on the thin linen square, but the colors were faded, the stitches unraveling.

"Leander won't tell me where his soldiers are," Miss Dujardin said. "He doesn't want anything to happen to them, so he's hidden them. I hate that."

"I saw a valise in the stable aisle," I said. "Have you packed Leander's effects in anticipation of being evicted?"

She nodded. "He has so little, and I do not trust Mrs. Danforth farther than I could toss you, my lord. Martha had no place else to go, and none of this is Leander's fault. If she turned us out, I wanted Leander to at least keep what little he has."

"I can send somebody to retrieve the valise," I said, "but what of your effects?"

"I can bundle up what I own in less than a minute."

She spoke from wretched experience, apparently.

"My inclination is to simply keep the boy," I said. "Take him back to Waltham House, send Mrs. Danforth a chilly note of explanation, and be done with her. She wants him gone, he's not safe there unless you hover at his elbow, and he knows it."

"What's stopping you? Mrs. Danforth begrudges Leander butter for his porridge, and he's learning from her how to hate. He never encountered the sort of meanness she's shown him until he came to her household."

"I hesitate to essentially kidnap Leander, because he's had enough upheaval in recent weeks, and I'd like to spare him another shock. I can have a stern word with Mrs. Danforth, and I will. The real problem is that as soon as I publicly acknowledge that Leander is a Caldicott, then his mother, whoever she may be, has influence over His Grace's household. She'll extort coin at least from the duke and make worse trouble for him than that."

Arthur had been discreet with Banter—very discreet—but Clothilda Hammerschmidt worried me. Polite society speculated about Arthur's friendship with Banter, especially now that they were planning to travel together, though polite society speculated about any passing triviality if it bore a hint of salaciousness.

Miss Hammerschmidt would not speculate. She would *accuse*. She'd *allege*. She'd create problems for Arthur and Leander both, and coin alone might not be sufficient inducement to shut her mouth, much less keep it shut.

Then there was Clarissa, who also needed money and whose relationship with Harry was the nearest I'd found to a mistress and her protector.

As a footnote to the above, Miss Siegurdson had had opportunities for intimacy with Harry, she protested her innocence vehemently, and she'd all but pointed a finger at some housekeeper I'd be unlikely to track down in years of trying. Helvetica Siegurdson was an exceedingly intelligent woman, and she'd have an ally in Her Grace of Ambrose if I gave any indication that she was among my list of maternal suspects.

"Take Leander home with you," Miss Dujardin said. "Send somebody for his valise. One more change of abode won't make that much difference at this point."

I wanted to kick something—Mrs. Danforth's Christian charity, for example—but the situation called for reason.

"Until I've sorted Miss Hammerschmidt out, taking the boy into the ducal household is ill-advised. I will speak to Mrs. Danforth when I return you and Leander home. Speak to her very pointedly. She has given me another week to get Leander settled, and I need that week. Then too, the boy will want to collect his soldiers."

"They are somewhere in the garden," Miss Dujardin said. "I know that much."

I knew precisely where his soldiers were, but that wasn't my secret to share. "You've never heard of a Clothilda Hammerschmidt?"

"She was a seamstress. Martha knew everybody backstage, and the wardrobe seamstresses were all friendly. Pansy said Clothilda came around yesterday, asking the housekeeper for Martha's dresses, but I had no idea... She claims she's Leander's mother?"

"Vociferously. She says she left him with Martha, the respectable widow who had a bit of a widow's pension coming in, though Clothilda contributed conscientiously to the household coffers too. Clothilda claimed that a widow with a baby was treated more kindly than an opera dancer with a baby would be."

"I cannot fathom... I cannot grasp such boldness. You must not let her have Leander, my lord. She'll sell him to a brothel, or worse."

"She might threaten, but he's the goose who can lay golden eggs for her, once I admit he's Harry's son. As long as there's doubt about Leander's paternity, Miss Hammerschmidt will tread carefully." A hope rather than a certainty.

"So you leave Leander and me with the Danforth creature while you do what?"

"My next step will be a frank talk with Lady Clarissa Valmond, who intends to decamp from London at first light. Tell Leander that he should be ready to collect up his soldiers on short notice."

"Right." Miss Dujardin stalked off in the direction of Hyperia and Leander, who were admiring the various fancy coaches parked around the square.

"Miss Dujardin?" I called.

She turned. "My lord?"

"One more question." I closed the distance between us. "Were you at the agencies this morning?"

Her chin came up. "And if I was?"

"They can't offer you much if you lack a character and references." Not quite what I'd meant to say.

"I know that, and if I didn't, they certainly made the situation plain to me."

"I had hoped when Leander came to Waltham House that you'd join him. Call yourself his nursemaid or his governess—he'll need both—but don't abandon him in strange surroundings." I'd made my plans plain to her on a previous occasion, but she hadn't agreed to those plans, had she?

Her expression turned not merely bleak, but desolate. "Sometimes a clean break is best." She hailed her charge and inspected his mostly clean hands, while I considered a question:

Best for whom?

~

"I will see if Lady Clarissa is in." The sniffy butler appropriated my card, set it on a salver, and decamped without so much as offering to take my hat. He had a slight limp and was at least six inches shorter than a regulation Mayfair butler should be.

Affordable summer help in London. At Valmond House in

Sussex, the staff knew me on sight and would have caught me up on all the latest household gossip on the way to the family parlor, rather than offer me the next thing to the cut *domestique*.

Lady Clarissa was sharing quarters with her brother, Viscount Reardon. His lordship was a gifted artist, flush with the success of his recent debut exhibition. Reardon came down the steps, his cuffs turned back, no morning coat, his blond hair sticking up on the right, and a faint odor of linseed oil wafting about his person.

"Lord Julian? What are you doing loitering in the foyer? Is Clarissa going out in this heat? Excuse my dirt, by the way. I didn't know we had a caller. Hanford!"

"I believe he's gone to see if her ladyship is in. I take it the painting is going well?"

"Splendidly." He rolled down a cuff, fished in his pocket for a sleeve button, and finding none, turned his cuff back again. "I took your advice and scheduled sittings only upon receipt of a retainer. I thought that would put people off, but it seems demanding coin made a spot on my calendar more desirable."

He was Clarissa's younger brother, which put him more than five years my junior. As the only son of the Earl of Valloise, Reardon had not served in uniform, not even in the local militia, and yet, his battle scenes were eerily realistic.

"You're still enjoying the work?" I asked.

"Interesting question. When I'm required to paint a specific person, the task isn't the same as when I can follow the inspiration of the moment, but both can be challenging. Mr. Osgood Banter will sit to me later this month. I don't know him well, but he's an attractive fellow. They make for easier subjects than the other kind."

Reardon was happy, and more to the point, he was earning much-needed coin. He would doubtless have waxed eloquent by the hour about pigments, light, and symbolism, but Hanford scuttled forth from down the corridor.

"Lady Clarissa will see you, my lord. I'm to warn you that she hasn't much time to spare."

"Clary's haring off," Reardon said. "Can't stand the stink of Town in summer, though I'm partial to eau de turpentine myself. Hanford, send a tray in to her ladyship when you've got Lord Julian situated, and for pity's sake, don't leave a caller cooling his heels in the foyer. That's what we have guest parlors for."

Hanford's expression went from haughty to the glacial stoicism of a junior officer receiving an undeserved dressing down before his fellows. "Yes, sir. My apologies, sir. This way, my lord."

Reardon waved us on our way and disappeared into the house's lower reaches. He'd violate eight standing orders of decorum by intruding belowstairs, but if he was at all akin to Harry, the staff would like him for it.

"You were infantry?" I inquired as Hanford led me down a shadowy corridor.

"Artillery. The French didn't get me, a mule tromped on my foot, then wouldn't get off. We should have forgotten all about besieging those Spanish towns and simply turned a herd of army mules loose on 'em."

"Would that Wellington had had your insight."

We shared a smile, and Hanford announced me correctly. Clarissa received me in the family parlor and rose from an escritoire to clasp both my hands.

"My lord, what a delight. An absolute delight. Hanford, we must have refreshment. Will lemonade do, Julian? Or are you still favoring meadow tea?"

"Cold meadow tea would suit. Any sort of mint. You're looking well."

She twinkled at me as only Lady Clarissa Valmond could. Her beauty was unconventional—dark hair instead of the favored fair locks, brows a touch too heavy, and jaw a bit angular. Rather than try to soften her appearance, she reveled in her differentness. Lady Clarissa had an arsenal of smiles, each one more intimate and memorable than the last, and she knew how to touch a man such that even an innocuous brush of her fingers on his sleeve approached a caress.

Harry had warned me against her charms, but I had yet to decide whether Harry was being protective of me or possessive of Clarissa. His admonitions had not flattered the lady, and that puzzled me too. To the extent Harry and Clarissa had had any sort of understanding, the arrangement had been on Harry's terms.

"You are too kind," Clarissa said, waving me to the second wing chair. "Looking well in this heat is impossible for any save a parakeet. I vow I've never endured a more oppressive summer." She accepted my proffered hand and settled onto the opposite seat with all the grace of a sylph.

"I hear you are abandoning the capital to return to Sussex, my lady. Will Reardon be escorting you?"

"Don't be catty, Julian. Reardon has moved his studio to Town, his commissions are all here, and honoring his commissions has become his *raison d'être*. Mama and Papa have returned to the seaside, and I will join them after a short respite at home. How are Waltham's travel preparations coming along?"

A typical Lady Clarissa prevarication, delivered with all the sparkling good humor in the world, though she'd also aimed a surreptitious glance at the clock on the mantel.

"Waltham would leave tonight if his solicitors permitted it."

Clarissa's vivacity faltered. "Society does that. Makes foreign shores look extraordinarily appealing. I've yet to see Paris myself. Tell me what it's like. You've been there, haven't you?"

She knew I had. She was being equal parts flattering and manipulative. Behind her warmth and smiles lay an agenda, though I had yet to divine the particulars.

"We can discuss Paris some other day, Clarissa. At the moment, I'm pressed for time and more than a little frustrated."

She made a face. "This has to do with Harry again, doesn't it? I've told you all I know, Julian, and the topic bores me. Harry was a war hero, taken much too soon, felled in his prime, and all that, but he's been gone for some time, and we were never as close as people thought."

"Because," I replied, "that was the point. For all the hostesses and hopefuls to think Harry was so smitten with you that, but for a nasty little war, you and he might as well be betrothed."

She tapped a manicured nail on the upholstered arm of her chair. "Old news, Julian. Harry paid me to keep up that pretense, to swan about on his arm when he was in Town and look smitten. I appreciated the coin I earned with my fawning, and Society was fooled. I wonder what's keeping Hanford with that tray."

I rose and closed the door, then resumed my seat. "I am up to three candidates for the post of mother to Harry's by-blow, if the boy is even Harry's in the first place. We have the late regimental widow, and now an opera dancer turned seamstress has come forth. She's threatening to make life difficult for His Grace. If she is Leander's legal custodian, difficult will be an understatement. I've also learned that Harry's domestic staff doted on him shamelessly that winter, though it's a toss-up whether the pretty cook or the devoted housekeeper favored him with her affections. I have only the cook's inferences to go on regarding the housekeeper, you see."

"Half the world doted on Harry. He was handsome, charming, well-heeled, and ruthless in pursuit of a goal. He considered himself doomed to become the duke one day and intended to have a fine time while he awaited his fate."

"He was aware that Waltham was unlikely to marry?" If so, that was news to me, and likely to Arthur too. Bad news.

"Abundantly aware. On Harry's twenty-first birthday, the old duke sat him down and made matters appallingly clear. Harry was to be fruitful and legitimately multiply, so Harry of course charted a path that did not include matrimony or the near occasion thereof."

"He did not marry you?"

"Julian, has the heat addled your wits?"

*Worry* was addling my wits. "Harry might well have procured a special license, though investigating that possibility will take some time. Easier to ask what you're hiding and why you're leaving Town when you can finally afford to frequent the shops for the first time in years."

She smiled blandly. "Perhaps I'm removing myself from temptation. I bought a few necessities, but I don't want to lose the habit of frugality. The estate has been neglected, the commissions could dry up as quickly as one of Reardon's portraits cures, and there's little company of merit left in Town this time of year."

"Your insults are usually more subtle, my lady."

"The heat," she said, gesturing languidly. "My wits wilt in the heat. You must admit, the countryside is a more comfortable place to while away high summer, and thus I will decamp on the morrow." A tap on the door interrupted that prevarication. "Ah, the tea. At last. Come in!"

Clarissa beamed at her butler.

He set the tray on the low table. "Will, there be anything else, my lady?"

"Not for the nonce. Lord Julian won't be staying long."

"Very good, my lady."

Hanford closed the door in his wake, which spared me the effort. Clarissa passed me a drink and sipped at her own glass while regarding me over the rim. The effect was more watchful than flirtatious.

Harry could be ruthless—Clarissa was right about that—but Clarissa had a ruthless streak too. She'd gone to great lengths to preserve her family from financial ruin, even to accepting coin from Harry to play the role of fiancée-in-waiting. She'd been a ferocious advocate for her brother's talent, and she'd kept the family seat functioning on sheer resolve.

"May I ask how Harry compensated you?"

She ran the fourth finger of her left hand around the rim of her glass and again allowed her gaze to stray to the clock. "He paid me. What other sort of compensation is there? Must you belabor the past at such tedious length?"

"I apologize for prying, but I'm trying to make sense of Harry's ledgers. I can find no indication of your arrangement with him in his account book. No invoices from jewelers or modistes, no exorbitant debts of honor. If he hid his payments to you in the undergrowth, so to speak, he might have had a similar arrangement with Leander's mother. I would not ask, except that Leander deserves to know the truth of his antecedents."

That had become *my* agenda. Clothilda Hammerschmidt's threats, Mrs. Danforth's cruel charity, Helvetica Siegurdson's evasiveness troubled me exceedingly, but my concern was more and more for Leander, who, of all parties, was blameless.

"Maybe, Julian, the boy and his mother will be better off if you simply put a roof over his head and cease meddling. Leander might be devastated by the truth. Did you ever think of that? Society loves a mystery, but you cannot allow even your departed brother any privacy. You must have your facts, and damn the consequences."

For Clarissa, that was a tantrum. She wanted the world to think her vain, shallow, and harmless, but she was, in truth, defined by determination to protect the interests of her loved ones. What could drive an attractive, privileged woman to extended feats of deception, even as she appeared to swan from parlor to music room to conservatory, not a care in the world?

Clarissa glanced at the clock for the third time, a breach of manners, even given that she found my errand tiresome.

"You're leaving this evening, aren't you?" I asked.

"Oh, perhaps. If I finish packing in time. Spares the horses the worst of the heat to travel at night, and there's so much less traffic at the tollgates."

After dark, fewer people would see a lady quitting Mayfair on short notice, without an escort. Something about my queries was driving Clarissa into a disorderly retreat. She was brave, tenacious, and much smarter than she wanted the world to know.

More cunning, as I'd recently learned in Sussex, and more devious.

My curiosity returned to a question Lady Ophelia had posed

more than once: Why wasn't Clarissa married? True, her family was pockets to let, in far worse straits than anybody knew, but she was an earl's pretty daughter. She was precisely the sort of bride a wealthy cit sought for his darling son, the socially well-placed half of what was usually called an advantageous match.

She'd not only failed to pursue such a course, she'd apparently discouraged all comers and contented herself with Harry's unflattering arrangement, followed by looming penury.

Why? *What* could inspire a woman raised to value the married state above all else to deny herself that solution?

These thoughts passed through my mind in the time it took Clarissa to circle her finger twice more around the rim of her glass.

She was trying for an annoyed expression and failing. Behind the feigned boredom and testy oratory lay a watchfulness. A vigilance. I'd kept relentless vigils on reconnaissance, observed French scouting patrols by the hour, noting their every move. I'd defied exhaustion, common sense, and my own self-preservation instincts to ensure the menace stayed far, far from my fellows back in camp.

Insight struck on the third pass of her ring finger around the rim of her glass. Clarissa wasn't motivated by a *what*. Her actions were inspired by a *who*.

"You did have a child," I said. "But was Harry the father?"

# CHAPTER NINE

"I need some air." Clarissa was on her feet and wrestling with the window sash in the next instant. "I am weary to death of this wretched weather, and the noise, and the smell. Reardon breathes his paints and turpentine as if they bear the scent of Elysium, but they give me the worst head."

She struggled to raise the sash, though humidity or disuse was defeating her efforts.

I joined her at the window. "Allow me."

She stepped back as if I'd brandished a knife, and I soon had both windows open. The breeze that came in was hot and smelled vaguely of the stable, and the whole business had likely been meant as a distraction.

Clarissa regarded me as if I, too, were some malodorous artifact from the muck pit. "You should leave, Julian. You are making outlandish accusations. I know you are concerned for the boy, but you insult me, and I cannot overlook that."

"If Harry trifled with you, then I offer the insult to my brother. Were he alive, I'd offer him a sound thrashing as well." I'd likely have to wait until Arthur had served Harry a proper drubbing first. "Whatever missteps you've made, *I have made worse.* I have no interest whatsoever in judging you, and your confidences are safe with me."

She rubbed her arms as if she were chilled in the midst of the oppressive afternoon. "I want you to go, but you won't leave, will you?"

She and I had already had one surprisingly frank discussion, wherein I had become acquainted with the extent of the family's financial woes and her efforts to solve them.

"You can tell me anything, Clarissa. You know I am no gossip."

Her ladyship rested her forehead against the raised window. "Don't you dare pity me, Julian."

Pride, the last weapon against despair. "Wouldn't dream of it. Let's finish our drinks, shall we?"

She straightened to fire off a glower. "Don't cosset me either."

"Perhaps that leaves *listening* to you?"

She subsided into her wing chair. "I suppose it does, at that. You cannot tell anybody. Not Waltham, not Hyperia West, and certainly not Lady Ophelia."

"Lady Ophelia has likely already pieced together any evidence for herself, and she can be the soul of discretion." Also a nattering featherbrain, to appearances.

Clarissa poured herself more meadow tea. "One would not think it, to watch her flitting about."

"Precisely the effect Lady Ophelia intends. She's been playing Society for fools for decades and deceiving me for much of that time as well. I've regarded her as a harmless, aging flirt, but she has a will of iron and a capacity for logic as incisive as it is well hidden."

"You admire her."

"I admire you as well." I'd said as much, when it had become clear that Clarissa had stood between her family and ruin, as she all the while pretended to absorb herself with the latest fashions. "Who was he, Clarissa?"

"Not even you need to know that, Julian. Another officer on leave. He'd come home in the autumn to recuperate from a wound, and I was... smitten. He knew Harry and apparently knew Harry's interest in me was tactical rather than romantic. He consoled me, I confided in him, we talked and talked and talked... Nobody had ever *listened* to me before. Not truly. I had turned down three suitors by then, and people thought it was because none of them was rich enough or titled enough. That was part of it, but so was... Those strutting peacocks talked *at* me, Julian. Not *with* me.

"A girl spends years being lectured in the schoolroom," she went on, "then it's deportment instructors and drawing masters, finishing governesses, and piano instructors... Nobody ever *listens* to her, and then she's to marry a man who continues the tradition."

Lady Ophelia would have been nodding vigorously at those sentiments, and Hyperia would have let silence portend her agreement as well.

"Your swain did more than listen, my lady."

"All I knew was that he was special, and he was mine, and he was going back to that infernal war. We took risks, but, Julian, I would take them all over again, given the chance."

I was pleased for her that she'd admit as much. "No regrets?"

"Not a one. Because he'd left the fighting before the army went into winter quarters, he felt he ought to return to Portugal immediately after the New Year. I didn't realize I was in difficulties until Harry asked me about it."

"Harry knew the extent of your involvement with this other fellow?"

"He guessed, though we were very discreet. I began to have to use the necessary with unusual frequency. Harry noticed that and noticed that food had stopped agreeing with me. I thought I was upset to think of my love gone away to war, but Harry recognized the symptoms."

Because he'd observed them before? I considered myself fairly well informed regarding female biology—sisters would inflict that education on a fellow—but that business about having to use the necessary more often... I'd not come across that previously.

"What did Harry do when he learned of your situation?"

"He did not offer to marry me, if that's what you're thinking. He was kind, practical, and ultimately self-interested, of course. His first concern was to ensure nobody thought the child was his. He offered to pay for me to visit a midwife, but not for the purposes of midwifery."

"To get rid of the baby."

She nodded. "The notion horrified me. By this point, the baby's father was at sea, time was of the essence, and I regarded the decision as one I had to make on my own. I hoped to marry him, but he hadn't been willing to bind me to a soldier's uncertain prospects, and I understood that too."

I myself had used that logic with Hyperia, and for less than noble reasons. "Then you did not accept Harry's offer?"

"To his credit, he did not harangue me. Just put the option before me, noted the risks attendant to any path I chose—risks to my life—and said he wished his friend had exercised more restraint."

"Then Harry scarpered hotfoot back to Spain himself, so you had not even Harry's dubious friendship to lean on?"

"Something else sent him back to Spain, Julian. He did not scarper. Harry always spoke glowingly of a soldier's life, but I know now he was painting a fiction of bonhomie and silly pranks in camp. Cricket matches and impromptu hunts, regimental balls... He was lying, because it was easier on him to deceive those here in London than to let them in on the truth of his life at war. Easier on him and much easier on them."

I understood that too. "We colluded in a polite lie most of the time. Nobody back home wanted those in uniform to know how difficult things had become in Britain either. You nevertheless had a child to think of."

"I did. Harry returned to his regiment on short notice. He paid me in coin, Julian. Cold, hard coins that have no provenance and involve no signatures or bank transactions. He left me a hundred pounds. I'd never seen half that much in my life, and to have my own money... You cannot know what that meant."

What I knew was that Harry, having *failed to exercise restraint* himself, would take every possible measure to ensure Clarissa's problems did not become his problem. Had her situation been laid at his feet, he would have been expected to marry her, assuming the baby's father wasn't on hand to offer for Clarissa himself.

"You made arrangements for the child?"

"I missed the Season that year. Everybody thought I was pining for Harry, or—if they were less charitable—sparing my family the expense of yet another Town whirl after spending the winter in London. I went up north, and bided with relatives. Cousins on my mother's side. I had a daughter, Julian."

She smiled, a wistful expression very different from any I'd seen from her previously. Luminous, sweet, fierce... *joyous.*

"I *have* a daughter," she said more softly. "I named her Atalanta. She is magnificent. A complete hoyden. I live for the Glorious Twelfth. When all of polite society is off to the grouse moors and house parties, I spend two months with my daughter. She thinks I'm her godmother, her mother's cousin, but someday..."

Atalanta was a notably ferocious Greek heroine. "This is why you haven't married?"

"One reason. Grief was another. My beloved fell at Albuera. He had a letter from me before he died—his commanding officer returned the epistle to me. My darling knew I would not be left entirely alone should the worst occur, and I hope that gave him joy. Then too, my family was already in serious financial difficulties. It's one thing to marry a penniless earl's daughter and acquire some titled cachet—half the bankers in London wanted to match me with their sons—but quite another to accept that I'd bring the risk of scandal to the union as well."

Clarissa would not try to hide a daughter from her prospective husband. "Does Reardon know?"

"He probably suspects. I went north in late spring of 1811 to see cousins I barely knew. I was gone for nearly a year, and I return annually. Reardon doesn't ask, and I'm not about to burden my brother with my secrets."

I thought of Arthur and Harry, both muddling along with responsibilities they'd kept to themselves. "Reardon might surprise you. He's young, but not a complete gudgeon. You won't tell me who the father was?"

"He was from good family, good enough that they might... interfere, and while I trust you, what you do not know you cannot inadvertently acknowledge. I might tell Reardon. Maybe. Eventually."

And maybe not. "Think of it this way, then: Reardon is the girl's uncle, and he's in line for a title. If anything happens to you, she will need her titled uncle's influence and support."

"Nothing will happen to me."

Said every soldier ever to take the king's shilling. I patted her hand. "Appoint me as Atalanta's honorary uncle, then. Let your cousins know my direction and that you have taken me into your confidence. I am not exactly good *ton* myself, but I have some means, and I'm still, for the most part, received."

She blinked, she looked away, she clutched at the arms of her chair. "You mean that. You honestly..."

Oh drat and perdition. I passed her my handkerchief. "I am very likely Leander's uncle in truth, but the boy has been left to the tender mercies of fate for five years. A mother figure of some sort dying of consumption, a putative mother who sees him only as a means of extorting coin from a duke, his true mother possibly from the servant ranks and choosing her good name over his safety... I didn't even know I had a nephew, and *Harry, serving in time of war, didn't see fit to confide in me.* Children deserve better from us, so yes, I mean what I say about your daughter."

Clarissa dabbed at her eyes. "You can't tell anybody, Julian. Maybe when she's older, and she can bide with me from time to time, but not now. She wouldn't understand, and I can't... The Valmonds are still in difficulties, and Society grows more narrow-minded by the year."

In the general case, secrets made me uncomfortable. The French had damn near killed me, not in honorable conflict on a battlefield, but in a dank, malodorous prison, because I'd carried secrets. Harry had likely died guarding secrets, and then too, something in me rebelled at the notion that a child should have to *be* a secret.

"My lady, you must know that your movements have likely been noted. Unless you were in the habit of visiting these cousins in childhood, somebody will suspect." Lady Ophelia, for one. My mother might as well. The Duchess of Ambrose also struck me as shrewd enough to see the evidence and draw accurate conclusions. Hyperia's insights were often astonishingly astute.

"I can bear up under the weight of suspicions, Julian, but not scandal. Please, no more of that, after all I've been through."

Drat the woman, she looked ready to cry. "You have my word that I will do nothing to encourage gossip about your situation. Are you still intent on leaving Town?"

She folded my handkerchief into eighths. "You are poking old hornets' nests, asking all these questions. If you are asking about Harry, that will bring to mind that Harry was keeping company with me, and then you will add this child, Leander, into the ducal household. What does he look like?"

"He looks like a small boy. Darkish hair, a bit elfin or stubborn around the chin. Blue eyes. Not a biddable child, but not a brat."

"*I* have dark hair and blue eyes. My chin is adorably well defined. I am not particularly biddable."

That chin had acquired the slightest pugnacious angle. "Harry had dark hair and blue eyes too, my lady."

Clarissa's momentary bout of sentiment had passed, and I faced a seasoned negotiator, a woman worried about her reputation, and a mother concerned for her child.

I had negotiated with bandits, Spanish mules, and, on two occasions, with Wellington himself. "You don't want to be seen fleeing

Town without an escort, my lady. Bide here awhile longer, and I'm sure I can prevail on Lady Ophelia to accompany you back to Sussex."

"I wasn't planning on going to Sussex." She worried a nail. "Can you keep your distance, Julian? Don't call on me, don't take supper with Reardon in the clubs, don't drop by when Banter is sitting for his portrait?"

"I can keep my distance." I would *rather* keep my distance. I had too much else to do, and Clarissa's situation was delicate. "If you recall anything that might illuminate Leander's particulars, Lady Ophelia or Miss West can reliably and discreetly convey to me what cannot be put in writing."

"Very well, I'll bide in London awhile longer. Nothing will stop me from going north with the grouse exodus, though. Nothing on earth."

"I understand." I bowed over her hand and took my leave, trying to convince myself the interview had been a success. I had eliminated one person from consideration as Leander's mother, and that was progress.

I had also, however, learned that Harry's tidy little account book was at least in part a work of fiction, and that was not progress at all.

~

"Both children might be Harry's." Arthur offered that observation as we rode side by side down one of Hyde Park's secluded bridle paths. "He was damnably exuberant with the ladies."

The same notion had occurred to me, despite Clarissa's teary tale about a love lost on the battlefield. Clarissa was a skilled actress, but why lie about a connection that could only benefit her daughter, albeit discreetly?

Arthur's mood had reverted to the staid, taciturn older brother I'd known for most of my life. He and I had saddled up for a dawn hack as Osgood Banter had rolled out of Town to make a final inspection of the Osgood family seat in Sussex.

Their farewell in the mews had been short, perfunctory, and nonetheless hard to watch. How many such partings had they made, hands in plain sight at all times, lest somebody be watching from a nearby window?

"Harry was a flirt," I said, "but he was mindful of disease." Not mindful enough, in my opinion.

"Julian, what aren't you telling me?"

My horse, Atlas, enjoyed these dawn patrols, mostly because he knew they included a hearty gallop, and I wanted dearly to set my heels to his sides and send him thundering forward.

"Harry took a pragmatic view of his duties in Spain and Portugal."

"Spying is a dirty job," Arthur said. "A gentleman does not lurk behind hedges and so forth, but victory can depend on such under-handedness. I've made no apologies for the capacity in which you and Harry served."

Intelligence officers, scouts, reconnaissance officers. Polite fictions for the nasty business of cheating at war, in the opinion of many.

"I preferred to work in the countryside," I said, "and Harry could do that, too, but he wasn't as fit for the purpose as I was."

Arthur's mount, a great dark beast named Beowulf who turned into a shameless puppy if his neck was scratched just so, pretended to shy at a green maple leaf twirling down from above.

"Is there a point to these reminiscences, Julian?"

"Harry's best efforts were deployed in the cities and towns, in the garrisons, and even the larger villages. He was charming and inspired people to confide in him, while I was observant."

Arthur halted his horse, made the beast execute a foot-perfect rein-back, then allowed Beowulf to proceed. Not a scold, but a subtle reminder that a gentleman maintains his dignity in public.

"Harry was an accomplished flirt," Arthur said, patting his horse. "You agree with me. Both children might be his."

*Bollocks and botheration.* "Harry was willing to fuck in the line of duty. Got a certain satisfaction out of it, even. Liked the notion of literally and figuratively rogering the enemy."

"Distasteful." Three syllables imbued with a dukedom full of disgust.

"His behavior in this regard was utterly baffling to me. He gave no credence to the notion that if he'd shed his breeches for king and country, then his partner might well be slipping free of her chemise for the sake of *la République.* Or for the sake of keeping a roof over her head. Every gate out of a citadel is a potential point of entry for the enemy to breach that same fortress. That's obvious to any boy who plays with toy soldiers."

"You and he argued about this?"

"We argued about nearly every aspect of our role and mostly agreed to disagree. When the generals needed a lady charmed or compromised, Harry often obliged." Not always. Some women even Harry would not deceive, but I'd never been able to find a pattern to his choices, other than an unwillingness to despoil innocents.

"And thus we circle back to my conjecture," Arthur said. "Both children could be Harry's offspring."

"Clarissa spun a lovely tale about a fallen soldier, but I know the Valmonds have ties to France. They might still own land in France. I cannot rule out that Harry stayed close to Clarissa for reasons of state."

"Would he have ruined her for reasons of state?"

"He could have, but he did not. He gave her a large sum of money and kept his mouth shut, because ruining her would have been akin to befouling his own complicated, half-dishonorable nest. Nonetheless, his little arrangement with her curtailed her movements in Society."

The day was lovely. Overnight, the humidity had fled, and the air had cleared. London, for once, sparkled in the early morning sunshine, or this little corner of it did. I was loath to continue discussing Harry's sordid past, but I'd awoken with yesterday's developments much on my mind.

"Approaching poverty curtailed her movements," Arthur said, tipping his hat to a pair of ladies on matching chestnut mares. "I find that explanation to be the most credible. We have ties to France, cousins in France, land in France, when the French are inclined to recognize our title. Banter thinks I should have a look at the acres in Provence."

"Go in the spring. The season starts early that far south, and the beauty of those landscapes will stay with you for the rest of your life."

"I forget you were there."

"When I finally stumbled out of the mountains, I landed in Provence, and the warmth alone... Something about that region insists on peace, insists on calm and good cheer. The sunshine perhaps, or the spices. In summer, the air is redolent of lavender, rosemary, sage... good aromas. I ranged eastward, supposedly looking for a British unit traveling north, but mostly I was..."

"Recuperating?"

How to describe the transition from living like a wild beast to once again acquiring human tendencies? "Making a start on healing." Putting off my return to military rank, with all the questions and the killing attendant thereto.

Atlas rooted gently at the reins. *Time to gallop, please?*

I patted his neck. *Soon, my friend. I promise, soon.*

"What turned your thoughts in the direction of Harry's past?" Arthur asked.

"The money. Reconnaissance officers learned, almost by default, to watch who has money, who needs money. Who has bought a new coach despite a universally bad harvest? Whose womenfolk are accepting fewer and fewer invitations, despite an army of fancy servants still in livery? Harry paid Clarissa one hundred pounds in coin, Your Grace. Coin of the realm. Not a note of hand, bearer bond, jewels... and yet, I found no trace of that sum in his account book."

"Coin is discreet," Arthur said. "The aristocracy pretends actual money doesn't exist, but we value at least that aspect of it."

As did pickpockets, extortionists, and assorted other rogues. "Spying can be lucrative."

"We progress from the distasteful to the treasonous?"

"Not necessarily. If a fellow knew the British were advancing through a certain valley in a month's time, he could secure ownership of cattle in the valley at a reasonable price, then demand twice that sum from the quartermasters a fortnight later. The business required intermediaries, good luck, stout nerves, and so forth, but I know of at least one instance where Harry turned a profit based on what he'd seen on reconnaissance."

And I'd ripped up at him for that. Allowing personal motives to displace a focus on orders struck me as a slippery slope ending in a deep and fetid ditch.

"That's not treason?" Arthur asked.

"It's not selling secrets. The generals turned a blind eye. Otherwise, they'd have had a lot fewer competent spies. They even exploited the whole business. I was once sent thirty miles outside camp to discreetly buy cattle, supposedly in anticipation of a British advance in that direction."

"Meanwhile, your superior officers moved their troops along an entirely different route. The French were deceived, and some deserving farmer had a cozy winter."

"Precisely."

We rounded another bend, and again Atlas inquired as to when we'd be about the proper business of a morning hack. The path was straight enough, but another rider was ambling toward us a good thirty yards off.

*Not yet. Soon.*

"What does any of this have to do with Harry's progeny?" Arthur asked.

"Harry had to have kept another set of books," I said. "The hundred pounds to Clarissa, and other payments made to her, came from nowhere. Harry accounted for his officer's pay in the records we have, but his schemes in Spain were apparently going into a different account or some hoard of coins we know nothing about. Clarissa's arrangement reminded me that Harry had his little side projects, and they are not accounted for in his ledgers."

"Buried treasure. Who else but Harry would have left behind buried treasure? And you are right. He was a Caldicott. He would have kept some record somewhere, though might that record not be in Spain?"

"He paid Clarissa in London and offered to cover other expenses for her as well."

Arthur glanced up the path, but the other rider was still fifteen yards off. "He wouldn't have told you, because you would have sermonized at him, but he should have told me. Lady Clarissa was a damsel in distress, and Harry had to return to Spain. He should have put me wise to the matter. That he didn't suggests he was confident the child could not be his."

I assessed that reasoning and, to my relief, found it sound. "Papa told Harry you were unlikely to marry. A twenty-first birthday gift of an unwelcome truth, apparently."

"I told Harry long before that. Felt I owed him honesty. Quaint notion, given all you've disclosed about his activities in Spain."

That was Arthur being flustered. He'd known that Harry and I had served in an unconventional capacity, but not exactly how unconventional. How ungentlemanly.

The lone rider advanced toward us, and a shivery feeling came over me before I could make out his features in the shadow of his hat brim.

*Not this again.* "You see him?" I asked Arthur quietly. "He goes by St. Clair now."

"We have not been introduced."

"Would you like to be?" St. Clair had been the last person to see Harry alive, as far as I knew. Arthur had mentioned previously bringing Harry's remains home for a proper burial, and that meant somebody would have to ask St. Clair where those remains had been interred.

I would rather not be that somebody.

"Get it over with," Arthur muttered. "He will vote his seat one of these days, and public rudeness is denied me by my station." His tone said that private rudeness was another matter entirely.

I angled Atlas slightly across the path. St. Clair took the hint and drew his horse to a halt.

He even nodded cordially. "Lord Julian, good day." He did not so much as look at Arthur, which was both shrewd and polite of him.

"St. Clair, an introduction is in order. Waltham, may I make known to you the right honorable Lord St. Clair. My lord, I present to you His Grace, the Duke of Waltham."

Arthur's civility toward Harry's murderer should have knocked St. Clair off his damned horse. Yes, there had been a war on, which was all that allowed St. Clair to continue drawing breath.

After an instant's pause, St. Clair executed a mounted bow, removing his hat completely. "Your Grace." He held the posture for a moment, then straightened and placed his hat back on his head. His behavior was correct and—drat the man—seemed sincerely humble.

Arthur nodded curtly and nudged Beowulf forward.

I had to wait for a moment for Beowulf to pass St. Clair's horse, and I used that time to study St. Clair. He wasn't sleeping well, and despite his military bearing and exquisite manners, the encounter had unnerved him. The evidence was in his eyes, usually so bleak and unreadable.

I should have been cheered to see my enemy out of sorts, but the business had unnerved me as well. I caught up to Arthur, who'd kept Beowulf to the walk.

"He's just a man," Arthur said. "I want him to be a leering, sniveling rat, a reeking pile of walking excrement, but he's just a man, and apparently not a very happy one."

"Likely doomed, despite some sort of order from on high that he's to be allowed to live out his days in peace."

Arthur glanced over his shoulder, though St. Clair was already lost to sight. "Let's get in a gallop before the sun rises any higher, shall we? And don't let me win. Make Bey work for his oats for a change."

Atlas won by a length, and I hoped Arthur hadn't let us win. When we gave our noble steeds a loose rein and turned them in the direction of the park gates, I saw St. Clair on a slight rise. He had dismounted, and made a lonely figure in the morning light.

I hoped—in vain—that I'd seen the last of him.

# CHAPTER TEN

"What are we looking for again?" Atticus posed the question as he peered up the cold flue in what had been Harry's bedroom on Dingle Court.

"A ledger book," I replied, "or some sort of tally sheets. A journal, possibly, and it might not look like an accounting. In winter, hiding something up the chimney would have been a dicey proposition, but that just means you should have a look anyhow."

I reverted to old training, making a mental grid of the room and starting my visual inspection in a corner of the ceiling. No signs of disturbed plaster, no irregularities in the molding. Harry's bedchamber had been comfortable—Dingle Court was traditionally a mistress's abode—but many notches below the grandeur on offer at the ducal residence.

And now, the place having gone years without refurbishing, summer morning light revealed a fading establishment. The half-rolled-up carpet, once a strikingly rich swirl of peacock hues, was turning pastel, the bed hangings had long since been taken down, the blue lace curtains had been victimized by moths. The side of the bed frame closest to the windows had faded while the side facing away from the windows retained a hint of its old beeswax shine.

Cheadle and his footmen ought to take the place in hand.

Harry had been nearly as tall as I am. Hiding something overhead would have occurred to him, but the room's architecture didn't lend itself to such a handy solution.

"Nothing up the chimbly," Atticus said, shaking a paw grimy with coal dust.

I tossed him a square of linen. "Remind me to allot you some plain handkerchiefs. A gentleman should never be without. Use your clean hand to tap the walls."

He transferred a considerable quantity of dirt from his fingers to my handkerchief. "Why am I thumpin' the walls?"

"A well-made structure is reinforced at regular intervals. You should find a pattern. Tap across that wall, and the sound will change every two feet or so. That's where a supporting timber, or stud, has been placed to keep the building upright. Ceilings and floors are reinforced with joists. If you tap along, and the sound changes where it oughtn't, you might have found something." A slow process, usually a last resort.

"And then we'll knock down the wall?" The boy apparently liked that idea.

"And then we will assess the wainscoting, but the general idea with a hiding place is to exploit the spaces already available, not create a racket hacking into walls or destroying the chimney."

I turned my attention to the dressing closet, looking for false bottoms in the empty wardrobe and clothespress, tapping the walls, and generally getting nowhere.

"Shame ain't nobody livin' here," Atticus said. "Alley is wide enough for carriages. Quiet street, plenty of trees, has a garden."

Not a garden, a rioting patch of weeds, wild flowers, and a few maples that could no longer be referred to as saplings. Such neglect was unlike Arthur.

"Say a prayer that Harry didn't secret his papers in that garden."

"He were here in winter. Digging up frozen ground is a right pain in the arse."

"The kitchen hearth would be on an outside wall, and the ground along that wall wouldn't freeze. The heat from the flue would have warmed the soil to a good depth, given that the kitchen is belowstairs. Gardeners know that and sometimes put their cold frames in such locations."

Atticus left off rapping the wall to the rhythm of "God Save the King." "Where do you learn such things?"

*From being a pest like you long ago.* "I asked a lot of questions. I paid attention. We'll have to search the damned kitchen."

"I like kitchens."

"You like food and warmth and biding where I can't see what mischief you get up to. You like eavesdropping on the gossip in the servants' hall."

Atticus fisted his hands on his hips. "I learn things that way. Mr. Banter will be back next Wednesday to commence sitting for his portrait. Did you know that?"

I knew I was searching for a needle in a haystack, and Harry had been better at hiding needles than keeping his pizzle out of sight. I could not sit on the bed to have a think—the mattress had been removed long since, lest the mice take untoward notions—but I could pace.

"What is your most precious possession, Atticus?"

"According to you, me gentlemanly good name, 'cept I ain't a gent."

"According to you?"

He pushed dark hair from his eyes and surveyed me as I perambulated about the room. "I have a locket. Was me mum's. I don't wear it, because the pickpockets might get it, and 'sides, it's a locket. She give it t' me when I were little."

I was abruptly ashamed of my question. At the foundling homes, illiterate mothers would leave a token with their babies—a bent penny, a twist of braided ribbons—some unique identifier such that when the mother "got back on her feet," she could, in theory, redeem her baby from the care of the charity.

The ribbons crumbled to dust, the babies died, and the sorrow never ended.

"You will have to show me the locket sometime," I said, examining the mantel and pilasters. "If we take it to the shops on Ludgate, one of the jewelers might recognize it as his own handiwork."

"And then what? So he made a little bit of pretty years ago. Don't mean nothing."

"If he made the piece on commission, he might have a record of who ordered the work, and that gives us the start of a trail that might lead to your family. Where do you keep the locket?" Atticus's antecedents were mysterious. His previous employer had more or less purchased him at a tender age from one of the London poorhouses, taken him to the shires, and turned him into a general dogsbody belowstairs.

He had no education, no known family, and few manners, but he was a quick study.

"I have a box under me bed. We all do. Look under a fella's bed, and you're asking for trouble."

Even at fancy public schools, that rule held, mostly because a boy could claim no other patch of real estate in the whole establishment save the space beneath his bed.

The ropes had long since been removed from the bed frame I now beheld, and the floorboards below appeared entirely regular. I nonetheless heaved the bed frame aside and used the heel of my boot to tap along the floorboards.

"Odd sort of dance, that," Atticus said, shoving the tattered curtains away to perch on the windowsill. "Somebody only half looked after this place. These curtains woulda been pretty once."

They were ghostly now.

"I'll have a word with Cheadle." The boy was right—the carpet had been only partially rolled up, such that the portion left lying flat on the floor would be more faded than the rolled-up part. The curtains should have been taken down and stored with lavender or camphor sachets. The bed frame should have been dismantled and stored in the dressing closet, or some other place where sun could not work its evils on the wood.

I completed a circuit of heel-tapping. "Nothing."

Atticus hopped down from the windowsill. "Off to the kitchen?"

Kitchens were busy places. In winter, the footmen might have preferred to sleep near the cozy hearth, rather than shiver the night away in their garret dormitory. The cook would have been up well before dawn to put bread in the oven, and the housekeeper's quarters were often immediately proximate to the kitchen.

Then too, Harry ought by rights to have never trespassed below-stairs. A bachelor's temporary quarters—particularly Harry's temporary quarters—would have been no citadel of protocol, but still, he'd have been *noticed* on every foray into the servants' domain.

Searching the whole house could take days, and I did not have days.

Leander did not have days. Clothilda Hammerschmidt might have already begun whispering in the ears of the penny press about a downtrodden seamstress taken advantage of by a ducal son, her child scorned by his wealthy relations.

When I'd taken Leander and his nursemaid back to Mrs. Danforth's after our outing, I'd had a discussion with their hostess regarding the inappropriateness of using corporal punishment on grieving children. Her reaction had been tight-lipped and resentful.

"What?" Atticus asked as I continued visually probing the room. "It's a bedroom. Fer restin' and rompin'. Some people read their Bible before they go to sleep. Some people say prayers on their knees."

Not Harry, though he had been a voracious reader, mostly of newspapers, another spying habit.

I studied the relics of habitation yet remaining in the room—the half-rolled-up carpet, the bed frame, the blackened hearth, the tattered curtains. The dingy windows let in a gloomy version of morning sunshine, but on a winter night, if Harry were inclined to read, he'd need...

The only sconce in the room was on the wall opposite the windows, and that made sense. Other illumination would be provided by the fire in the hearth and by candles on the mantel or bedside table, though where...?

"The bed wasn't near the outside wall in the middle of winter," I said, shifting to regard the inner wall, the one adorned by the lone sconce. "The bed was away from the chill of the windows, directly beneath a source of artificial light. Somebody moved the bed around to make a start on rolling up the carpet."

I crossed the room and resumed heel-tapping. Within a minute, I'd found the loose floorboard. I used the knife I carried in my boot to reveal a space between joists, and to my fierce satisfaction, that space held an oilskin bag.

The tar coating had cracked at the seams, and the lot was covered in dust, but the contents remained secure.

"Love a duck," Atticus whispered, looking over my shoulder. "Will ye look at that."

I took the bag to the window and eased the drawstrings open. Harry had troubled to stash some sort of scent bag in with his journal, still faintly redolent of thyme. I set that aside, set aside a sizable cache of coins, and withdrew a slim leather-bound notebook such as I was still prone to carrying with me at all times.

Harry hadn't bothered to encode his entries, but he'd used only initials and dates to record most transactions. From Mr. LHS £3 received on Dec. 11. To Mme B £2 disbursed on Dec. 17. To Ld TS £7 paid on Jan. 5. From Visc Ht £15 received on Jan. 23. To Mme B another £5 on Feb. 5. On and on, the entries ran, until the end of February, when they abruptly stopped.

"Well?" Atticus asked. "What's it say?"

One name had been spelled out near the bottom of the last page and underlined. I had the sense that Harry was preparing to leave

Town and reminding himself to tend to that bit of business before he took ship.

"My brother variously paid, was paid by, and ended up owing a small fortune to, one of London's most fashionable madames. He was also doing business with a few courtesy lords and at least one viscount."

"Leander's mum was a fancy piece?"

I wanted to put my hand over Atticus's mouth, but he'd leaped to the most reasonable conclusion.

"If so, she could afford to do better by her boy than to entrust him to an ailing military widow." Then too, the professional ladies took precautions against conception, precautions far from foolproof. More to the point, Harry had not favored brothels, fancy or otherwise.

"I don't care for the nunneries," Atticus said, moving away. "They'll snatch a boy up, will he, nill he."

"They won't snatch you. You're in Waltham livery, more or less." Modified to allow him the sartorial glory of a London tiger's striped jacket.

"The whores pay attention to that?" Clearly, it had never occurred to Atticus that a badge of office could afford protection.

"Their livelihood depends on keeping powerful men happy. Waltham is very powerful, when he's of a mind to be. If you prefer that I drop you back at the house, I'm happy to oblige, but I'll be traveling on to Mrs. Bellassai's establishment."

Atticus wrinkled his nose. "I'll go with you, and I'm keeping me jacket on."

~

Mrs. Bellassai's might have been any fine home in Mayfair, right down to the dignified butler at the front door, matching footmen in the parlor, and fresh roses on every sideboard. I'd left Atticus cooling his heels in the mews—extensive mews, around back, of course—

where a coin to the grooms had ensured the lad would be kept out of trouble.

"My lord, a pleasure." My hostess made me a proper curtsey, though I was somewhat surprised to find her awake before noon.

"Mrs. Bellassai, thank you for receiving me."

She gestured to a tufted sofa done up in imperial purple. The parlor was well appointed—silk on the walls, a Mediterranean coastal landscape above the mantel—but she'd chosen bolder colors than those typically favored in fashionable Society. Violet and burgundy with splashes of emerald and peach.

Unusual, while Mrs. Bellassai herself embodied Renaissance perfection. She was the dark-haired angel of serene gaze and flawless complexion who knew exactly how to wear a decolletage that only hinted at her abundant charms.

"A man, particularly a titled man, calling on me during daylight hours provokes my curiosity," she said, taking a seat in a matching wing chair. "How is your dear brother?"

As opening salvos went, that one whistled by mere inches from my self-possession. The number of souls who'd refer to Arthur as a dear anything... I counted myself, Lady Ophelia, Hyperia at a stretch, and Banter. Beowulf, if apples were involved.

"His Grace is thriving, thank you. He's preparing for extended travel on the Continent, and the prospect of a change of scene seems to have lifted his spirits."

"Good. He is too serious by half, and travel broadens the mind. He's taking Banter with him?"

The question was not how she knew these things—Arthur and Banter had made no secret of their plans whatsoever—but why she bothered to impress me with her knowledge.

"A journey shared is a journey made more interesting," I said. "Shall I convey your good wishes to Waltham?"

"You need not. He knows he has them. A lovely man, and no, I've never had occasion to appreciate his amatory prowess. Do not be disrespectful. Waltham supports a certain charity that I also favor, and he supports it generously." She held up a hand. "Do not pry. His privacy matters to him and to me."

"His privacy matters to me as well," I said. "As it happens, my visit is occasioned not by Waltham, but by my late brother Harry."

Her manner became less fierce and more gracious. "My condolences on your loss, my lord. Lord Harry had a streak of daring that boded ill for his longevity."

"He had a streak of bad luck. Might we leave it at that?"

A footman bearing a silver tray stood in the open doorway. Even in this house, I would have expected the noon hour to have merited no more than the everyday service.

"Come in, Peter. I will pour out."

Peter left the offerings on the low table before Mrs. Bellassai, bowed, and withdrew. He was gorgeous, though dark-haired and an inch or so short of the requisite six feet.

"His twin is named Paul, and the uncle who raised them is a Dissenting preacher. They assure me that my coin out-preaches their uncle's theology. In a few years, they will return to the shires with full pockets, and I will miss them sorely."

I had never been introduced to Mrs. Bellassai, but a night in her establishment was considered a rite of passage among young men. Forever after, they could casually allude to that sophisticated bit of self-indulgence as if it had become their second home.

*Mrs. Bellassai serves the most excellent sangria...*

*Mrs. Bellassai's establishment favors good cotton sheets, none of this silk nonsense...*

*The ladies at Mrs. Bellassai's play better chess than you do, my good fellow...*

And so forth.

That streak of daring, or simply curiosity, might have sent Harry through Mrs. Bellassai's doors initially. Something else had kept him doing business with the lady.

"Tea, my lord?" She picked up the silver pot and poured a cup, the angle of her body perfectly mimicking the graceful curve of the spout. The scent of jasmine wafted up, delicate and soothing.

"Please. A dash of honey."

She fixed my tea and passed it over. "How are you getting on? One heard the most alarming rumors."

"Thank you for your concern. I am not back to one hundred percent, and I might never be. I am glad to be alive."

"Good. Harry would not want you to mope. A moping man with your great advantages would be an offense against God. Put the nightmares behind you."

How many nightmares had she put behind her? I heard a trace of an accent in her words, not French, to which I was acutely attuned in all its many dialects, though Italian didn't strike me as a perfect match either. I wasn't quite as knowledgeable of Spanish dialects, but I could rule out Basque.

"The blue spectacles are intriguing," she said, taking up her tea. "You might start a fashion."

"The blue spectacles protect my eyes from bright sunshine. I will apologize in advance for taking up a less than genteel topic, but I am in something of a hurry."

She sipped placidly. "You do not want to be seen at my humble establishment?"

"I do not want a young child, possibly Harry's son, to disappear into the stews, where his own mother might hold him for ransom."

She set down her cup. "Explain."

I gave my report as succinctly as if Wellington himself were attending the recitation, and Mrs. Bellassai appeared to attend me closely.

"Harry would not have frolicked with an opera dancer," she said, putting several sandwiches on a plate and passing it over. "Eat. You are too thin, and yes, we will feed the rascally little familiar you brought with you."

"The hospitality is appreciated." The sandwiches weren't the usual polite gesture involving a dab of butter and a hint of ham. Some

creamy cheese had been applied with a generous hand, and the ham
—lightly smoked—was abundant as well.

"In my experience, Harry would frolic where he was told to," I
said, "provided the direction came from a general or senior colonel.
Harry's battles were not typically waged amid smoking cannon and
charging cavalry."

"One surmised as much. Nor were yours."

I hadn't the aptitude for the sort of skirmishing she invited. Harry
had doubtless confided in her. She and Arthur apparently had some
sort of attenuated connection, and thus she had the advantage of me.
I was a supplicant, and she was a woman inured to male
importuning.

"In any case, Harry's activities here in London might well have
included fathering a child. The putative mother has died, and the
boy's antecedents on all sides are proving difficult to establish. I'm
trying to deduce whether Harry kept a regular mistress during the
winter of 1810-1811, and if so, who she was."

Mrs. Bellassai wrinkled an aquiline nose. "Parliament left us no
peace that year. My ladies were unrelentingly busy. Lord Harry was
home on leave. His last extended leave in London, if I'm not
mistaken."

"You are not."

She munched a sandwich, and I waited. How much would she
tell me? How reliable would her information be?

"Harry was still keeping Lady Clarissa Valmond at his side that
year," Mrs. Bellassai said. "And he asked me about how to deal with
an unplanned conception. I gave him some names, but I doubt that
child was his."

"Lady Clarissa says not, and your instincts support her. Why?"

"Harry was vain. If the child had been his, he'd have been proud
of himself. He would have married Lady Clarissa—they understood
one another quite well—and gone right back to Spain."

"Harry might not have been aware this child was conceived," I
said. "And then he was hard to locate once he returned to Spain."

Impossible to locate for weeks on end, at least from a distance. "I did, however, find this secreted in his previous London quarters."

I withdrew the notebook from my breast pocket and passed it over. Mrs. Bellassai flipped it open and perused the contents. She might have been a librarian trying to decide how to shelve an obscure manuscript, and yet, even engaged in that academic exercise, she was attractive.

"He should have destroyed this," she said, handing it back. "There you see evidence of his arrogance. Such a record could cause many problems, not the least of them for you and your dear brother."

"Was Harry a blackmailer? Courtesy lords and a few peers are noted among the transactions."

"He did not blackmail anybody. I would have gelded him for such foolishness, but he did accept payments and make payments about which I asked few questions. Some were payments directed by his superiors. Others were..."

"On his own initiative?"

She poured us both more tea. "For want of better terms, yes. My job was to convert sums paid to the currency of Harry's choosing. An establishment such as mine is paid in the coin of many lands and occasionally in jewels or other valuables. I am regularly in possession of foreign currency, and I occasionally convert pounds and pence into dollars or francs. My ladies send money home, and they hail from all over."

"You were Harry's banker?"

"His currency broker and sometimes his banking assistant. He'd send me money from Spain—or wherever he was—and I would do with it as he directed. That all stopped about three months before he died, but then, I often didn't hear from him for several months."

"Harry moved a lot of money in a short space of time," I said. "Did any of those funds go to a particular woman?"

"You'd have to ask his banker, my lord, or his solicitors. Harry had a significant amount of cash at his disposal, and many of his expenses would have been paid in coin. Even his men of business would not have known of those transactions. For a ducal heir to support a by-blow, though, wasn't a matter Harry would feel compelled to hide."

He'd save his coin for matters more deserving of discretion, in other words. "Harry never mentioned a child to you, or a particular woman other than Lady Clarissa? No regimental widow or domestic who'd caught his eye?"

"He could be discreet, else he'd never have lasted in his chosen profession, would he?" She held out a plate of cakes, and I took one. She took two.

"He could be convincingly mendacious," I said. "Not quite the same thing as discreet." The sweet turned out to be some sort of cream cake-biscuit combination. The base was mild cheese—sheep or goat, perhaps—flavored with lemon and garnished with orange zest. A hint of spirits came through the sweetness.

I'd had this distinctive dessert once before, and the richness had been nigh overwhelming at the time.

"You don't ask my opinion," Mrs. Bellassai said, "but I am supposed to be an expert on the male of the species, so humor me. Lord Harry seemed caught between a boy's rebellion and a grown man's respect for duty. He suspected he was to become the duke, and while being a duke should carry certain responsibilities, the status itself is enviable. Harry nevertheless resented that he wasn't to have any choice in the matter, and that resentment occasionally elbowed his better nature aside."

"Your theory has merit," I said slowly. "Harry could be both astonishingly selfish and very kind." He'd been kind, in his fashion, to Clarissa. Also selfish toward her.

"And now he is dead, and you are concerned for a child that might not even be his." She polished off her second cake with a relish some would call unseemly. "If the boy is Harry's, then Harry did not know of this child when he left England. He might have made some provision for the lad at a later point, but I doubt the situation had come to Harry's notice during that endless winter. The bankers should be able to tell you more."

Her assessment of the situation was more knowledgeable than my own. This unconventional call had borne some fruit.

"I'm off to Coutts and Company, then. Wish me luck."

"Coutts?" She dusted her hands and rose. "I know Waltham banks there, as does half of Mayfair."

"My grandfather switched our accounts to Coutts more than fifty years ago. He believed the Scots have a knack for managing money."

She licked her thumb, and that gesture, which should have been seductive, struck me as simply human, appealingly human, and not in the least flirtatious.

"Fine for your grandfather," she said, "but this was Lord Harry, and coin he'd find difficult to explain to the family ciphers. He kept his funds at Wentworth's. Good luck getting any information out of them. I keep my money there, and I would trust the discretion of a Wentworth banker over that of any priest or solicitor."

Wentworth's was a relatively new organization. The clientele was not exclusive, and the owner was some dour fellow from the Yorkshire dales. His institution appeared to prosper at a time when banks regularly failed.

"I'm off to Wentworth's, then. My thanks for your hospitality."

She curtseyed properly. "Give my regards to His Grace."

I bowed and should have taken my leave. Nonetheless, I hesitated. I was unlikely to cross paths with her again, and she was, by some lights, an expert.

"Mrs. Bellassai, have you ever known a man to lose his capacity for..." I gestured vaguely in the direction of the floor above us, "disporting, without any apparent physical cause?"

She returned to the tray and helped herself to another cake, which I accounted an act of consideration for my dignity.

"Yes. Frequently, in fact, but men don't generally speak of it with other men. My ladies are occasionally called upon to attempt to remedy matters, but that seldom helps and can make the situation worse."

"What does help?"

She bit off half the cake. "Time and love, if a man is lucky to have both."

Good God. A madame was not supposed to know how to pronounce the word *love* with that much innocent sincerity.

"I have shocked you," she said, taking a sniff of the uneaten half of her sweet. "The day becomes memorable. By 'love,' I mean the things a man delights in doing, the people he adores to be with, the books he relishes on every reading, the home he treasures... These all nourish his spirit, and it is the spirit that often affects the humors. Tell this man whose humors are at low ebb to recall how to love and be loved, and the rest might well right itself."

"I'll tell him."

"You will remember me to the duke?"

"I will convey your personal and kind regards, and my thanks for your hospitality." I left her eyeing the tea tray and saw myself out. That last little exchange should have mortified me. I was instead encouraged.

I had lost much during the war. Self-assurance, confidence, some arrogance—might as well be honest—and a dear brother and countless friends. But I had not lost the ability to love, to enjoy life, to treasure what mattered. If anything, going to war had made me more appreciative of the many blessings in my life, and thus I had reason to hope my manly powers would someday be restored to me.

I collected Atticus from the mews, where he was raptly observing a game of dice while consuming a meat pie.

"Are we for home?" he asked around the last mouthful of his feast. He took up the perch behind me on the curricle and waved farewell to his new best friends.

"We are not." I gave the horse leave to walk on. "You can tell no one where we've been, you little scamp. The occasion calls for discretion."

"Somebody should write a discreet song about the meat pies Mrs. Bellassai serves. Was beef, not mutton, and had lots of cheese in it and taties. I could eat three of 'em at one go."

"You cannot mention the meat pie either. You'd hurt Mrs. Gwin-nett's feelings." Cook was sensitive about her art, and one crossed her at peril to one's digestion. "We're off to pay a call on a banker."

"You skint, guv?"

"If I were short of funds, that would be none of your business, provided your wages were paid timely. I am not short of funds, but I am investigating Lord Harry's finances, and the trail leads to a banker's doorstep."

"Somebody could make a fortune off those meat pies. Feller would visit Mrs. B for her kitchen if he wasn't inclined for other reasons."

"Hush your rude mouth, child, or you will be walking home."

"I could handle the ribbons."

"This is not Beecham, and I said hush. I need to think."

"About what?"

*Incorrigible boy. Dear, incorrigible boy.* "About why Harry relied on a lady from Corsica to handle some very delicate transactions for him."

"Corsica? As in the Corsican Monster? Don't nobody like to be from Corsica these days. I wonder if those meat pies were some Corsican treat?"

I could not be sure of my theory, but the sweets on the tray— *fiadone*—were a distinctive Corsican treat—and Mrs. Bellassai's faint, charming accent had hinted of the Corsu tongue.

Gracious powers, what had Harry been mixed up in, and did it have anything to do with a small, orphaned boy?

# CHAPTER ELEVEN

"This way, my lord." Quinton Wentworth, the bank owner himself, turned on his heel and expected me to follow like a well-trained footman. He was a big, dark-haired brute, and all the excellent tailoring in the world could not disguise the hint of Yorkshire lurking in his diction or the pugnacity lurking in his posture.

He showed me to an office that struck a balance between gracious dignity and countinghouse practicality. The desk by the windows was large and elegantly appointed with silver standish and pen set, though no documents had been left in plain sight on the blotter. Fresh roses adorned the sideboard—he had that in common with Mrs. Bellassai, did he but know it—and the carpet bore an exquisite pattern of intertwined flowers in subdued hues.

This office, on the bank's upper floor, was noteworthy for two qualities—quiet and cleanliness. Everything gleamed, from the windowpanes to the silver appointments, to the brass-topped andirons, to the vase holding the roses. The quiet resulted from solid construction, abundant upholstery, and the man who owned the entire premises.

Wentworth didn't chatter, and he likely did not suffer chattering from his employees. His gaze was watchful, and if I'd had to characterize him with a single word, I'd have been torn between *vigilant* and *serious*.

"What can I do for you, my lord?"

No small talk then, thank the celestial powers. "Answer some questions regarding my late brother's circumstances."

Wentworth took up an abacus from his desk, tipped it to the side, and set it on the mantel. "Shall we sit?" He gestured to a pair of chairs before a cold hearth. "I assume you refer to the late Lord Harry Caldicott?"

"The same." Did *Arthur* do business with Wentworth? I did not dare inquire. "It has come to the family's attention that Harry might have left offspring behind, but details are few and unreliable. The child is about five, suggesting conception occurred during the winter Parliament brangled over the Regency Bill. Harry would have been in Town for several months, but he left us no indication that he'd become a father. I am looking into his finances in hopes of finding evidence that he supported his progeny or the child's mother."

Wentworth regarded me with a gaze that had likely intimidated every clerk, teller, and charwoman on the premises. I regarded him back. One didn't serve under Wellington without learning how to bear up under a parade inspection.

"A man's financial matters are confidential," Wentworth said. "I know nothing of a child and would not tell you if I did, absent permission from Lord Harry to do so."

"A man's financial matters are confidential," I said, "but upon his death, his estate does not enjoy the same privilege. Cases in Chancery are regularly bruited about. Harry left a will, and it did not mention assets held at this bank."

Wentworth's scrutiny shifted to the windows, which had been cracked to let in a warm breeze. "Wills generally don't list accounts and funds individually, particularly not the sort of wills the military demands of its officers. The language is general—'to my oldest son living and legally competent at the time of my death, I bequeath all my right, title, and interest in any property, real or personal, tangible or otherwise, as well as any future interests in property or goods that might develop, to be used for the benefit of my surviving dependents as he sees fit...'"

"You've read a lot of those wills."

"Thousands, thanks to the Corsican's bloodlust and the patriotism of England's young men. I'd rather never read another. I did not read Lord Harry's will."

"Your recall is that precise?"

Wentworth didn't smile, but those cold eyes admitted of some warmth. "I have no doubt the good fellows at Coutts were privy to the will. His lordship wanted discretion from me, else he'd never have graced my humble establishment with his coin."

Harry and his damned intermittent bouts of discretion were driving me barmy. "I don't care if Harry supported eight opera dancers, four charities, a brothel, and a gaming hell. I simply need to know if he made any arrangements that suggest he was providing for any progeny."

I was sufficiently frustrated that pummeling a few answers from Wentworth held some appeal, except that he could doubtless out-brawl me without breaking a sweat. He was not a man to trifle with, which was probably why Harry had reposed some trust in him.

Wentworth rose, slid open a panel in an Italianate credenza behind his desk, and extracted a folder bound in black ribbon. He perused the contents and resumed his seat.

"Other than this one account, I cannot discuss the specifics of your brother's financial affairs with you, but his instructions were that upon his death or protracted disappearance, I was to turn over to you or His Grace of Waltham all funds held for him under this account, to do with as you saw fit, provided you came to me making inquiries regarding same."

And Wentworth, years later, recalled those directions word for word. "You were not to notify us of the funds?"

Wentworth consulted his files again. "I was not. You've presented yourself, I personally know you to be Lord Julian Caldicott, and I hope you will accept a bank draft before you leave so I can consider this obligation to your brother fulfilled."

"We haven't been introduced, Wentworth. How can you vouch for my identity?"

He set the file aside. "One does not wish to give offense, but you enjoy a certain notoriety, my lord. The blue spectacles, the pale locks, the rumors of captivity and worse. London loves to talk, and bankers often profit by listening carefully."

He was both delicate and direct. I liked Quinton Wentworth, which sentiment would doubtless appall him, and I grasped why Harry had chosen to rely on Wentworth's discretion.

"In the course of your listening, did you ever hear mention that Harry had a child?"

"I did not, but then, I would not. I am not received, except by peers in need of credit. They tend to prefer a chance encounter on a quiet bridle path, followed by a meeting in the library of some accommodating friend of common birth. In desperate cases, I am invited to call upon solicitors who act for a party who must not be seen talking terms with me."

He was telling me, with no shame whatsoever, that he was something of a pariah. "I am received reluctantly," I said, "but only because nobody dares to offend my brother. You're better off being valued for the service you can render and turning a coin or two off it. The great privilege of twirling down the room at Almack's turns out to be more tedium than thrill."

"I would not know." A greater load of indifference was never carried by four words, and yet, I sensed he was curious about the goings-on at those subscription balls. Curious in the manner of a banker rather than a bachelor, but curious nonetheless.

"How much did Harry leave behind?"

Wentworth named a sum that frankly astonished me. "I invested the principal in the five-per-cent market, and thus we've seen some appreciation, though the interest and the disbursements kept pace for the first few years."

"Disbursements?" Now we were getting somewhere, now that I'd admitted my own cool reception in Mayfair.

"His lordship instructed me more or less quarterly to disburse the interest in specie to a certain posting inn, to be held for receipt. His lordship apparently made other and further arrangements at the posting inn. I received no final instructions upon his lordship's death, and thus I've held the money in trust, as per the terms of the account."

"Which posting inn?" He did not have to tell me, and given that Harry had been gone for some time, the information wasn't likely to gain me much.

"The Swan."

"Which Swan?" Half the pubs that weren't named The George were named The Swan.

"North of Hyde Park, along the Oxford road."

A decent neighborhood, one any footman or undercook could frequent safely. "You're certain of the amount?"

He smiled, a fleeting, piratical glint of amusement. "I lack confidence in God, king, fate, and human kindness, but of my numbers, I am certain. Will you accept a bank draft, my lord?"

"May I see Harry's instructions?"

Wentworth leafed through the file and passed me a single page. Beneath paragraphs of tidy copperplate, I noted Harry's slashing scrawl.

*In the event of my death or protracted absence, such as that term may be interpreted by the bank officer signing below, I direct that any sums held in my name in this account be disbursed to either His Grace of Waltham or Lord Julian Caldicott, should they ask in person for same,*

*to be put to whatever use the recipient deems best in the circum-*
*stances. To these directions, I do affix my hand and seal...*

No mention of the child or of a woman. *Thank you, Harry, for*
*creating more questions than answers—again.*

"Might we simply move the funds?" I asked. "From Harry's name
to mine? Leave them in the cent-per-cents for now. I have no idea
what use is best in the circumstances, in part because the circumstances remain befuddling."

Whatever direction Wentworth had been expecting, it wasn't
that. "You're sure you don't want to take the money with you?"

I rose, which had Wentworth on his feet as well. In a fair fight, I
might make him work for victory, but I wasn't at my best. He'd
pummel me flat and show no mercy.

"It's not my money. It's Harry's money, earned I know not how,
though I suspect the purpose was to see to the child's welfare."

"But you don't know that, my lord. You're off to the Swan?"

I should be, but Atticus had been racketing about with me for
hours, and the day was once again growing miserably hot.

"When the heat has eased, I will pay a call on the Swan."

"Talk to the women," Wentworth said. "Tell them a boy has been
left orphaned. The proprietor will keep well away from the affairs of
a lord, but the women might tell you something if you can look harmless enough."

He extended a hand with perfectly manicured nails, and yet, his
palms were calloused. I shook—the least courtesy I owed a fellow
pariah—and he saw me to the mezzanine above his bank lobby. The
place was busy in a pleasant sense, thriving ferns and ample skylights
giving it an oddly genteel air.

I descended the steps, aware of Wentworth's gaze upon me until I
quit the establishment.

Atticus was loitering with the curricle in the shade, and I could
see he was flagging. His temples were damp with sweat, and he was

probably thirsty. I climbed aboard, unwrapped the reins, and passed him my flask.

"We're for home," I said as Atticus gulped away. "Get you out of the heat and put a few questions to my dear brother."

"You still don't know if the lad is your nephew?" Atticus asked, capping the flask and passing it back. "Does it really matter?"

"You, of all people, my boy, know that it does."

He remained uncharacteristically quiet for the duration of the journey home, while I pondered the most important piece of information Wentworth had conveyed, despite all his posturing about confidentiality and discretion.

Throughout our discussion, I had not referred to Leander by name or gender. I'd used generic terms—the child, progeny, offspring —but Wentworth had referred to *a boy* left orphaned. I held the pieces of a larger puzzle than I'd known even a day ago. I was nonetheless certain that use of the more specific term from the likes of Quinton Wentworth had been intentional.

I was equally certain that Wentworth knew firsthand about the lot of orphaned boys, and his knowledge was bleak indeed.

~

I found Hyperia and Arthur in the back garden, a half-empty pitcher of lemonade between them. A plate adorned with a few breadcrumbs suggested they'd also enjoyed some sandwiches. Hyperia's call was doubtless intended to distract Arthur from Banter's absence, though I was pleased to see her on any occasion.

"I've had an interesting day thus far," I said, sitting in a wrought-iron chair to remove my spurs. "We found a ledger of Harry's, and that took us to a discreet establishment owned by Mrs. Bellassai."

"Interesting woman," was Arthur's sole comment. He lifted his chin in the direction of the footman who'd appeared in the shade near the door. The fellow came forward to collect my spurs and hat.

"Lord Julian will want some sustenance," Hyperia said, "and he'll want to do justice to this lemonade, if you would please fetch another glass."

"I'd also do justice to some meadow tea," I said, glad to be rid of my hat, but keeping my spectacles on my nose. "Mrs. Gwinnett's special recipe, if she has any made up."

"Very good, my lord." The footman bowed and withdrew.

"Was Mrs. Bellassai helpful?" Hyperia inquired, now that we were less likely to be overheard.

"She was." I explained the role she'd played as Harry's currency broker and all the questions raised by the coin Harry had traded in. "Some of the payments, according to Mrs. Bellassai, were made or collected at the behest of Harry's superiors."

Arthur's jacket was unbuttoned, a concession to the afternoon heat and to his regard for Hyperia. "What sort of *behest*? Official? Unofficial? Personal? I have never cared for *behests* in the general case."

"Probably some blend of all three that those superiors would disavow to even their confessors." Now that I was sitting in the shade, fatigue crashed over me like a phalanx of galloping French cavalry. "We need to do something with Dingle Court, Your Grace. Whoever tidied it up after Harry's departure did so in haphazard fashion."

"I never had need of it. When I decamp for the Continent, you can have the house done over, rented out, or sold. You will have my power of attorney to act for me in all regards."

"Put Cheadle to the challenge," Hyperia said. "He'll relish a proper project. I'm surprised he hasn't seen to it previously."

Arthur glanced at the door. "Harry left in something of a hurry that year. Recalled to Spain on urgent business, or fleeing London for reasons he would not confide in me."

"Or could not confide in you," I murmured. "Or pretended he could not confide. Perhaps he was simply trying to put distance between himself and Lady Clarissa before her situation became the latest scandal."

"Plausible."

We suspended conversation upon the arrival of the footman with a tray. Mrs. Gwinnett had sent up a whole pitcher of her signature meadow tea (mostly mint, spent black tea leaves, a dash of honey, and I know not what else). She had also—bless her for all eternity—provided a tray of sandwiches, along with a dish of sliced pickles and a plate of cherry tarts.

"She spoils you rotten," Arthur muttered when he'd dismissed the footman. "I get tepid lemonade sporting a bouquet of lavender and flowers. You get a feast. The tea is chilled, isn't it?"

I took a sip. "Slightly, not enough to curdle the digestion. Please do help yourself."

He tossed the garnish gracing his lemonade into the lavender border, swilled the dregs of his glass, and poured himself a full serving of meadow tea. "Miss West, some tea?"

"No, thank you." Hyperia took a pickle instead. "Jules, what else did Mrs. Bellassai have to say?"

"She has no specific knowledge of Leander's antecedents, but said Harry would not have taken up with an opera dancer. I agree with her. He was too wary of disease."

"He certainly spent enough evenings at the opera," Arthur observed. "One assumed..."

Hyperia helped herself to another pickle. "Harry probably wanted you and everybody else in polite society to *assume*, but Mrs. Bellassai's perspective adds another sliver of doubt to Miss Hammerschmidt's claim."

"Doubt won't matter to the penny press," Arthur retorted. "I begin to fear that my travel plans will have to be moved back. How will it look if accusations against Harry come to the fore just as I'm leaving for extended travel? Those accusations redound to the discredit of the family, and that reflects upon me."

Hyperia set the plate of tarts before Arthur. "Before we get to redounding and discrediting, you should both know that I made a pass through some of the better employment agencies. I was looking specifically for Mrs. Bleeker, Harry's old housekeeper, or L. Fielding, the footman dispatched to Dingle Court that winter. I had no luck in either case, but I also asked after Miss Dujardin."

I paused between my first and second half sandwiches. "In what regard?"

"She told you she'd been to the agencies when we went to pick up Leander for his outing with us. I was curious as to whether she sought employment as a governess, nurserymaid, companion... She's quite well spoken, and she might long to be done with the whole drama surrounding her charge."

"What sort of post is she seeking?" I asked.

"She isn't seeking any post, at least not from the agencies where I inquired, but then, domestic work in Town this time of year isn't plentiful. She might have been trying for the lesser strata—the cits and merchants who don't leave London for the shires in summer. Different agencies serve different clientele. I can start on the more plebian establishments next, if you like."

"We aren't prying into the nursemaid's affairs," Arthur said. "If this Mrs. Bleeker kept house for Lord Harry Caldicott, she could look higher than cits and shopkeepers. I'm surprised the footman isn't racketing about somewhere, too, though. He was in ducal service, and he'd be sought after for that reason alone."

"Unless Harry turned him off without a character for snooping?" I was tired, and tired of Harry and his games. "Mrs. Bellassai sent me on to Harry's banker."

"What could the old fellows at Coutts have to add?" Arthur asked.

"Not a thing. Harry had entrusted some personal funds to Wentworth's. I spoke with Mr. Wentworth himself, who is not an old fellow. Harry's accounts included a small fortune from which he regularly directed Wentworth to make disbursements."

"To Miss Hammerschmidt?" Hyperia posed the question with a shudder. "Please tell me that woman did not have her hooks into one of Wellington's best spies."

"Wentworth erred on the side of discretion, though by indirection, he offered confirmation of our suspicions. He believed Harry had a child—a son—and that the funds were to be used to look after the boy and his mother." I further conveyed the banker's suggestion that I speak to the women at the Swan.

"I keep some funds with Wentworth," Arthur said when I'd finished my report. "He handles certain charitable matters for me."

"Mrs. Bellassai entrusts her coin to him as well," Hyperia said.

Both Arthur and I regarded her with masculine astonishment. In proper conversation—which this admittedly was not—Hyperia shouldn't acknowledge that Mrs. Bellassai drew breath. That Hyperia knew where Mrs. Bellassai kept her money was beyond inexplicable.

"Don't look at me like that. Mrs. Bellassai contributes generously to the foundling homes. I've had occasion to cross paths with her because I support the same ends. The charities won't accept her money, so she relies on intermediaries to see to her donations. I am sufficiently dull and unremarkable that my donations are welcome anywhere."

Arthur peered into his drink. "She relies on multiple intermediaries, apparently."

Hyperia grinned and saluted with her glass. "Your secret is safe with me, Your Grace."

"I am surrounded by intrigue." I appropriated the plate of cherry tarts from their perilous location at Arthur's elbow. "I don't care for it. Your Grace is not to change any travel plans just yet. I will get to the bottom of Leander's situation before heroic measures are called for. When we are finished here, I am off to the Swan to make further inquiries, unless you lot have other plans for me?"

"I've asked Miss West to look in on the nursery," Arthur said, swiping two cherry tarts and rising. "A woman's touch is in order, and I'm beginning to think the sooner we get that boy under this roof, the better all around."

Hyperia took a tart as well. "And if Leander is not a Caldicott?"

The same question I would have posed.

"Mrs. Bellassai, Wentworth, the ledger book, Clarissa... Nobody has refuted the possibility that the boy is ours," Arthur said. "I ask myself, what is the worst that can happen if we take him in, and he's not Harry's son? Miss Hammerschmidt can plague us for money like a drunken uncle on remittance. She can go to the press and malign us as a family. What else can she do?"

Hyperia stated the obvious, and did so gently. "She can take the boy, produce falsified baptismal records establishing her as his legal guardian—records she well knows how to procure—and hold him hostage or consign him to a very bad end."

Arthur considered that possibility for the duration of one cherry tart. "Then Jules must collect the lad sooner rather than later. Drop in at the Swan, then relieve Mrs. Danforth of her unwanted guests. I am getting an itchy feeling about this whole business."

He was eyeing the plate of tarts with larceny in his heart when a rock landed two yards down the walkway. I moved without thinking to put myself between Hyperia and the garden gate.

"Fetch the rock," I said to Arthur, who merely raised a dark brow and, for once, did as he'd been instructed. "There's a bloody note wrapped around the thing." Rapidly retreating footsteps sounded in the alley, but I wasn't about to quit my post.

"Language, Julian," Hyperia murmured.

Arthur unwrapped a torn piece of foolscap from about a chipped chunk of brick. "Could have broken a window with this thing."

"These matters abide by a certain protocol," I said. "Breaking a window becomes destruction of property and is more likely to involve the authorities. The pickpocket or flower girl tasked with delivering the note waited until the grooms in the mews had their backs turned and voices were coming from the garden. The messenger would have accepted the task from some other ignorant third party, and pursuit would be pointless."

Arthur frowned at the paper. "One shudders at the things you know. 'Do right by the boy, and soon. Or else.'"

"I would not have thought Miss Hammerschmidt literate," Hyperia said. "That has to be her way of forcing the matter."

"She could have found a scribe in any tavern," I replied, "if the note came from her. She also claimed to know her letters. Mrs. Danforth might have penned this as an indirect eviction notice."

Hyperia took the paper from Arthur. "You'll get jam on it, and now I have an itchy feeling too. Best fetch the boy, Jules."

I wanted a wash first, and a nap. The nap was wishful thinking. "Let's have a peek at the nursery. And we'll need accommodations for Miss Dujardin too. Leander is attached to her, and as far as I know, she hasn't taken another post yet."

"I'll see you at supper, then," Arthur said, fishing a folded piece of vellum from his pocket. "Though this came for you by messenger. No reply needed, apparently. Miss West, good day." He bowed, she curtseyed, and I read the note that hadn't been hurled over the garden wall.

"Healy says I'm to look in on a certain Lieutenant Palmer at Horse Guards." I passed Hyperia the note, which said only that.

"You put Healy up to chatting with his military chums?"

"The prospect of calling at Horse Guards holds little appeal." I dreaded dealing with Horse Guards as deeply as I'd dreaded facing Arthur after Harry's death, which was precisely why I'd delegated the visit to Horse Guards to Hyperia's brother. "Waites served in India. I thought a few casual questions were worth asking. Somebody might recall a detail about Martha—her papa's congregation, where she and Waites married, which cousin or sister she was returning to here in London. Even a maiden name might tell us a lot."

"And Healy more or less flung the job back in your lap. Shall I have a word with him?"

I was hot, tired, and frustrated, but Horse Guards wasn't the underworld. My fellow officers had had a year to call me out, insult me to my face, and otherwise make their opinions of me known. Some had been rude, others distant, and still others had doubtless slandered me in absentia.

None of which mattered when Leander's situation was becoming urgent.

"I'll call on this Palmer fellow," I said. "Healy isn't as well acquainted with the situation as I am, and asking a few questions won't take me long."

Hyperia looked like she wanted to argue, but she chose instead to trudge with me up through the stuffy house to the even stuffier third floor.

"For pity's sake, let's open some windows," she said. "The whole building will thank us, and for that matter, the attic windows should be opened to create a draft from below." She set about raising sashes and tying back curtains while I did likewise.

This nursery had not figured prominently in my childhood. My father and, more especially, my grandmother had believed that country air was healthier for growing children. London had been a mysterious, busy place where Papa and Her Grace disappeared to be even more important and grown up than they were at Caldicott Hall.

"Whose bear is that?" I asked, taking from the mantel a toy somebody had stitched together out of brown velvet.

"I made it for Leander," Hyperia said. "The body is easy, but getting the head bear-shaped took some refining. The nose makes all the difference. I chose a bear because he already has a horse, and one needn't bother with a mane and tail for a bear."

The air stirred, bringing a hint of relief from the heat. Hyperia surveyed the appointments like a general looking over her gun placements the day before battle. We were in the playroom, which was abutted on one side by the nurserymaid's chamber and on the other by a dormitory outfitted at present for a single child.

"He'll be lonely here," Hyperia said. "I don't like to think of him being lonely."

Neither did I. "Mrs. Bellassai struck me as lonely." I hadn't planned to say that, but to Hyperia, I could say almost anything. "She makes friends of her footmen, or something like it. She approves of Arthur, though I don't think she held Harry in such high esteem."

"My sentiments toward Lord Harry veer from 'one shouldn't speak ill of the dead' to 'the dead ought to have behaved better if they sought to merit unrelenting postmortem praise.'"

"I don't know what Harry sought, other than to avoid becoming the duke." I wanted to take Hyperia in my arms. The impulse was unexpected but, upon reflection, understandable. My efforts to solve the mystery of Leander's origins were bearing all the wrong fruit—more questions, more riddles, more indications that Harry might have been up to no good.

In Hyperia's embrace, I invariably found solace and joy, however fleetingly.

I had no sooner formed that thought than she delivered the sort of swift hug that could serve the same purpose as a whack to the back of the head.

"I want you to get to the bottom of Leander's situation so you and the boy can both have some peace." She stepped back when I wished she hadn't. "Carry on, Jules. I'll have the housekeeper make up the governess's quarters for Miss Dujardin. Please do let me know when you have the child settled. You might also consider grabbing a nap. You're looking a bit peaky. No need to see me out."

She patted my chest, passed me the bear, and swanned off, though I ought to have escorted her to the front door. I sat on the toy chest that doubtless held some relics of my past—and Harry's. The family crest had been carved into the lid, which was ridiculous.

I would not nap, but I would take a few minutes to sort through the day's events. Not the Harry- has-created-a mess part, but the how-is-Julian-holding-up part. I was learning to avoid the forced marches and feats of stamina I'd taken for granted in Spain.

I was still far too easily overtaxed, and I did not recover from excessive exertion anywhere near as quickly as I once had. So I perched on the toy box and mentally prepared to pay a call at Horse Guards—heaven defend me—then drop in at the Swan, and finish my sortie with a surprise raid on Mrs. Danforth's citadel of violent, grudging charity.

I wasn't looking forward to any of those tasks, and yet, the day had held a gift for me too.

"There's hope," I said to the room at large and to the stuffed bear in my hands. "Mrs. Bellassai says with time and love, there's hope, and she likely knows of what she speaks."

I put the bear on the mantel, offered him a slight bow, and went off to find soap, water, and fresh linen.

# CHAPTER TWELVE

"Healy West says you were asking about a fellow named Waites," Second Lieutenant Palmer said. "Served in India, died of a fever."

Palmer was that ageless article, the career soldier of middling rank. Because he'd been billeted to Horse Guards, rather than sent home on half pay, I put his age past forty, but he might well be closer to thirty or fifty. Years in India took a toll on English complexions, as did years in Spain.

Palmer was paying that toll plus interest. His blue eyes were especially vivid against the weathered parchment of his skin, and his hair wasn't graying so much as the sun had leached away what little color he'd been born with.

He was tallish, though his posture was slightly crooked.

"I'm inquiring about a Lieutenant Waites and his wife." I had not been invited to sit, but then, every chair in the cramped room was full of file boxes and stacks of loose papers. Palmer occupied a desk that struck me as too low for a man of his height.

"Let's walk," he said, abandoning his chair. "My hip does better if I don't sit for too long."

The last thing I wanted to do—the very, very last thing—was patrol the corridors of Horse Guards during business hours.

During any hours.

Though Palmer, for his part, probably didn't want to be seen ambling along the street with me, which left the worst option—the vast, level parade ground, where the sun would be painfully bright, and I would be on display from every compass point.

"You served with Waites?" I asked as we set off down the hot, dim corridor.

"If you can call it that. We were largely idle, until some prince or other decided he'd rather not have Britain tell him what to do." Palmer set a limping pace, and when we reached the end of the hallway, he executed a lopsided about-face and started back the way we'd come. "Waites didn't last long. Never saw combat."

"Do you recall anything of his wife?"

"Won't forget that one. Martha. Army life is hard on the wives. Some of the officers in India prefer the local culture. Most of them took local wives or mistresses. The British wives were supposed to tolerate that without actually accepting it. Mrs. Waites wasn't high in the instep, if you know what I mean."

We rounded a corner, and I was abruptly faced with one of the myriad men whose path had crossed mine in Spain. Captain... No, not captain. Ensign. I rummaged around in my memory. A short name, one of those trade names. Cooper, Smith, Harper... He was blond, going from solid to paunchy, and still sporting a mustache about which he'd been inordinately vain.

While my mind had known I was likely to encounter such men here of all places, the reality was unnerving. My legs wanted to run, my belly wanted to heave, and a clammy sweat trickled down my back.

Surprise in the ensign's eyes turned to shock, then disgust.

*Draper*, that was it. Ensign Hugh Draper. His nicknames had alluded to a proclivity for disrespecting women. He'd apparently come up in the world despite that failing, and he'd finally made lieutenant.

"Who let you in?" Draper sneered.

"I did," Palmer replied. "You have a problem with me, Draper?"

"I have a problem with *him*."

That was my cue to shove Draper in the gut, slap a glove across his jowls, or otherwise take the rancid bait his insult offered. He personally had no quarrel with me. We'd not even been in the same regiment. He'd been artillery. I'd been infantry or occasionally cavalry.

He wasn't worth my life, and I wasn't about to become a murderer for the sake of his vanity.

"This man," Palmer said evenly, "told my colonel that to send our sharpshooters through the mountains to establish camp ahead of the artillery and infantry would be rank foolishness. My colonel listened to him, and everybody got to camp safely, including both of my brothers. Colonel Blanton hated to have his plans questioned and loathed taking the slower route through the valleys. Others were not so fortunate as to heed Caldicott's intelligence on that same campaign, and they aren't here to complain about it."

I had all but forgotten that argument with Blanton. I'd been exhausted past any regard for protocol, manners, or etiquette. Blanton, looking at a map, had decreed that the shortest distance between two points was a straight line. Artillery might not be able to travel that straight line, but elite British riflemen for damned sure could, and then secure the destination that much faster.

The colonel had never attempted to explain straight lines to a mountain that topped eight thousand feet. He'd never tried to make summer uniforms and rations suffice at that elevation, where little vegetation grew, and less water—other than snow on the north-facing slopes—was to be found, but bandits abounded.

He'd listened, though. That time, my shouting and swearing hadn't been in vain.

Draper's parting shot was to treat me to one more silent,

disdainful perusal, then to proceed past us, chin up as if on business for Wellington himself.

"Pity we couldn't tell the French where to aim," Palmer said mildly. "What did you want to know about Mrs. Waites?"

We resumed walking, or limping in Palmer's case.

"Any detail you can recall. Where was she from? Did she ever mention a maiden name? A village back home? A cousin or sister in London?"

"She was lively," Palmer said. "The other ladies couldn't abide that, a woman who managed to be happy in the heathen climate. A woman who was glad to be away from English winters and the stink of coal. I had the sense Mrs. Waites wasn't from London, but she'd spent enough time in the Great Smoke to want to be quit of it."

"One of the many who come to Town looking for work and find only misery and dirt?"

"Not that bad, but a land-on-her-feet type. She would have made a good soldier."

We executed another about-face and were again heading back to Palmer's office. "Is it possible she was ill, Palmer? A consumptive who found relief in a warmer climate?"

He stumped onward for several yards. "Yes, now that you mention it. She had the complexion—the pale complexion and the pink cheeks. Redheads sometimes do, but in hindsight... She would occasionally take a poor turn when the weather changed. She didn't want to go back to England, I know that, but Danforth was adamant that she not marry one of the other junior officers, to the disappointment of every fellow at the fort."

"Danforth?"

"Lieutenant colonel. I didn't serve under him, but his lookout included what to do with widows."

His lookout, or his lady wife's? "Do you know anybody who did serve under Danforth?"

Palmer paused outside his cramped, stuffy office. "Bennet's still around. I see him occasionally on the parade ground at the beginning or end of the day. He'd recall Danforth."

"Chat him up, please. General impressions of Mrs. Waites, incidents of note, that sort of thing." I gave Palmer my direction, and because he had not asked, I also acquainted him with the larger parameters of my mission—an orphaned boy, questionable antecedents, Mrs. Waites's claims, and my brother's confusing legacy.

"Damned war," Palmer said. "The shooting ends. The battles and misery go on."

I thought of his unexpected defense of me and of Draper's retreat. "The battles and misery don't go on forever, at least not the part we can blame on war."

He lowered himself carefully to his chair. "True enough. Another six months, and I can retire. I'm grateful for my post, but I will be more grateful to see the last of it. Best of luck, milord."

"Same to you."

I made my escape by virtue of a dingy set of backstairs and emerged into the brutally sunny expanse of the parade ground. The space was level, wide open, and graveled, about as far from the uneven terrain, poor visibility, and stink of a battlefield as a site for military maneuvers could get.

A former tiltyard, where Henry VIII had staged violence for his royal entertainment.

I hurried on my way, though I spared a thought for Martha Waites. She'd been ill even in India—consumption could take forever to kill its victims—and Mrs. Danforth had condemned her to return to London's cold and coal smoke. Martha's great offenses had been a blithe spirit and a pretty face.

She'd turned in her extremity to the very person who'd doubtless condemned her to a shorter life endured in London's foul air. Perhaps she thought Mrs. Danforth owed her, or perhaps she wanted her nemesis to witness her death.

Not all battlefields were characterized by cannon and cavalry, and some heinous blackguards wielded jasperware instead of pistols.

~

The women at the Swan recalled only generalities.

Every three months for about two-and-a-half years running, a young lady had arrived to retrieve a parcel from the "hold for receipt" correspondence entrusted to the innkeeper. She came alone, and she came within a week of the parcel's delivery.

One day, the lady had arrived to collect the quarterly epistle, but no epistle had awaited her.

The timing coincided loosely with Harry's death, and the description of the parcel's recipient was vague. Youngish, though not a girl. Trim, rather than skinny. Decently clothed, no widow's weeds, no fancy veils or attempts to disguise her identity. Tallish, but not a maypole. The innkeeper's niece recalled the woman as fair, but she'd worn bonnets, and thus hair color had not been noted.

Mrs. Waites, Helvetica Siegurdson, and Clarissa fit the description, though for all I knew, so did Lady Clarissa's lady's maid or any number of Mrs. Bellassai's employees.

Clothilda Hammerschmidt, while short, could have enlisted Martha Waites to collect the funds for her.

I climbed into my curricle and took the reins from Atticus. "No progress. In three years, the trail has gone cold. The ladies wanted to help but had little to offer by way of details."

Beecham was in the traces, and that good fellow was content to continue dozing until I gave him the office to walk on.

"Years are a long time in London." Atticus shifted back to his perch behind the bench. "In the country, nothing happens, and folk sit around recalling everything forever. When the dog had twelve puppies and they all lived. When somebody's cousin ran off with the squinty-eyed curate twenty years past. London... It's different here. Too busy. No time to sit and recall anything."

In London, Atticus was apparently paying a bit more attention to his diction—at times.

"Wentworth came around the Swan after the last packet was

leaves filled the borders. Gold thread among the blue, red, and green gave the whole a luminous quality.

Such an article was fit for brandishing at a fellow's court presentation. I held the linen to my nose and caught nothing but camphor in the scent, though a hint of Harry's preferred cedar shaving soap would not have surprised me.

"Mighty fancy," Atticus said, peering over my shoulder. "Too bad about the initials, or it would fetch a pretty penny on Rosemary Lane."

"This might well be the boy's sole inheritance from his father. Somebody had sense enough not to sell it."

Mrs. Waites, perhaps. Miss Hammerschmidt would have long since pawned such an item to cover her tab at the nearest gin palace. Miss Dujardin was clearly the guardian of Leander's legacy now, though why hadn't she mentioned this item to me earlier?

"What's with all the lions?" Atticus asked.

"Those are griffins. A cross between a lion and an eagle. We've discussed them before, and they relate to the Caldicott family crest. Give Beecham his water, please."

Atticus watched while I replaced the contents of the valise. "Somebody had some new duds."

Atticus well knew to whom the clothing likely belonged. "See to the horse."

He picked up his bucket and bustled off while I set the valise back in its corner and took another look around. A stable, like a garden or pantry, often had stories to tell to the observant. Something was amiss, or perhaps Mrs. Danforth's staff was in the habit of deserting their posts.

On a hook behind some horse blankets, I found a cloak tied up into a bundle such as shepherds, drovers, and other humble travelers fashioned. I thrust a hand between folds of fabric and extracted a little tin of lemon soap. Hard edges suggested I'd find Miss Dujardin's few books, along with her hand mirror and comb.

Like a good soldier, Miss Dujardin had been ready to break camp on a moment's notice.

I replaced the bundle and crossed to the garden gate. "Atticus, don't wander off. We might need to leave in a hurry." A general caution. I had no reason to suspect disorderly retreat would be required, but no reason to trust Mrs. Danforth's continued hospitality either.

The funds Wentworth had been holding, if they were known to Leander's mother or those posing as his mother, made the child a financial prize. Arthur and I were not legally compelled to use that money for the boy, but the implications were enough to provide grounds for a lawsuit, with all the endless scandal and expense that would entail.

I had a quick look around the garden—deserted—and decided to eschew the front door. I took myself down the steps to the kitchen, and all the quiet of the stable and garden was replaced with uproar and pandemonium.

"Be ye a robber?" a half-grown girl asked. Her cap was askew, and a damp semicircle of dubious hue discolored her apron. "We ain't got nuffink worth stealin', unless you count Cook's buns."

Cook, a robust woman of middle years, ceased chopping scrubbed potatoes, while a maid of some sort wept into an apron. A young fellow who might have passed for a footman tried to console her.

"We didn't hear the bell," Cook said. "House is at sixes and seven. Who be ye, sir?"

"Lord Julian Caldicott, come to call on Master Leander. Your stable lads were not in evidence, and I gather there's been some sort of general upset."

"They took 'im!" the lachrymose maid expostulated. "The sweeps got 'im, I tell you. The lad's little and quick and strong. The sweeps stole 'im."

The footman patted her shoulder ineffectually while the sobs grew louder. Another fellow, older and clad in the sort of rough garb I associated with a man-of-all-work came down the steps that led to the garden.

"No luck so far," he said, "but the lads will want some supper. We've searched the nearest squares and asked at every kitchen door on the street. Who's he?"

The itchy feeling coalesced into pure, black dread. "Lord Julian Caldicott, at your service. I take it Master Leander is missing?"

"The sweeps got 'im or the coalman," the maid wailed. "Little boys go down the mines and never come up. Me cousin says it 'appens all the time. The Navy will steal a lad for midshipman, and 'e were just a wee mite. Them molly 'ouses is forever snatching up sweet little lads, and Leander is ever so sweet."

The Navy had ceased impressing even grown men, to the best of my knowledge. The threat of a French blockade had been eliminated, and the high seas were much safer than in years past.

The other listed threats were all too possible.

"Somebody take me to Mrs. Danforth, please."

The older fellow glanced at the cook. This was her domain, and she was the appropriate authority to issue any orders.

"Bella, cease your caterwauling. Jones, take his lordship to see Missus, but button yer jacket afore you set foot abovestairs. Ask Missus if she'd like supper moved back, and tell her Griffith reports no luck."

Jones offered Bella one more consoling stroke of his hand over her shoulder, then he buttoned his jacket and produced a set of gloves from a pocket.

"This way, sir, er, milord." He began jogging up the steps, but slowed his pace as he neared the landing.

"New to service," Cook said. "We always get 'em when they're new to service."

When their wages would be lowest. I followed Jones up the steps and was shown to the fussy parlor.

"Don't bother with a tea tray," I said. "You have more important things to worry about."

"Sweeps haven't been in the neighborhood, sir. Bella's just a little nervous."

"The sweeps would hardly go hunting in the same location where they're working, would they? They'd leave their brushes and ladders at home and look far afield for their climbing boys."

Leander was the perfect age to take up the profession, and the sweeps might get a good two years' service from him. Sweeps typically begrudged their lads good tucker in an effort to keep them small and nimble as long as possible, but then, after a year or two, most of the boys were suffering from sooty warts, bad lungs, or worse.

"He'd run from the sweeps, sir. Miss Dujardin told him that if ever strange men tried to befriend him, he was to run and yell bloody murder all the while."

"And if, instead, a friendly, pretty woman approached him and asked him to hold her dog for just a moment in exchange for shiny coin?"

Jones swallowed and glanced away to the west, probably the direction of his much-missed, and much less criminally inclined, home shire.

"Please fetch Mrs. Danforth," I said, "and let Miss Dujardin know I'm on the premises."

"She and Pansy are out looking with the rest of us, sir. Inquiring of the neighbors and asking Vicar to put the word out."

*Splendid.* If the boy had been abducted, a general alarm would do more harm than good. Witnesses would leave their posts to join in the search, evidence would be disturbed, and accurate recollections would become harder to elicit.

"Then please fetch Mrs. Danforth and tell the other lads they're to report their findings to Griffith, with whom I will confer in person. You, Griffith, and the rest of the staff are to take supper before we decide next steps."

"Aye, sir. I mean, milord." He reached up as if to tug at a cap, remembered to bow, and marched off.

Mrs. Danforth made me wait another five interminable minutes before presenting herself, and those five minutes entirely obliterated my patience.

"Well, he's gone," she said without offering me so much as a greeting. "Despite your dithering and lording about, you will no doubt blame me, and after all I've done for the boy. I barely knew his mother, and yet, I opened my home to her and her brat and even saw to her final arrangements. I am not so lacking in Christian charity that I'd—"

I advanced on her and came close enough to see the face powder that had caked in the creases around her mouth.

"When did you last see him?"

She took a step back. "I endeavor not to see him or hear him."

"Believe me, ma'am, he prefers to avoid you as well. I don't suppose you hit him again?"

She looked away.

"Did you?"

"Of course not."

Maybe not, but she'd apparently come close or threatened the lad. "When did you last see him?"

"He was belowstairs again, on the back terrace, maybe an hour and a half ago. Dujardin was nowhere in sight. He claimed she was using the jakes, and I wasn't about to investigate that allegation. Children lie all the time, boys especially, and then they grow up to be cheating, dishonest..."

"Enough." The late Lieutenant Colonel Danforth had failed to earn his wife's respect. That was hardly my problem, much less Leander's. "Did you chase the boy back up the steps?"

"I indicated that returning abovestairs was in his best interests, then went off on my charitable calls."

I detested bullies, and that thought alone preserved me from delivering to Mrs. Danforth such a lecture as would leave her fearing for her immortal soul, her reputation, and her safety in dark alleys.

"Get out of my sight, madam, and you'd best hope we recover the lad hale and whole, or I shall become the flaming arrow of justice that ignites the pyre of your social damnation. That is not a threat. That is my solemn oath."

She sniffed and gave me her back, nearly colliding with Miss Dujardin at the door. They moved around each other, an odd little dance of mutual loathing that put me in mind of pugilists at the start of a match. Miss Dujardin had been crying, but her bonnet was tied in a tidy bow, and her gloves were spotless.

"My lord, you've come. You got my note, and now you've come. Please say you'll find him."

"I will move heaven, earth, and any available parts of hell in that very effort," I said, bowing slightly. "What note?"

"I saw that woman lurking about, the seamstress who claimed to be Martha's friend. She was loitering in the alley this morning, and then I saw her again by the pub when Leander and I went to the park this afternoon. She made me uneasy, and I thought... I sent you a note, and now you're here."

Bloody, bollocking hell.

"We'll find him, and your sharp eyes mean the search just narrowed to manageable proportions." I adopted a brisk tone and directed Miss Dujardin to be seated.

As we wasted precious minutes reviewing her recollection of the day's events, I mentally inventoried who and what I knew of London's theater community and where Clothilda Hammerschmidt could temporarily hide a small, very frightened boy. Atticus had followed Miss Hammerschmidt to a gin palace two streets from Covent Garden, which, unfortunately, narrowed the possibilities not one bit.

# CHAPTER THIRTEEN

"We have a line of scent to follow," I informed the ranks of Mrs. Danforth's employees as they took their supper at the kitchen table. "Miss Dujardin has seen a certain personage of dubious intent in the vicinity of this house earlier today, a Miss Clothilda Hammer-schmidt, a seamstress who works for the theaters."

The teary maid, Bella, glowered at her tankard of ale. "She come around looking for dresses, she did. Most outlandish bonnet I ever did see and demanding what she 'ad no claim on, like the pope claiming the New World."

"The very same woman," I said. "We have reason to believe she means to hold Leander for ransom, and of all things, she claims to be his mother."

"Baggage," the cook muttered. "What sort of mother never comes around to see her lad when he's bidin' barely a half hour's stroll from Drury Lane?"

"Excellent point," I replied, "but I cannot at present refute her claim, and if Leander is illegitimate, she is his legal custodian."

"She is not his mother," Miss Dujardin said from a perch on the raised hearth. "Martha would have told me, and the only times I can recall Miss Hammerschmidt looking Martha up was when Miss Hammerschmidt was between jobs and without coin. She never took an interest in Leander."

"Be that as it may, Miss Hammerschmidt and Lord Harry were occasionally seen together during his last winter in London. She will fabricate all manner of documents, eyewitnesses, and other proof. My intention is to simply appropriate Leander from her care."

Miss Dujardin, still in bonnet and summer cloak, worried a nail. "Leander will become a shuttlecock."

"Yonder lord's brother is a duke," the footman, Jones, observed while buttering a slice of bread. "Good luck winning a match in the courts against such as that."

"That's not the point," Miss Dujardin snapped.

I had never heard her use such a sharp tone. Not on me, who'd occasionally vexed her sorely. Not on Leander.

"Miss Dujardin, I suspect you are in want of sustenance and certainly in want of something to drink. I am off to pay a call on an acquaintance who might know where Miss Hammerschmidt bides. Jones is right that my brother is a duke, and more to the point, I was a reconnaissance officer serving under Wellington. I will track Leander from St. Giles to purgatory to the ninth circle of hell if necessary to bring that child safely home."

My audience did me the courtesy of allowing my stirring declaration to go unchallenged, but Leander did not, at present, even have a home. I collected my hat and walking stick and took the steps up to the garden. Evening was descending, and I shuddered to think where Leander might spend the night.

The child had not had an easy time of it. No father to speak of, his mother ill—if Martha Waites had been his mother—then gone from his life. Racketing from pillar to post, tossed on the cruel charity of the Danforth viper, and now this.

I sank onto a wooden bench, overcome not by fatigue of the body precisely, though I was tired, but by a sense of hopelessness. I had left the boy here, where he'd not been safe, even after Mrs. Danforth had taken out her wrath on him. She'd likely done that on purpose, striking the child because she could not vent her frustrations on me.

And then that nasty note. As sparrows flitted about in the maples along the alley, I wondered if Mrs. Danforth hadn't summoned Miss Hammerschmidt in a fit of pique. Mrs. Danforth would not want the likes of Miss Hammerschmidt to darken even her back garden gate, but I'd already underestimated Mrs. Danforth's ill nature once.

"Thank goodness you're still here." Miss Dujardin emerged at the top of the kitchen steps. "Cook said you should eat something. These meat pies are cold, but they are meat pies. Plenty of beef and made just this afternoon."

She passed over a linen bundle. The poor woman still had not taken the time to remove her bonnet or cloak.

I rose and accepted the proffered bounty, feeling the day's exertions in every joint and sinew. "Considerate of her and of you. I forgot to tell Griffith not to resume searching. We know now that Leander hasn't wandered off."

Miss Dujardin paced off a few steps, pivoted, and stalked back to me. "I thought Leander's worst problem was avoiding Mrs. Danforth, then Bella started bleating about bordellos and coalmen. I have never been so frightened in all my life, and there's nothing I can do. Might you post a reward?"

"I can." Though a reward would bring all manner of false witnesses out of the sewers and hedges. A hue and cry would also do exactly what Arthur hoped to avoid, and create a tempest of talk just as he and Banter were trying for a prosaic departure for the Continent.

My sense of failure mounted, such that if I did find Clothilda Hammerschmidt in the warren of London's feculent slums, she would deem me her worst nightmare incarnate. To extort coin from me or the Duke of Waltham was dirty tactics, but a venerable strategy in any war fought on the battleground of public opinion.

To involve the child she claimed was her son...

"She's not his mother," Miss Dujardin said again, resuming her pacing. "No sort of mother would treat her own offspring thus."

"A desperate mother might."

"Miss Hammerschmidt has work, you say, at the theaters. She'd have us believe her admirers once included a ducal heir. She had no need to do this."

Those were sound arguments, and yet, I played devil's advocate. "Perhaps that life has exhausted her capacity for human decency. People can be pushed too far." Had Harry somehow been pushed too far? He'd certainly been involved in questionable undertakings while on leave in London.

Miss Dujardin cast herself onto the bench I'd vacated. "What excuse would you make for Mrs. Danforth, my lord? She has a roof over her head, some regular income. She can afford this house and a staff—a full, mostly idle staff—and yet, she begrudges a child his porridge. She'd have tossed poor Dasher to the ragman if Leander hadn't insisted he either keep the horse in his very hands or hide it in my room."

Despite the miasma of despair clouding my mood, my mind seized on the detail of the stuffed horse.

"Where is Dasher now?"

"Not in my room. I checked. Checking became a habit because I do not trust Mrs. Danforth to spare the child even a ratty old toy. She needed us gone, my lord. To use the language of my betters, Leander and I are not good *ton*."

I wanted to ponder the horse and the significance of its absence until the sun had set and the seasons had changed, but darkness could only aid Miss Hammerschmidt and give Leander one more thing to fear.

I took out my notebook and pencil and scribbled a few words in French. "Can you have Bella or Pansy deliver this to His Grace?" I passed over the note and, as an afterthought, wrote another. "That one is for Miss West, who dwells with her brother on Ainsley Lane. They will be as concerned for Leander as I am."

I let out a whistle, which would signal Atticus to get Beecham ready to depart. A handful of oats, another offer of water... We had a long evening ahead of us.

Miss Dujardin rose and collected the second note. "I should have insisted you take in Leander a week ago. I will never forgive myself for putting deference to your station above his welfare."

"You did not steal the boy, miss. You did everything in your power to keep him safe in enemy territory while I dithered over legalities and ancient history. If anybody is to flagellate himself with guilt, let it be me. I'm an old hand at it."

Her smile was wan, but reminded me that Miss Dujardin—did I even know her Christian name?—was a pretty woman. Not in the overt, sensual, *grande horizontale* manner of a Mrs. Bellassai, but in a quieter, sweeter manner.

I very much wanted to pay my call on Alexander Newton in hopes the playwright might know where Miss Hammerschmidt bided, but I needed to sort out a few pertinent details.

"As I understand it, you came into the garden earlier today to heed the call of nature. Leander ventured downstairs on his own in pursuit, or perhaps to keep you in sight. Mrs. Danforth says she caught him wandering again and gave him at least the sharp side of her tongue, if not another smiting. Would he have brought his horse along on such a sortie?"

Miss Dujardin slanted a perplexed look at me. "I did not come into this garden this afternoon, my lord. I stay abovestairs with Leander to the greatest extent possible. I've started teaching him French out of sheer boredom."

Mrs. Danforth claimed she'd caught the boy on the back terrace. She wasn't about to lie for him, which meant Leander had been lying to her when he'd said he'd been following Miss Dujardin to the garden.

The rows facts and columns of observation weren't adding up correctly. "How did you know he was missing?"

"We typically nap in the later afternoon. It's too hot to tarry in the park at that time of day, though I try to get him there most mornings if his lessons go well. I attempt a second round of lessons after our nooning, but after that... I know he doesn't sleep some days, but he plays quietly in his room while I have a lie-down. Routine can be a comfort when a child has known a lot of upheaval, and that quiet time in the later afternoon was a fixture of our days."

"And when you went to check on him, he wasn't in his room?"

"Correct. I'd left him alone for maybe half an hour at that point."

This recitation made little sense, given Mrs. Danforth's version of events. "Then he took up his prized horse, braved the lower floors on his own, crossed paths with the dreaded Mrs. Danforth on the back terrace, and told her a great bouncer regarding your whereabouts." What possible motive could he have had for risking another skirmish with his own personal dragon?

"Leander can tell a fib when it suits his purposes. He's not the sort of child who lies clumsily. That he's good at dissembling alarms me, though he deploys the skill as a last resort."

Miss Dujardin certainly knew her charge well, and she had taken on far more of the governess's role than that of nursemaid. I ought to ask her when she'd last been paid, but that discussion could wait.

When I had periodically gone absent from Caldicott Hall as a boy, nobody had assumed I'd been abducted. They had instead concluded I'd run away from home, a puerile rite of passage apparently, or they conjectured that I'd become stuck atop a haystack or in some venerable tree.

"What of Leander's soldiers?" I asked, naming the possessions the boy might well prize as highly as his stuffed horse. "Are they in their proper garrison?"

Miss Dujardin glowered up at the house. The windows reflected the slanting evening light, like blank eyes, and a raven marched about in an attic gutter.

"I still don't know where his soldiers are, my lord. He won't tell me. He says they are safe, where the enemy can't capture them. That he has to hide his toys, what few toys he has left..." Miss Dujardin rubbed a hand across her forehead. "I cannot bear this. I cannot bear the pass we've come to."

And yet, bear it, she would. I moved around to inspect the space behind the rain barrel and found nothing. The battlefield established earlier in the week was deserted, though under the lavender border, I found a skeleton force of three.

I hunkered to study the few pieces remaining. "He took his artillery and cavalry and left a trio of sentries posted."

"He might have split up his forces, put some here and some there, lest somebody find one of his hiding places."

I collected the sentries and put them in my pocket. "When would he have had time? You are with him when he's away from his room, and while *I* know he slipped his forces into the lavender bed when I was on hand to distract you, on subsequent trips to the garden, you would have watched him closely."

Miss Dujardin stared up at me. "What are you saying?"

"He was not kidnapped." The realization brought both relief and renewed terror. "He has struck out into the world on his own, and we have less than an hour of full daylight before he's alone after dark in London."

Miss Dujardin looked up at the sky, her expression utterly bleak. I knew how she felt, beyond despair, and into the realm where tears and profanity were pointless.

"God help him."

"First," I said, "we need to dispatch those notes, then we need to review all the places he might try to reach on his own."

Miss Dujardin stared at the two pieces of paper in her hand. "He never goes anywhere without me, and we have only been in London proper since Mrs. Danforth took us in. I have no idea... I have no earthly idea where he could be."

Neither did I, but suffice it to say, locating the boy had gone from just barely possible back to unspeakably difficult, and we had roughly one hour in which to find him.

~

A search of the alley and stable took up twenty minutes and yielded no results. Miss Dujardin had agreed to remain at the house in case any reply arrived from Hyperia or His Grace, though no reply had been needed in either case.

I simply wanted to get her off her feet. The night might be long, and she was already on her last nerve.

"The lad used to ask me about the pub," the footman Jones said as the shadows in the cobbled alley grew more ominous. "The Hare and Dog is right around the corner, but I don't guess Miss ever took him inside."

Women worked in pubs and, in some cases, would patronize them, but rarely without a male companion.

"What about the church?" Griffith asked as two lanky grooms made short work of evening chores in the stable. "Lad got drug to services regular enough."

"Miss Dujardin inquired of Vicar," I replied. "I assume the curate would have done a cursory inspection of the pews and loft."

"But not the graveyard," Griffith retorted. "Many a boy's played hide-and-seek in a graveyard."

"Not after dark," Jones observed. "Not without his mates."

Leander, as far as I knew, had no mates, no friends at all.

Throughout this discussion, Atticus had been patiently stroking Beecham's neck and shoulder. The gelding was dozing with a hip cocked. Atticus looked drawn to me and more than a little anxious.

"You should get back to Waltham House before the light's gone," I said.

"You might need me to hold the horse."

"The horse will stand until kingdom come, lad. Be off with you. Tell His Grace we've made no progress, but will continue to search."

Atticus got a look in his eyes that boded ill for my good manners. "Search where, yer worship? You done searched the alleys, the neighbors' yards, the nearest squares, the church, and halfway to perdition, but you ain't found him. He mighta piked off to begin with, but by now, somebody has snatched that boy, sure as Beecham farts when he trots."

I was assailed by the fact that I'd overlooked the obvious. I was trying to find a boy, a boy new to London and one with few allies. Atticus was such a boy, though he had the benefit of perhaps twice Leander's years.

"Where would you suggest we search?" I asked. "Don't turn up pugnacious on me now. I am asking in all seriousness."

"Pug-what?"

"Difficult, bellicose, contrary. *Where would you go?*"

He stroked the horse's neck again. "To the park, I s'pose. You can breathe in the park, and it's quiet. More like the country. People are happy there. They play with their dogs and chase balls and feed the ducks. London has one pretty, happy place, free to all, it's the park."

"Lad's gotta point," Griffith said. "Miss was forever taking the young master to Hyde Park if he'd made a good try at his studies. Got him out from underfoot too."

"I like the park," Jones said wistfully. "I go every half day. I try to walk along Park Lane if I have time after divine services."

I recalled Leander wheedling for an outing to the park, and Miss Dujardin standing firm. The park was a reward and a refuge. An oasis of freedom, fresh air, and safety—from the boy's perspective.

"Where else might you go, Atticus? If you didn't know your way to the park, where would you go?"

He shook his head. "I know how to get there, and if I didn't, any passing stranger would be able to tell me. Everybody knows how to get to Hyde Park, and it's barely a quarter hour's walk from here."

"Very well. To Hyde Park." The obvious next step, and I had missed that too.

We had enough light left to dash to the park and make a start on a search, no more. "Jones, please fetch Miss Dujardin. She'll know the boy's favorite haunts. Griffith, you and the grooms go ahead on foot. Send the men searching along the banks of the Serpentine and the

Long Water. As hot as it's been, Leander might have taken a notion to go wading."

A potentially fatal notion.

"I'm coming too," Atticus said. "You can order me home all you please, but I'll just go to the park and hunt for the lad on me own."

I wanted to hug him and to send him packing. "Up you go, then."

Miss Dujardin bustled out of the house not five minutes later, bonnet ribbons neatly tied, gloves on, her velvet reticule in hand.

I roused Beecham to a smart pace, and we were soon tooling down Park Lane toward the entrance nearest Apsley House.

"Where do we search, Miss Dujardin?" I asked as Beecham clip-clopped along.

"Along the water. Leander loves the ducks and geese. We sometimes helped ourselves to a handful of grain when the grooms weren't looking, and Leander delighted in the racket the waterfowl made in pursuit of a treat."

The grooms and Griffith were already patrolling the paths along the waterways.

"Did you stick to one bank or the other?"

"The northern bank is our preferred haunt. We never wander as far as Kensington Gardens. Leander is getting too big and too dignified for me to carry, and the walk home always takes twice as long as the walk to the park."

The boy's father should have been on hand to piggyback him home, as my father, despite his lofty title, had occasionally transported me home from picnics at Caldicott Hall.

And if not Leander's father, then a devoted uncle should have been pressed into service.

I drew the gelding to the side of Park Lane and brought him to a halt. As I leapt down, a female sort of person sashayed past the curricle, her perfume a hyacinth pollution upon the evening air. Her hems were modest enough, but her decolletage was in danger of losing the battle with gravity, and her hair was done up in a ridiculous confusion of ringlets and braids. She passed into the park, where she doubt-less intended to ply her trade.

"We'll need torches if we're to search much longer," Griffith said, trotting up on my right. He made a valiant effort to ignore the endow-ments of the woman parading along the walkway, while the two grooms trailing behind him succumbed to a bout of ogling.

Had I been that fatuous when my manly humors had been more in evidence? That stupid? I daresay I had been, and on more occa-sions than I was comfortable admitting.

"Fetch some torches." I passed him over a few coins. "Tatts should oblige. Tell them a lad's gone missing."

Miss Dujardin and I made another pass on foot along the north bank of the Serpentine. We explored a few side paths, but as we were without illumination, and those paths became increasingly haunted by the park's criminal and commercial denizens, I decided the time had come to send Miss Dujardin to safer surrounds.

"I don't want to go back to Mrs. Danforth's," she said when I put my concerns to her. "That woman looks at me as if this is my fault, and it is, but it's not all my fault."

"If you will blow retreat, I can more easily approach certain parties who regularly do business in the park in the evening hours. You will be comfortable at Waltham House, or I can send you to Miss West."

A presumption on my part, but I was confident Perry wouldn't let me down.

"If you find Leander, you'll take him to Waltham House?"

"Directly."

"I don't want to go."

She cared for the boy, clearly, but the time had come for plain speaking. "You will slow me down, Miss Dujardin, and as the hour advances, seeing to your safety will become an increasing hindrance."

I braced myself for argument and pleading—more wasted time—but Miss Dujardin studied the dark mirror of the water's surface, then squared her shoulders.

"I'll go to Waltham House."

*Thank the merciful powers.* She trundled off with Griffith's escort, and I accompanied them as far as Park Lane. Atticus was minding the curricle and yawning about every thirty seconds.

I passed him my flask. "How were the meat pies?"

"Not as good as Mrs. Bellassai's, but good enough. I saved one for the lad, like you told me to."

Shadows were forming into patches of darkness. A few of the more conscientious households along the street had already lit their streetlamps. Atticus drained my flask and shook the dregs into his mouth.

"If you were facing a night in Hyde Park, Atticus, and alarming sorts of people were occupying more and more of the paths and getting up to mischief behind the hedges, where would you hide yourself?"

Atticus capped my flask by banging his fist on the cork, then passed it back to me. "Not in the bushes, that's for sure. Bushes got bugs in 'em, and gents and dogs like to piss on bushes."

"Along a building, then?" Hyde Park had a few. Sheds, gazebos, arches, memorials...

"Rats like to scurry along buildings." Atticus yawned again. "Lad's probably catching a nap on some bench or in a tree."

"The trees are too large to lend themselves to climbing."

"No, they ain't. Some fine climbing trees down this end of the Serpentine, along the short bank, just off the path."

"How would you know such a thing?"

He grinned. "How'd ya think, guv?"

I tousled his hair. "Rotten boy. Don't you dare eat the last meat pie."

I jogged back the way I'd come, yelling at the two grooms to follow me. When I reached the point where the path diverged along the long northern shore of the Serpentine and the short eastern side of the lake, I took the eastern path and sent Griffith's minions on to the next clump of trees along the northern bank.

"Leander, I know you're up there. There's a meat pie in it for you if you come down now, lad. Miss Dujardin is most concerned by your absence without leave, and I daresay Dasher is hungry for some oats."

My heart sank when the only response to my call was a squirrel scampering across the path.

Well, damn. What had I expected? The boy had probably been snatched up within a quarter hour of passing through Mrs. Danforth's garden gate. I subsided onto a bench that sat in near darkness and tried to make my tired mind think of next steps, possibilities, anything productive.

A small, thready voice floated down to me through the gloom.

"The trouble is, sir, I'm stuck, you see. And when I try to get unstuck, I get more stuck. I'm hungry and thirsty, and I have to wee, but mostly I'm s-stuck."

*Thank God.* Thank God and all His angels, and thank my canny, stubborn little Atticus too.

I sprang up from the bench. "Fortunately for you, rescue is at hand. Shake a branch, and I'll have you down in no time."

"I really do have to wee."

"Two minutes, lad. Just hold out for two more minutes."

He managed, bless the boy, but it was a very, very near thing.

# CHAPTER FOURTEEN

"I will pay for this day's work." I accepted a brandy from Arthur, not because I wanted a brandy, but because Arthur was being gracious. Thus did shy dukes settle their nerves.

Miss Dujardin was tucking Leander in up in his aerie. I'd sent notes to Hyperia and to the Danforth household. Atticus had received a hero's welcome in the stable and kitchen, as well he should have. I'd asked for a tepid bath to be prepared for my dusty self, but given the late hour, nobody—least of all myself—was moving with any haste.

"You found him," Arthur said, saluting with his drink. "That is all that matters."

We sat outside the library's French doors, no sconces lit, no footmen hovering. I was worn out as only a long day of indecisive battle could leave a soldier weary in body and spirit.

"Finding Leander is not all that matters," I replied, setting my drink aside, untouched. "We still don't know the boy's antecedents."

"He's Harry to the life at that age. Not something you would know. We have likenesses, somewhere. We were all immortalized in Her Grace's sketchbooks."

Arthur had watched in silence when Miss Dujardin had been reunited with her charge. She had not wept, but the boy's puerile dignity had come completely unraveled, and that had nearly undone me as well.

Poor little mite. Poor, brave, reckless little mite. "Leander and I are due for a talk, when he's feeling a bit more the thing. When I retrieved him from the park, he was too busy inhaling a meat pie and fretting that he'd be made to do endless sums."

"An unkind fate indeed." Arthur's tone reminded me that he did sums by the hour. By the day and week too. In his absence, that task would fall to me. I liked tallying and toting up. I'd found such work restful when I'd been recuperating among the quartermasters.

"I don't particularly care who Leander's mother is, Jules. The Hammerschmidt woman won't try to steal him out of his cot, and if that cook—the one with the Viking name—tries to claim him, I will have a word with Her Grace of Ambrose. If anybody has the temerity to inquire, Mrs. Waites had the honor of bringing him into this world."

A fine plan, if one was a duke and could quell gossip with a raised eyebrow. As soon as that duke's back was turned, the whispers would resume at even greater velocity.

"The boy deserves to know the truth, Arthur. Who one's parents are is not a detail in this life." I sipped my brandy, needing the fire in my gullet. "I don't suppose you know who my father is?"

"Your father was His Late Grace of Waltham, as far as I know. You'd have to take up the discussion with Her Grace, and I'd say she owes you those answers."

"Perhaps you'd opine to that effect in your next weekly report to her?"

"I might, at that."

I was learning to read my brother, and in Arthur's silence, I heard enormous relief. Leander's situation had cast a cloud over Arthur's travel plans—and over his heart—and now that a departure date had been set, Arthur was allowing himself to look forward to the occasion.

I, by contrast, was looking forward to long weeks at Caldicott Hall, the beauty of the English countryside in autumn, the peace and deep quiet of a rural winter...

"The boy will come down to the Hall with me," I said. "Safer for him there."

"Healthier too. Show him all of Harry's old haunts. You never did say where you came upon the lad."

"Stuck ten feet up a tree." A metaphor, that.

"Harry was always part monkey. Once I explained to him that nobody looks up, he started on his career as a spy. He was always sizing up this or that tree for climbing potential, and then he began on the porticoes and gazebos. Took years off Papa's life with his acrobatics."

"I have visions of you parading around the nursery in miniature full court regalia. How would you know about the privacy to be had in trees?"

He sipped his drink. "Leander is not the first Caldicott boy to run away from home. We can get his name changed by deed poll before I leave for Calais."

"Changed from what? We have no proof of his present name, and the legal types generally like to start there."

Arthur set his glass beside mine. "You won't let this go."

"Can you forget you are the duke?"

"I intend to give it a damned good try, thanks to you. All my life, I've known what lay ahead. Papa made sure I held no illusions. I'd have little privacy, few real friends, many dilemmas. No matter what choices I made—to ignore petty poaching or enforce the letter of the law, to support this cause or decry that one—I'd be judged vociferously. For the next year, I hope to set all of that aside and be... myself."

My brother and I shared a burden of loneliness I hadn't been able to see clearly because I'd been so wrapped up in my own troubles. Banter's company was doubtless a comfort, but the title also made Banter's company a greater risk.

"The boy will know a version of the same burden you do, Arthur. Whispers will follow him from the schoolyard to the churchyard, into whatever profession he chooses. The talk will affect how he sees himself, what doors open to him and which slam in his face. His Grace was my father of record, and even the great edifice of legal, ducal legitimacy has been no shelter against the looks, the asides, the jokes in poor taste."

I'd chosen reconnaissance in part because those duties meant less time spent in the officer's mess, less time in camp, less time idling about on leave with the men who were my inferiors in one sense and my irrefutable betters in another.

*Leander is just a boy,* I wanted to shout. A small, frightened, helpless boy. Shrewd for his age, likely of necessity. A competent liar, Miss Dujardin had said, and that broke my heart. I had learned deception at a young age as well.

I'd learned to pretend the name-calling didn't matter. To put on a convincing show of indifference when the young ladies passed me over at the tea dances for the spares of lower rank. To act as if the hostesses invited me for my competent dancing and charming small talk, rather than out of fear of offending my mother.

"You are tired," Arthur said. "I am tired, for that matter. You are the hero of the day, and yet, you insist on fretting. Go to bed, Jules. 'Take therefore no thought for the morrow... Sufficient unto the day is the evil thereof.'"

"Matthew, chapter six." A deportment manual Mrs. Danforth ought to be made to memorize. "We must deal with the Danforth woman, or she'll be every bit as persistent in her attempts to extort money from us as Clothilda Hammerschmidt on her most tenacious day."

"That reminds me. Your trip to Horse Guards bore more fruit. A note arrived from some friend of Healy West's. Somebody recalled a few facts regarding the late Lieutenant Colonel Danforth. He was a lecher and a drunk, not much liked."

"Neither would have disqualified him for military service." Though Danforth had made an enemy of his own wife.

"He was given the choice of selling up or a dishonorable discharge. Something to do with a colonel's pretty young wife."

"Then he was a fool, and the military can tolerate only so many fools among its officers." The news ought to spark in me some compassion for the fool's widow, but she'd struck a child simply because he'd been unable to fight back. *Hell hath no fury...*

Arthur finished his drink. "Get up to bed, Jules, lest you fall asleep out here and take a chill to go with your unhappy mood. I will call on Mrs. Danforth in person. She will dine out on that miracle for years. I will inform her that I have purchased the lease to the dwelling she so graciously made available to my nephew."

I considered that tactic, which had much to recommend it, though we still did not know for a certainty that Leander was our nephew. "Have you purchased the place?"

"By this time tomorrow, I will own yet another Town property I do not want and become responsible for all of its repairs and maintenance. She's likely late on the rent and will communicate her ongoing displeasure with the shutters and flues to me personally. Some people derive all manner of joy from complaining."

Arthur was not one of them. I did not want to join those ranks either. "Deed the place to her, Arthur. Thanks for her charity, appreciation for her generosity. She will be bound by your largesse to speak well of you and thus of Leander."

"That is..." Arthur rose. "That is... I do like it. Deprive her of her victimhood, her martyrdom—she is nothing remarkable without it— and she will be truly furious, not simply bitter. Diabolically noble of me. Jules, you might find you have a flair for the ducal role after all."

He jaunted off to bed, or to pen his daily epistle to Banter, who likewise sent missives up from the country with faithful regularity.

If Mrs. Danforth was given a roof over her head and the prospect of a secure old age, she might part with a portion of her ire. I did not particularly care how she dealt with her windfall, provided she spoke no ill of Arthur or Leander, ever.

I followed Arthur into the house, because he'd been right: Another quarter hour sitting in the dark, and I'd have succumbed to the sheer weight of fatigue. Better by far to fall asleep in the bath. I had loose ends to tidy up on the morrow, and inertia would see me through that day. The day after tomorrow, though, I was likely to be completely useless.

I might manage to show my nephew some of the lesser-known details of the battle plan Wellington had adopted at Waterloo. Might let him sit on a pony for his first ride up and down the alley.

But was Leander truly my nephew? That question prevented me from slumbering in the tub and even kept me awake when I'd found the great and glorious comfort of my bed.

~

I rose in the morning, stiff, sore, and well aware that I owed Hyperia a report, despite Healy West's interdiction on my socializing with his sister. First, I had another party to interview, however reluctant he and I might both be to even acknowledge each other.

I'd awoken with the birds, the habit of an officer behind enemy lines, one with miles to cover before the worst heat of the day. I was still tired and also famished in an I'll-deal-with-that-later way, but I made myself take tea, toast, and eggs in my room. I left the house shortly after first light.

Atlas was happy to be under saddle and set a brisk pace for the park. We'd even managed to canter a bridle path or two before I spotted my quarry. He stood on the same hillside, reins in hand, his horse patiently awaiting further orders.

I kept Atlas to the walk as we approached. St. Clair merely watched us. If the eyes were the window to the soul, Sebastian St. Clair's soul was an impenetrable abyss of silence. His gaze put me in mind of an old battlefield, still haunted, perhaps never to return to the province of the living.

"Lord Julian, good day."

He did not bow, but I took his greeting for a willingness to parley. I dismounted a good eight feet from where he stood.

"St. Clair."

"You found the boy?"

How could he possibly...? But then, St. Clair was supposedly living on borrowed time, and I figured near the top of the list of those who'd be justified in killing him. He doubtless kept a close eye on me and many others.

"He's safe and sound, biding at Waltham House. Is he Harry's son?"

"That's good. Good that you found him."

The relief seemed sincere, and I was reminded that St. Clair had been a boy stranded in France when the Peace of Amiens had come to an abrupt close. I shoved that recollection far to the side.

*"Is he Harry's son?"*

St. Clair's horse, who was of a height with Atlas, nudged at his owner's arm. St. Clair stroked the beast's ear gently. "Why would you expect me to know such a thing?"

"Two reasons. First, you were apparently the last person to see Harry alive. If, God forbid, I am taken from the mortal realm in a situation of extremity, I hope my dying sentiments will be to commend my love to my family. Second, if Harry had a son—a boy you've apparently taken some interest in—then you'd have used that knowledge against my brother. You made it your business to know a man's vulnerabilities and exploit them."

"Of course I did. I had to get results, or my superiors would have resorted to that time-honored diversion of torturing the prisoners."

*"You* tortured me."

St. Clair was silent for a time, gently petting his horse.

Part of me wanted to wrap my hands around his throat and choke the life from him. But there he was... scratching his horse's ear while the horse made sheep's eyes and tilted his head at an undignified angle. One could not commit murder—or even take revenge—against a fellow who was merely showing his mount some affection.

I couldn't, apparently. Not on this fine summer morning in the midst of Hyde Park's peace and verdure. Bad form and all that. Then too, I was tired.

So abidingly tired.

St. Clair produced a carrot, broke it in two, and passed me half. Atlas was wiggling his damned lips before I'd accepted the bribe—or peace offering. The morning air was soon full of the sound of horsey mastication, though I well knew St. Clair was using the delay to organize his thoughts and choose his tactics.

"Physical torture is problematic for many reasons," St. Clair began, as if embarking on an exegesis of some verse from Proverbs. "The first and most glaring difficulty is that the results are generally useless. Torture makes liars of the most honorable men. Why damage a fellow to the point that he will tell any falsehood, no matter how outlandish, if it's what his tormentors want to hear? Torture also has the disagreeable risk of resulting in death. If the victim guesses wrong about what information is sought, if his constitution isn't up to the challenge... you see the difficulty."

So rational. While Atlas crunched his carrot, I envisioned backhanding St. Clair off his feet. I wasn't the walking weapon I'd once been, but my bitterness made Mrs. Danforth's look like the village militia bumbling about the green by comparison.

And yet, I wasn't merely tired, I was exhausted. Backhanding a man of St. Clair's proportions onto his backside would take considerable strength.

"You broke men's minds rather than their bodies."

"What is broken up here,"—St. Clair tapped his temple with a black-gloved hand—"can heal. What is broken in the body often lingers, providing an unrelenting echo of the original wound."

"So you starved me, half froze me, and denied me water out of concern for my wellbeing. How considerate of you, and entirely beside the point. Did Harry speak of a son, of children in the general case?"

"He did not, and I have no reason to lie to you about this, my lord. If anything, I am motivated to serve your cause."

"Because you are such a philanthropist among men. Of course." I was getting angry, or trying to, but my temper wasn't much interested in obliging me. St. Clair would deal graciously with my anger—like Arthur deeding a house to Mrs. Danforth—and I would find no satisfaction in being humored.

More to the point, my rage, much like my manly humors, seemed to have deserted its post. No doubt, three evenings hence, pretending to appreciate another brandy, I'd feel the fullness of my ire, but watching the sun rise over stately maples and the calm expanse of the Serpentine... I could conjure only annoyance and weariness.

St. Clair produced another carrot and repeated his ritual of sharing. "I am the last of my line. Because of my station, the French allowed me a choice of starvation in a parole town or joining *La Grande Armée*. Not out of compassion, but because they delighted in the thought of an English baron's son—the baron himself in later years—being made to serve the Corsican. French humor can be a subtle thing, *non?*"

His French accent, barely in evidence in previous occasions, was less subtle now, possibly by design.

*"Did Harry have a son?"*

"I believe he did, but I do not know of a certainty. He made no dying declarations, no convenient entreaty to me or the Almighty. He kept his own counsel, and he knew I held you elsewhere in the chateau. He could have bargained, he could have negotiated. He kept silent."

"You are saying he could have protected me by compromising his honor, but refused that course?"

"Despite all rumor to the contrary, I am a rational man. For the sake of my continued survival, my efforts at the chateau had to bear fruit. But by the time you and your brother were captured,

Wellington was moving through the passes. He was crossing the border, and the French army was in no state... I needn't recite particulars. I offered your brother options. He chose his own course."

The sun turned the dewy grass into a sparkling green wonder, the birds sang, equestrians offered one another cordial greetings, and footmen chatted while walking dogs for nearby households. A lovely morning, and Harry wasn't here to see any of it.

"Did Harry bargain for my life?" I hated that I'd ask, but realized that St. Clair wanted me to have this discussion with him. St. Clair might or might not have information regarding Leander, but the topic of Harry had to be aired first.

That Harry's ghost troubled what passed for St. Clair's conscience gratified me exceedingly.

"Lord Harry did not bargain for your life, perhaps because he knew your death was never my objective. He trusted your ability to come through any ordeal I could devise, and you have. He kept his own counsel, but at the last, he was a man with deep regrets. I have no proof, but I have experience of men facing death, and Lord Harry Caldicott struck me as a fellow with much to mourn."

"We all had much to mourn." Also much to be grateful for, though I wasn't about to admit that to St. Clair.

"True, but some griefs are harder to bear than others. I, for instance, am under an unwritten death sentence, but I have been given a reprieve. I am certain that once I have a healthy, legitimate son in my nursery, my days upon this earth will be brought to an end."

"Because English honor is a subtle thing, *non?*"

"*Précisément.* As is English justice. I will never live to see my son grow up. I will be denied the chance to explain my choices to him at moments when he might receive my words with compassion. I will never have an opportunity to beg, if not his forgiveness, then his understanding. I will never hold a grandchild in my arms. My torment now is to know and mourn my fate.

"The woman who marries me," he went on more softly, "had best include widow's weeds in her trousseau, if any such woman I can find."

I would not, in my most drunken imaginings, have seen the potential for this patch of common ground between Harry and his killer.

"You think Harry had the same regret—that his son would never know him?"

"I do. I have no basis in fact for this conclusion. Intuition and reflection alone suggest it to me. I am sorry I cannot be more help."

"But you are not sorry you killed my brother."

St. Clair offered his horse one final pat, then swung up into the saddle with the athleticism of the born equestrian.

"*I killed no one.* Your brother essentially ended his own life and took his secrets—military and personal—with him. He had his reasons. I beg you to accept them and let the matter drop. I did not kill him, though I don't expect you to believe that. Nonetheless, if my opinion means anything, that boy is Lord Harry's son. Good day."

St. Clair departed, keeping his horse to a sedate walk.

Had I put a bullet in his back, he might have thanked me, but I knew then, if I hadn't known before, that the gun that fired such a bullet would not be mine.

And that was a relief beyond words.

≈

I had barely regained the saddle before Hyperia, mounted on her elegant mare, emerged from a break in the trees. She waved her groom off as soon as she spotted me, and that was a relief too. I wasn't up to small talk and subtle innuendo, not after my exchange with St. Clair.

"Is that who I think it is?" she asked, gaze following St. Clair's progress along the hedgerow.

"Sebastian St. Clair, Lord St. Clair. I think he comes out here of a morning in hopes somebody will use him for target practice."

She swung her gaze to me. "The war is over. His title is ancient. His auntie dotes on him."

Of the three considerations, the last was the one that likely kept him from stealing a march on his assassins. If St. Clair was the last of his line, then that auntie had no other family, no other benefactor.

"St. Clair knows things," I said, turning Atlas to toddle along beside Hyperia's mare. "Things about Harry. He claimed Harry took his own life rather than divulge any secrets."

"Then Harry chose the lesser of two dishonors," Hyperia murmured, "or perhaps St. Clair was speaking metaphorically. By keeping his mouth shut, Harry sealed his own fate. St. Clair offered him another option, but Harry refused to compromise."

"St. Clair's style is more irony than metaphor." We chose a path between stately maples, and already the shade felt good. "Murder was also not St. Clair's style, though his guards and superiors had a less refined sense of how to encourage a prisoner to talk. He believes Leander is Harry's son."

"Does St. Clair *know* that, or was he sharing a hunch?"

"An informed and educated hunch." Or knowledge disguised as a hunch.

The horses moseyed along. If I hadn't been in Hyde Park, where what remained of polite society was likely to come upon me, I might have dismounted, propped my backside against a handy tree, and dropped straight off to sleep.

"You are not satisfied," Hyperia said. "What additional stone could you turn, Jules? You've been to rubbishing Horse Guards, and that cannot have been a pleasant errand. Now you've confronted the author of your worst nightmares and consulted him on private family business. Arthur would be appalled that you sought out St. Clair."

No, he would not. He'd suggested it, in fact, and allowed me to introduce him to St. Clair. "Are you appalled?"

"Quite—at Harry. A son is not a trivial matter. That child has been on this earth for years, a Caldicott by birth, for all we know, and Harry could not see fit... I know Harry could be rackety and that he was involved in delicate matters, but to simply abandon the boy was disgraceful."

"Unless he wasn't Harry's concern."

Hyperia had a point. No other explanation fit with Harry's behavior, and yet, Harry had been sending money to some female regularly after he'd returned to Spain.

We rode along in silence, the conundrum of Leander's paternity and Harry's behavior gnawing at me. Hyperia's presence was nonetheless a balm to my soul. I could not imagine discussing St. Clair's revelations with anybody else.

"Maybe Harry didn't have time to tend to Leander's situation as he ought to have," Hyperia said. "He never took extended leave after that interminable winter. I don't even recall seeing him in Town again."

"He claimed he'd nipped up to London on his next leave, but I didn't go with him. He might have been meeting with an informant in Portsmouth."

Hyperia drew her mare to a halt at a shady bend in the path. "Harry kept secrets from even you and Arthur. I don't like that. You were not only a fellow soldier, you grasped the particulars of Harry's role. Arthur is a peer, the head of the family. Harry should not have left his brothers such a mess."

Atlas had shuffled to a stop as well. He'd had his brisk canter. He'd worked out his fidgets. He wasn't exactly dragging me off in the direction of his morning oats, but his business in the park had concluded for the day.

"Let's walk for a bit," I said, dismounting and coming around to the mare's side. "It's a pretty morning, and I meant to call on you when I was finished with St. Clair." I might never be entirely finished with St. Clair, but thanks to the very tangle Harry had left behind, I'd made progress in that direction.

"I planned to call on you on my way home." Hyperia freed her knee from the horn and slid into my arms. "Better that we meet here. Leander should have you and His Grace to himself today, I think."

I wrapped Hyperia in an embrace a shade too close to be considered a mere hug. She reciprocated with surprising ferocity.

"I was afraid you'd take on St. Clair in solo combat," she said, arms around my waist. "Jules, I would have come with you to call on him."

"I was afraid I'd lose my nerve. I've dreaded the sight of him, heard his voice in my nightmares. In the mountains, I'd imagine him stalking me, and when I wanted to quit, to lie down and give up, dread of him kept me moving. He was a devil on two feet, with his polite English and relentless civility. Such coldness isn't human."

Hyperia bundled closer. "And now?"

"He's broken. Something in that man—his heart, perhaps—cannot heal. Will never heal. I should be glad. I should gloat. He is tormented, and I should delight in his misery."

I could admit these things with Hyperia in my arms, and I could admit one more truth. "I don't think he killed Harry, not even metaphorically. I think Harry did himself an injury, on purpose. A mortal injury."

Hyperia eased back enough to look me over. "Will you tell Arthur?"

The next question, which she had the grace to spare me, was even more fraught: Would I someday tell Leander?

"I will tell Arthur what St. Clair claims to be true about Harry's death, but whether Arthur believes St. Clair is another matter."

We walked along the verge, leading the horses, until we came to a clearing with a single bench sitting in sunshine.

"Good grazing," I said, unwilling to give up Hyperia's company just yet. "Will your mare behave?"

"If there's grass at her feet, she'll bide patiently enough."

Atlas would not leave my sight without my permission, and that, too, would keep the mare from galloping off. We loosened girths and tied up reins, then took the bench and let the horses snack. Six different etiquette authorities would doubtless have been offended at our behavior and our horsemanship, and a dozen more would have chastised me for taking Hyperia's hand when we were side by side on the bench.

"The boy will need his things," Hyperia said, turning her face to the morning sun.

"When I found him, he had the cavalry stuffed in one pocket, the artillery in the other. He took Dasher's mane between his teeth to get up the tree."

"He will need his clothing, Jules. The boy needs trousers and shirts and linen. He might have a prayer book, a lucky robin's egg, a pretty pebble."

Right. Practicalities. One of the many reasons I treasured Hyperia West was because she kept hold of the practicalities.

"I'll fetch them."

"Has he told you why he piked off?"

"Mrs. Danforth apparently threatened him again." Except that wasn't quite right. As best I could reconstruct matters, Mrs. Danforth had interrupted him when he'd already been intent on eloping. "Leander and I need to have a talk about his order of battle."

Hyperia rested her head on my shoulder. "Does he ever mention his mother, Jules?"

"He does not."

"Ask him about her too."

We sat in the morning sun, and I let the enormity of recent events wash over me. I'd faced down Horse Guards. I'd skirmished, or something like it, with St. Clair. I'd found a missing boy despite all odds to the contrary, and I'd preserved my family from scandal. Successful missions, and yet, I'd failed to find the truth of Leander's antecedents.

"You're still fretting, aren't you, Jules?"

"Ruminating. Nothing urgent." And as long as Hyperia was content to stay with me hand in hand on that bench, everything—every other single consideration in the known universe—could wait.

# CHAPTER FIFTEEN

Before the park filled with nannies and children, before the sun got too high in the morning sky, I saw Hyperia home, and to blazes with her brother's offended sensibilities.

Time spent with Hyperia had steadied and fortified me. She'd given me orders too—retrieve Leander's effects from Mrs. Danforth's mews—and I was ever one to obey her commands. That I craved and delighted in her company, irrespective of the manly humors that had gone absent without leave, reassured me.

I yet lacked the courage to inquire into the particulars of her regard for me, but that conversation lay ahead of us.

Mrs. Danforth's grooms were lounging about, having already tended to morning chores. They inquired politely after the little lad and asked me to remember them to him. I wanted to think well of these humble, hardworking men who'd assisted in the search for Leander. A cranky, unsettled part of me wondered if they'd have been as solicitous of a boy who lacked ties to a ducal household.

My mood was stubbornly suspicious, and that, I knew, was a result of having failed not Arthur, and not even Harry's memory, but rather, one small child.

I gathered up the sentries yet on duty amid the lavender border, retrieved Leander's valise, and collected Miss Dujardin's bundle. Atlas dealt with the awkward burdens philosophically, and we were soon trundling up the alley behind Waltham House.

Breakfast—a proper, leisurely breakfast taken while perusing the morning paper—loomed as a benediction. I'd spend the day half dressed, wearing house slippers, catching up on correspondence, and likely enduring a call from Lady Ophelia.

Godmama was not one to let grass grow under her dainty feet when there were sermons to be delivered and gossip to be collected. If she distracted me from revisiting my earlier exchange with St. Clair, so much the better. I'd look in on the nursery, too, of course.

And some arrangement had to be made for Miss Dujardin.

She was more than a nurserymaid. A governess's wages, at least, should be offered to her. She knew enough French to start the boy on the rudiments, and in Caldicott fashion, we'd soon have him chattering away in my grandmother's tongue.

I took the valise and bundled cloak into the garden and set them on the wrought-iron table. A gentleman did not pry into a lady's personal affairs, but Miss Dujardin might have some artifact of Leander's origins among her possessions without knowing it. That elaborately embroidered handkerchief might have a twin. An old toy of Harry's, a book, a curio given to Mrs. Waites...

I was debating whether to snoop through Miss Dujardin's belongings when the lady herself emerged from the side terrace and scuttled down the path that led to the alley.

"Good morning, miss."

She froze, then turned slowly. She wore her bonnet and cloak and had her burgundy velvet reticule in her hand.

"I believe I have something of yours." I held up the bundle, then set it back on the table. "Let's have a look, shall we?" Where the hell had she been going, and had she informed anybody of her departure? Her furtive air suggested she'd been on the point of a clandestine departure, a thought which tried my already overtaxed patience.

I opened the knot fastening the bundle. If she made a dash for the alley, I'd catch her at the gate. She appeared to resign herself to that truth and came back up the walkway.

"My things," she said. "You found them."

"Any good soldier is ready to break camp on a moment's notice, and you apparently trusted the grooms not to steal from you more than you trusted Mrs. Danforth. Let's have a seat, shall we?"

I posed the question and waited for Miss Dujardin to make her choice.

She stopped a good two yards away. "Sometimes a clean break is best, my lord."

"So you said on a previous occasion, and yet, you did not abandon Leander then. Why pike off now?"

She shook her head. "Not your concern."

"You haven't a character or references of any sort. Is that why you couldn't apply to the agencies for a new post?" My imagination, which had been a sluggish and sullen creature since I'd found Leander, stirred to life.

"My lord, what are you talking about?"

"Miss West went to the better employment agencies, hoping to find word of one of the staff who served at Dingle Court all those years ago. She also asked after you and learned nothing. If you sought a new post in London, you did so at the lesser establishments. I would have written you a character sufficient to make the archangel Gabriel jealous of your prospects, but here you are, skulking into the alley at an hour when His Grace and I should still be abed."

"Nobody will hire me without a character," Miss Dujardin said slowly. "That is correct."

So where had she been on that half day? What had compelled her to leave the boy more or less undefended in enemy territory?

I opened the bundle on the table and began setting the contents in full view.

"My lord, this is unnecessary. I did not steal Mrs. Danforth's silver."

"She has only plate, I'm guessing." The tin of lemon soap sat next to the brush and mirror. The lemon hair tonic came next, then the books—stain removal, medicinals for female complaints, *The Book of Common Prayer*. "You made a clean sweep, gathered up everything except the boy himself."

She flinched. The reaction was so minute, I might well have missed it had she not been holding as still as a rabbit who hears the hunter's tread on an upwind path.

A rabbit, prey. Fast but vulnerable. "You meant to steal away with him." She'd been ready to break camp and had readied Leander for the same exercise. Ready to leave London. "Why?"

"I should be going."

I could turn up all lordly and imposing, or try to. Arthur was far more accomplished at such theatrics. Instead, I pulled out a chair and attempted sweet reason. If I was tired, she had to be nearly numb with overwrought nerves and harried fears. To steal the boy... no coin, no friends, nowhere to go. A desperate, doomed gambit, and she'd apparently concluded as much.

"Did you know, Miss Dujardin, that I am a bastard?"

Ah, I'd surprised her. She left off staring at the potted morning glories trailing up their lattice and looked at me in some consternation.

"I beg your pardon?"

"One doesn't use such vocabulary in the presence of a lady, I know, but here I stand, and the term applies. Leander and I will have that in common."

"I know his situation, my lord." Stated with an encouraging hint of impatience.

"And now you know mine, yet you still entrust that child to my care. His Grace will soon decamp for the Low Countries and is not expected back until next year. If you walk through that gate, you leave Leander entirely subject to my whim. If you trust me that far, don't you trust me enough to tell me the truth?"

Never had a woman gazed with more longing at a set of nursery windows. "You will be kind to him. You will keep him safe."

"I will be the most conscientious guardian a child ever had, but the legalities will be stymied by the fact that I don't even know the boy's real name. His Grace wants to give Leander the Caldicott name, but that means going through the deed poll rigamarole, and there again... we don't know Leander's true name. I believe you do, and I am humbly asking you to share it with me."

"Waltham is a duke. He can make up any name for Leander he chooses. Nobody will gainsay him."

"Leander might. I am a man grown, with every privilege imaginable, abundant blessings, and more reasons for gratitude than you can count, and yet, my own father, whoever he is, has never acknowledged me. That still has the power to wound, Miss Dujardin, to wound deeply. Your abandonment will hurt the child even more deeply. He won't get over it. He won't understand *someday*."

Mostly to allow her some dignity, I considered the small collection of effects on the table. Soap, hair tonic, a few aging books. She hadn't taken old Aesop. He was likely in Leander's valise at this point. The other offerings...

"You are not a nursemaid by trade or training," I said, picking up the little tome on removing stains. A laundress might have such a book, though she'd have learned its every secret before she turned twelve if her mother and aunties were laundresses. "You were a housekeeper."

I picked up the hair tonic, uncorked it, and sniffed. The lemon scent was powerful, though it would not clash with the soap in the tin. Why use any hair tonic at all when a lady's crowning glory was nearly always under a cap or a bonnet, particularly this lady's?

Even indoors. "You are lightening your hair, and you chose a lemon soap to try to disguise the fact." Why do that?

"Stop," she said, plunking her reticule on the table and taking the chair I'd proffered. "Please just stop. I think it best that I leave, and you have no right to paw through my things."

They were her things, and I had no right, so I ceased. I took the chair next to hers.

"Among Leander's possessions," I said, "I found an elaborately embroidered handkerchief that bears my late brother's initials as well as devices from the Caldicott coat of arms. An intimate item or one a father might want to pass on to his son. Proves nothing, of course, but it does raise questions."

She began repacking her bundle, so I marched on.

"Your reticule is made of the same fabric from which a handsome little Sunday coat was sewn for Leander, and sewn recently. The coat looks to fit him well, with seams designed to be let out as he grows. The same with the trousers and shirts. Somebody sewed him what amounts to a new wardrobe."

"Martha was a seamstress. She knew how to ply her needle."

"Martha was dying. Did she spend her last weeks stitching Leander's new shirt? I think not. I think you took the last of your good dresses and chemises and fashioned him a wardrobe to take with him into the next phase of his life. Then you hid the results of your hard work lest Mrs. Danforth demand goods in exchange for board."

Miss Dujardin paused, the hair tonic in her hand. "She would have sold me and Leander both, she's that angry with life."

"And probably with the compassionate God she professes to worship, but she is not my concern, and Dujardin is not your name." *The Book of Common Prayer* had told me that. I'd thought the article used, but it was old enough to have been owned by Miss Dujardin since childhood. The initials on the inscription, whatever they were, did not include a *D*. "Perhaps you are not Miss Dujardin, but rather, Lady Harry Caldicott?"

"Will you hush?" she replied, rising. "Will you please, for the sake of my nerves and all that is decent, just hush?" She jammed the last of her possessions back into the bundle, jerked the knot tight, and stood. "Tell Leander I love him and I will write when I can."

"Tell him yourself." I rose as well, and I was debating whether a gentleman could physically restrain a lady intent on making some heroic, cork-brained sacrifice, when a small boy launched himself from the house, pelted down the terrace steps, and lashed his arms around Miss Dujardin's waist.

"You can't go, miss. I knew you planned to leave me, but you mustn't go."

Arthur stood at the top of the steps, holding a tattered stuffed horse and looking very severe, as if that would make any difference to a small boy trying to prevent his world from crashing down on his innocent head.

Leander burst into heartrending sobs, Miss Dujardin took him into her arms and sat with him in her lap, and I breathed a heartfelt sigh of gratitude.

My reinforcements had arrived, and just in the nick of time.

~

While Leander snuggled in Miss Dujardin's lap with no more dignity than a puppy, I cleared the table of evidence. Arthur surrendered Dasher to his owner and busied himself finding a footman to order about while Leander regained his composure.

My own composure was none too steady, and yet, Miss Dujardin and I were nowhere near through with our discussion.

"Breakfast al fresco," Arthur said, joining us at the table. "Just the thing on a fine summer morning. Do you know, I have a horse too? I can't keep him with me at table, but he's a grand fellow, and I'm sure he'd enjoy making Leander's acquaintance after breakfast."

God bless my dear brother, taking the situation in hand. Whether Arthur had risen to the occasion on the strength of ducal discipline, patriarchal politesse, or the sheer decency of a good man, I did not care. To see that child so upset, so terrified of abandonment by the one person he'd been able to rely on during a short and uncertain life...

*God damn Harry*. Whatever his reasons and excuses, as I watched Leander sniffle into Miss Dujardin's handkerchief, I was almost glad Harry was dead. A growing heap of coincidences, hunches, and circumstantial evidence found his lordship guilty of a very poor and irresponsible sort of fatherhood.

I situated Leander in his own seat, using the valise to boost his little backside. He tucked into jam and toast and went into raptures about his hot chocolate, though the idea of enjoying such a beverage in the middle of high summer eluded me.

It hadn't eluded Arthur, who'd even remembered to have some ground nutmeg brought to the table. Miss Dujardin watched His Grace sprinkling the precious spice atop Leander's treat, her gaze unreadable.

"Because the occasion is special," Arthur said, adding a dash to his own chocolate and touching cups with Leander. "The prodigal is safely returned."

"Will I have to go back to Mrs. Dumbforth's?"

Arthur became absorbed with garnishing his own chocolate, though his shoulders twitched.

"You will not," I said. "Not ever. Your home is with us now. His Grace will soon be traveling on the Continent, so you and I will have to rub along as best we can until he gets back."

"And Miss too. She'll rub along with us." Leander regarded Miss Dujardin across the table, a chocolate mustache at variance with the solemnity of his gaze. "She won't go now, will she?"

"Leander," Miss Dujardin began very gently. "I know it's hard—"

I put my hand over hers. "Miss Dujardin was merely thinking ahead," I said. "She knew Mrs. Danforth was growing testier by the day and that *something could happen* to anything left in the house. She bundled up everything of value, and then I arrived without an invitation, and you mistakenly took matters into your own busy little hands. I'm sure Miss Dujardin was simply off to retrieve the luggage this morning before Mrs. Danforth could find it."

Leander wanted to believe me. I could see that in his eyes, so like Harry's, but so hopelessly innocent.

"Miss? Were you thinking to get the luggage just now? I saw you packing your bundle days ago, when I should have been napping. I wanted Aesop, and you were crying. You wouldn't leave me, would you?"

The morning acquired the sort of heavy stillness found only in high summer. The very air felt weighted as Leander licked his top lip and waited.

"I was off to snatch our luggage away before you finished your breakfast," Miss Dujardin said. "Lord Julian has the right of it."

Two grown men, one boy, a stuffed horse, every eavesdropping servant, and the very birds in the trees breathed a sigh of relief.

"Lord Julian fetched our things," Leander said. "You don't have to go back there either, miss. Not ever."

Arthur took up the chorus. "And thanks be to heaven on behalf of all concerned. Have you finished your chocolate? Well, then, make your bow, and I will introduce you to my horse. Come along."

To my surprise, that combination of good cheer and authority worked. Leander scrambled down from his perch and collected Dasher from where he'd been grazing on cherry cobbler near the teapot.

Leander stopped two steps down the path. "I forgot to ask to be excused."

Arthur made a get-on-with-it gesture.

"Miss, may I be excused?"

"You may. Try not to get dirty, and you will wash your hands when you come in from the stable."

"Yes, miss." Leander reached for Arthur's hand, then hesitated. "I don't know what to call you, sir."

Arthur looked from the boy to me. I nodded my agreement.

"Uncle Arthur will do, and that's Uncle Julian. He might be the slightest quarter inch taller than me, for now—I'm not quite done growing—but I am older and wiser. Please do bear that in mind. My horse is named Beowulf, and his friends call him Bey. He's partial to apples. He should just be finishing his oats by now."

They departed, Leander kiting along at Arthur's side.

"You will stay?" I asked. "I'm asking for all of us, not least for Harry."

Arthur and Leander disappeared through the gate, and Miss Dujardin rose. She walked off along the spent roses and gave me her back. It took me about fifteen seconds and the sound of one discreet sniffle to realize the poor lady was in tears.

I snatched the nearest table napkin and passed it to her. She surprised a year off my life by throwing herself into my arms and weeping as if she'd been denied admittance to heaven. Her tears were all the more upsetting for being muffled against my shoulder, while heat rolled off her, and her grip on my arm became painful.

I could not have stopped this storm if I'd been to Mount Olympus born, nor would I have tried. The woman had every right to cry. She wept on, and I held her, knowing all too well what it was like to wander a hostile landscape, no hope of ever finding a safe haven.

"He'll hear me," she whispered when the worst of the cataclysm had passed. "He mustn't hear me. He saw me crying... Oh, God. He ran away because of me."

Was she speaking of Leander or Harry? Did it matter? "The child is safe, and right now, he's under the direct supervision of the man fifty-third in line for the throne. Or maybe forty-seventh. I forget, and it keeps changing. You hardly ate a thing."

She eased away, dabbing at her eyes. "I'm not used to good meals anymore."

"Then we must reacquaint you with the habit. Let's sit, shall we? Beowulf enjoys callers, but Arthur's patience has limits."

"He's a duke." This was said with some consternation. "I knew that, but the reality is hard to grasp."

"Waltham finds himself facing the same conundrum and bears up manfully, for the most part. Please assure me you won't try to leave at the first opportunity."

We resumed our seats, and I waited for an answer that mattered a very great deal.

"I planned to take Leander with me at first. When I should have been applying to the agencies, I was looking over coaching routes and fares. I even considered taking ship. My French is good, and the Continent is rumored to be very affordable."

And if Leander hadn't run away, would he even now be enjoying his first sight of Calais? Informing any passenger on the packet's deck that he had to wee?

"I want Leander to be safe," she said quietly.

"I want him to be safe and happy, insofar as life allows us either boon. He was safe and happy in infancy, wasn't he?" I poured her a cup of tea, the universal restorative. I poured the same for myself as well.

"How do you know that?"

I gestured to her reticule. "You wore velvet. Leander developed a taste for nutmeg. He's learning to read. You have books. Your library has been whittled down, but that you'd haul those books about... Other women might have tossed them, but to you they were proof of better days. You were Harry's housekeeper on Dingle Court, weren't you?"

Those ledger entries hadn't recorded expenditures on behalf of Monsieur Beaujolais, but rather, Madam Bleeker or Millicent Bleeker, and the ambiguity on Harry's part had likely been on purpose.

"I was Lord Harry's housekeeper, and then I was something else entirely. Harry was as surprised by the whole situation as I was. I'm the usual cautionary tale. Raised in a vicarage—Martha and I had that in common—taught to work hard and mind my betters. Then along came Harry Caldicott, and twenty-five years of common sense, regular sermons, and good intentions went right up the bedroom flue. He was a force of nature, and I suddenly understood why smart women do very foolish things. I am comforted to think he was in the grip of something similarly unprecedented."

She sipped her tea, and I wanted to kick Lord Force of Nature in his cods. "He returned to Spain without marrying you, though."

"He did not realize Leander was on the way. Neither did I. I got a letter to him, though. He'd let me know how to do that. I was under the impression he had a gambling problem. He said he had enemies—serious, dangerous enemies—and the way he said it... I believed him. Please tell me he wasn't lying to me for his own convenience."

"He was telling you the sober, horrid truth about the dangerous-enemies part." That those enemies could have found him in London, and he'd never breathed a word of the danger, angered me.

"He left in a hurry," Miss... Mrs. Bleeker said. "He went everywhere in a hurry, which is why when he wasn't in a hurry..."

"He made quite an impression. Harry was complicated. If he set aside all of those complications to spend time with you, then he was acting on sincere sentiment, and taking a significant risk to do so." While an *affaire de coeur* would not have been a matter of first impression with Harry—or second or fifth impression—he'd clearly been smitten.

My words seemed to put something right for Miss Dujardin—or Mrs. Bleeker... Miss Bleeker. *Leander's mother.*

She ceased frowning at her tea and took a bite of Leander's unfinished cherry cobbler.

"Harry regularly sent money," she said. "More than enough to live on comfortably. I saved what we didn't need—once a parson's daughter, always a parson's daughter—and when the money stopped, I didn't worry at first. I assumed there had been a problem with the post or something. Martha and I took in mending, we sold a few things, but the money never resumed. Then I learned that Lord Harry Caldicott's name had appeared on the casualty lists, and I..."

"Martha was your sister?"

"Cousin, and by then, her health was delicate. She'd come to live with us, though she still took in work from the theaters."

"Hence Miss Hammerschmidt's scheme to assume maternal honors where Leander was concerned. Martha must have let a few details slip to her old friend over a nip or two of gin."

Far too many details, apparently.

"Martha was dying. I try not to judge her, and she was the one who came up with casting ourselves on Mrs. Danforth's charity. Martha had known her ages ago and had run into her outside some millinery shop. We had nowhere else to turn, and Martha was insistent. She did not want to die in the poorhouse, and I could not blame her. She claimed Leander as her son, took on the destitute-widow role, and I was left with the job of nursemaid."

"A desperate measure indeed. Why not come to us?"

Another pause while a second minuscule bite of cobbler disappeared. She'd learned to ration even so small a pleasure, thanks to my philandering brother.

"Harry said it wasn't safe for his family to know about Leander. He said you'd be watched, and his enemies would use Leander to get at him."

"Harry's worst enemies were in France and Spain." I put this gently. She'd have no way of knowing where the threats originated, because Harry had misled her, probably telling himself that was for her own safety.

"Not all of his enemies were abroad, my lord. Harry was a trusted officer, I know that, but he had enemies in London too. He managed to see Leander on three occasions. I never knew Harry was coming and didn't recognize him when he'd show up at our back door. He was a tinker, a rag-and-bone man, a poor émigré, and then he was a ghost."

"Harry is gone," I said, "and still you did not come to us."

"Are Harry's enemies gone?"

I thought of St. Clair on his lonely hill and of his knowledge that Leander had disappeared. If St. Clair wished the boy harm, he'd had years to achieve that purpose, and St. Clair had a diabolical gift for achieving his purposes.

"The war is over," I said. "Harry engaged in what is vulgarly termed spying. He was captured by the French, and he went to his grave without divulging Leander's existence. Those enemies, if they survived, would gain nothing by harming Leander now, and they would rouse a lot of inconvenient ghosts."

She was silent, finishing her tea and taking the last microscopic bite of cobbler.

I tried to put myself not in her worn and weary boots, but back into my own tattered cloak that miserable, frigid spring when I'd bashed about on the slopes of the Pyrenees. Starving, freezing, more than half mad. I recalled clearly when some shepherd in the lower elevations had sprung up from the bank of a stream, and instead of asking the first human I'd seen in weeks for directions, instead of greeting him, I'd pelted back up the slope and hidden away for another week.

"You were frightened," I said. "Too many bad things happened in succession, and you came to believe that Harry's family was not to be trusted either. Harry didn't trust us. Didn't even tell us of the boy's existence. You convinced yourself that we'd either toss you and Leander to the gutter, or keep the lad and send you away, never to see him again."

She'd been operating on the logic of survival, never assuming a benevolent outcome, never trusting without proof, and not even then. In that state, all luck was bad, nature was vengeful, and society became the handmaiden of injustice.

"It wasn't safe," she said softly. "To trust you, to come here, to present myself without evidence, without marriage lines. I have Leander's baptismal lines, but I did not name Harry on them. He chose the middle name. He gave Leander that horse and named the wretched beast after his first pony, but that's not enough."

Leander's laughter drifted across the garden, so like Harry's, so bright and sweet.

"You did not stitch Dasher into existence?"

"I did not. The handkerchief is my work. I do well with embroidery, and I could afford the thread then. Harry brought the horse along on his last visit. Leander was only a few months old, too young to play with a stuffed toy, but it was something from his father. Harry created a silly little production out of placing Dasher in Leander's cradle and making me promise I'd take as good care of the horse as I did of the boy. Leander slept through the whole nonsense." She blinked several times. "He was such a good baby, and he's a very good boy."

"Thanks to you. He's also a Caldicott, thanks to Harry, and I believe we can prove that, if you are amenable."

She turned luminous eyes upon me, and in their depths, I saw the thing that had kept Leander safe, the thing that even Harry's desertion and death and Mrs. Danforth's cruelty hadn't been able to extinguish.

I saw hope.

"I am amenable."

# CHAPTER SIXTEEN

The stable had worked its magic on uncle and orphan. When they returned from their morning call upon the equine dignitaries, Leander was perched on Arthur's shoulders, hands fisted in His Grace's hair. Arthur was smiling as if...

I had never seen my brother exude such warmth of spirit. He was in quiet transports, delighted, agog with joy. Tonight's letter to Banter would be long and effusive.

"I met Beowulf," Leander bellowed. "He likes me! He's very tall. Uncle Arthur says Bey is a horse of dis.. dis... Uncle, what was the word?"

"Discernment. Beowulf is a horse of great discernment and refined sensibilities. Down you go." He hoisted Leander up off his shoulders, held him aloft until the boy was kicking and giggling in midair and demanding to be put down this instant—or *Miss won't let you have any pudding*—and then set the lad on his feet.

Leander was flushed and beaming, and so, for those with eyes to see, was Uncle Arthur. I slipped Dasher into the chair behind me.

"I believe the stated agenda," Arthur said, "calls for a certain little Cossack to wash his hands." His Grace took up a piece of jam-slathered toast and gave half to Leander. "Uncle Julian might like to take that same Cossack for his first ride later this morning, before the heat grows too fierce."

Between bites of toast, Arthur had just laid down a challenge in the favorite-uncle sweepstakes, while Miss Du—what were we to call her?—Miss was blinking again.

"Simmons," I said to the lurking footman, "please take yonder Cossack and his plunder up to the nursery. See that he washes his hands and changes into boots. Tend to nature's call, if necessary. Master Leander and I will be mounting up in a half hour or so."

Leander looked to his mother. "Miss?"

"One doesn't wear slippers in the saddle, Leander. Your uncles and I will be here when you come back down."

"You promise?"

"I promise I will be here."

"I promise as well," Arthur said, munching his toast.

I put my hand over my heart. "The winds of ill fortune, the cruel hand of fate, and the unceasing larceny of the local toast thief will not move me from this garden until next you grace us with your presence."

"Your Uncle Julian will be here too," Arthur said around his last mouthful of toast. "Be off with you, lad."

Leander—bless his stubborn, wonderful heart—looked to his mother.

"Wash your hands," she said. "Change your shoes. Shoo."

Her placid maternal authority reassured the boy as my silliness had not. He scampered off, leaving the footman to take up the valise and trail after him.

I explained to Arthur what had passed between Leander's mother and me while Beowulf had been holding his morning levée in the stable.

"You will bide with us," Arthur said in his best the-duke-hath-spoken tones. "You and the boy. Don't think to quibble when we've been denied his company for years, madam."

Now I had two brothers in need of a kicking.

"The matter wants some discussion," I said. "First, what shall we call you, ma'am?"

The lady resumed her chair. "Millicent is my given name. I am a Bleeker by birth, though I like the sound of Dujardin better."

Arthur and I took chairs, and now that he'd got the lady's back up, Arthur apparently had nothing to say.

"You are Leander's mother, correct?" I started with first principles, because a general agreement set the stage for more specific treaty terms to follow.

"I am."

"And Lord Harry Caldicott was his father?"

"Yes." She sat very straight. "No other candidates for the post pertain, if that's where you're going with this."

"It isn't. As Leander's mother, given that you and his lordship were not married, you are Leander's legal custodian. You should also know that Harry left a considerable sum more or less in trust for you and the boy." I named the figure Quinton Wentworth had recited half a lifetime ago. "Harry did not mention you or Leander in his will, but his terms with the bank put that money at your disposal."

Arthur shot his cuffs. "You should know something else."

I sent him a look promising him a pudding-less eternity if he intended to turn up all ducal and stupid on me now.

"Harry left us money?" Millicent said. "*That much* money?"

She'd posed the question to me. "The sums you picked up at the Swan were the interest. Don't ask where Harry acquired that fortune, because I don't know and I don't want to know. The money is yours."

Arthur sent me a look that told me to shut my nattering gob, or pudding would be the least of my worries.

"Harry applied for a special license too," Arthur said. "Julian dispatched a clerk to Doctors' Commons, and given that Harry was only in Town for a limited time, the search went quickly. Harry applied for the license and never retrieved it. He meant to marry you, and he meant for Leander to be legitimate."

Well, damn. If ever a brother had redeemed his memory…

Millicent simply stared at Arthur. "A special license. A *marriage* license?"

Arthur looked around as if somebody had forgotten to put jam and toast on the table. "A special license would have meant the ceremony could have been very, very discreet. The next thing to secret. Harry apparently never saw a chance to retrieve the license."

We sat in silence for a few moments, each of us doubtless rearranging our memories of Harry and our questions about his life and honor. He'd sneaked back to London on several occasions, but had not seen a way to fetch that license or go through with a ceremony.

Whose safety had driven his choices? His own? Millicent's and Leander's? *Mine?*

"Will that be enough?" Millicent asked quietly. "Will that application for a special license and the money be enough to prove Harry was Leander's father?"

She was thinking of legalities, and unfortunately, the bank account terms were too general to be of any use, and the application for a special license wouldn't carry any weight either.

"We have something better," I said, sending up a prayer that my faith in Harry wasn't misplaced. "I hope you are up to a bit of veterinary surgery before Leander rejoins us, Millicent." I produced Dasher and subjected him to a few strategic squeezes. His left hind leg satisfied my tactile inquiries.

I took the knife from my boot and carefully split the stitching from fetlock to stifle. Sawdust spilled onto the ground as I extracted a rolled-up document about three inches by four.

"*I, Harold Merton Abershaw Wittingham Caldicott, do on this eighth day of December in the year of our Lord 1812, acknowledge as my son and issue that child whose birth is recorded as September 12, 1811, and who was baptized Leander Merton Bleeker. It is my specific and heartfelt wish that Leander be shown every advantage of his station as my beloved progeny and that his dear mother be accorded the esteem and affection she will always enjoy in my heart. Attested to on the date above by my hand and seal before these witnesses signing below...*"

I passed Harry's paternal decree to Arthur. "I suspect those witnesses work at Wentworth's bank," I said. "The names are legible enough. If we need to find them, we can."

Arthur scanned Harry's parting gift to us all and then passed it to Millicent. "And that is Harry's signature and the Caldicott seal. Harry could not have acknowledged the boy more clearly if he'd made an announcement on the steps of St. George's, Hanover Square."

Millicent studied the words on the paper. "Leander has hated calling me *miss*, but he never got it wrong. He hates it. I'm his mother, and he cannot abide that he hasn't been able to call me *mama*. He hasn't understood, and I haven't been able to explain, and this is all..."

She set aside the proof of Leander's paternity and began crying all over again. Arthur shifted to proffer his handkerchief and pat her shoulder, while I tidied up the injured Dasher and spared a prayer for Harry's soul.

*You old dog. You dear, damnable old dog.* I no longer wanted to kick him. I wanted to hug him, tightly, but I would have to content myself with hugging his son, gently and frequently, when the moments were right.

We'd name his pony Dasher, of course, and on long hacks at Caldicott Hall, I'd explain to the boy that his father had loved him— and the rest of our family—very, very much.

∼

"You'll need Lady Ophelia to manage the talk," Hyperia said. "You should call on her today, if you haven't already."

Hyperia was stitching embroidery onto a chemise or nightgown, adding flowers by the light of the morning sun. I'd called upon her— bedamned to Healy's nonsense—because after a week of Leander

settling in and Arthur trading voluminous dispatches with Banter—
I'd missed her.

And she apparently didn't intend to call on me.

"Godmama has been expected at Waltham House by the hour,
but I suspect she's giving us all time to consider options." Either that,
or Lady Ophelia was trying to keep us in ignorance of her latest
adventures.

Hyperia speared her needle into a corner of the fabric and set her
hoop aside. "What will you tell the world?"

"About Leander?"

"About Leander and Millicent."

"Arthur at first wanted to claim Leander as his own son. He said
that would open more doors, but Millicent wouldn't hear of it. She
claimed any door that would open to a duke's by-blow as opposed to
the by-blow of a ducal heir wasn't a door worth passing through."

"Let's get some air, shall we?" Hyperia rose, and I had no choice
but to comply. I could not read her mood—discontented, not
precisely annoyed—but I entertained the possibility she wasn't glad
to see me. Was she expecting a call from Ormstead, perhaps?

I escorted her into the garden, a peaceful enclosure that
embraced the house on three sides. We'd have privacy back here.
Since our interlude in the park, I'd had the sense she was avoiding
me. If the lady was giving me my congé, she'd do so where we
wouldn't be overheard.

"Have you considered presenting Leander as your son?" Hyperia
asked.

"I have not. I am still considered a traitor by many, Harry was at
pains to acknowledge the boy, and I... I am resigned to not having
children, Hyperia. I will be—I am—the most devoted of uncles. My
sisters' children all have papas, and Arthur rather eclipses me for
consequence, but with Leander, I can take an active, avuncular
hand."

She slipped her arm through mine and guided me down a rose
alley that no longer sported any flowers. The greenery and thorns

wove overhead, providing shade and promising more blooms next year.

"Ironic, isn't it? You seize upon the opportunity to be a father figure to Leander, while Clarissa hides away the fact of her motherhood. Millicent treads a middle path, and the objective in all cases is supposedly keeping the child safe from society's cruelties."

"What of you?" I asked, feeling as a doomed prisoner must feel when deciding on the menu for his last meal. "I imagine you look forward to the prospect of motherhood."

She took a bench halfway down the rose alley and did not invite me to sit beside her. "I like children," she said. "Atticus is a darling, and I'm stitching some monogrammed handkerchiefs for him. You must explain to him that they are not for every day."

"I can do that."

The urge to pace rose in me like a caged animal's compulsion to map the metes and bounds of its captivity. I instead took up a lean against the support opposite her bench. A lone straggler from the late summer bloom was trying to bud out at about my eye level. Cut off from the regiment, struggling to find the sunlight amid all the foliage.

"About children..." Hyperia said. "Do you know why I never pushed the matter of a proposal from you, Jules?"

What was she going on about? "You understood that a man riding off to war isn't in a position to make commitments."

She rose and began fussing with the thorny new growth trying to encroach on the alcove around the bench. "I did understand. I also understood that you... that Arthur and Harry weren't married. That Harry was a soldier, too, and not as naturally cautious as you. Arthur was a confirmed bachelor even five years ago."

"You want children," I said, rather than prolong my torment. "I cannot give you children. Hyperia, if you want to marry Ormstead, just say so. You deserve to be happy, to be a mother. He's a decent fellow. This business with Leander and Millicent has to have brought to mind all that I might never be able to give you. I understand that.

You owe me nothing, though I hope we will always think well of each other."

*Don't leave me.* I felt exactly the desperation Leander must have experienced when he'd watched his sole anchor and refuge in life preparing to steal away. I felt even more strongly, though, a grown man's duty to bow to the demands of honor.

I loved Hyperia West as a man loves a woman, and that meant my happiness could not come at the expense of hers.

She left off weaving the roses. "What has Ormstead to do with anything?"

"He clearly fancies you, and he comes from a good family." I made myself say the next part. "He can doubtless give you children and will acquit himself enthusiastically to that end."

She stalked across the alley, boot heels rapping on the brick walkway. "Why do you use that phrase—'give me children'? Do you know what Harry gave Millicent?"

"A son." A dear, darling, lively, fascinating, brave, stubborn little boy.

"*Ruin,*" Hyperia snapped. "He ruined her, and the fact that for a time he sent money does not change her situation in the slightest. When the money stopped, she had to sell all her worldly goods, stoop to deceptions, cast herself on the mercy of unkind strangers. She was relegated to endless terror for her son, terror she faced only because *Harry had ruined her.* That he wanted to marry her, that he acknowledged the boy in some secret treasure map hidden from even Millicent's view... What if she'd died in childbed, Jules?"

A not-unheard-of risk. "A tragedy would have occurred."

"For her and for the child, assuming Leander survived. Not for Harry. He'd have been sad, perhaps, if he'd ever learned the truth, but he was too busy being a war hero to even tell her he'd acknowledged the boy... I digress."

"Ormstead won't ruin you. He will esteem you above all other women. He will give you his name. He will provide for you."

"My grandmother provided for me. I already have a name."

The obvious finally dawned on me. "You are angry."

She studied the knot of my cravat—a plain mathematical. "I suppose I am, but that's not the point I wanted to make. Why is this so difficult?"

I loved her, and even in the middle of this awkward, sad discussion, admitting that gave me joy. "Just say whatever troubles you, Hyperia. I've entrusted you with more confidences than I've placed in even Atlas. My worst fears, my nightmares, my doubts, my joys, my hopes. They all repose in your keeping." Not all of my hopes—I had some dignity left—but most of them.

She brushed my hair back from my brow, the sweetest caress. "You are right, Jules, I am angry. I have lost two cousins to childbed. My best friend from school took months to recover when her second came along less than a year after the first. *Came along*, as if babies just toddle up the lane by some spontaneous whim of the Almighty. I was not a saint while you were off making war."

"I have never been a saint."

"I am not a virgin," she said, glowering at me. "Not by half. At first, I thought there must be something amiss with me, because the whole business was the most awkward, uninspiring... Don't you laugh at me."

"I am not laughing." I wanted to hug her, to tell her that her sentiments were likely echoed by many a bride on her wedding night. My sisters had doubtless felt some of the same consternation. In my present state, I could even agree that copulation was an odd business on a good day.

"I was unimpressed," Hyperia said. "Even when I came across a fellow who seemed to know what he was about, I still could not believe that such an undertaking was counted as worth a woman's freedom, her personhood, *her life*."

Good God, Hyperia spoke the domestic equivalent of treason. "Just how much adventuring have you done, Hyperia? The matter can take some study."

"I am invisible, Jules. Not a diamond, not an heiress to great wealth, not titled. I am agreeable, and I draw no notice. I armed myself with all the sponges and tisanes and whatnot. I was careful, and I was curious, and then I was..."

"Disappointed?" What was she trying to tell me?

"Bored. Puzzled, then furious. Women are not stupid, so we must be kept in ignorance. We are to remain chaste until marriage, and then it's too late to decide the reward isn't worth the sacrifice. Not *nearly* worth the sacrifice. A few minutes of pawing and panting, even skilled pawing and panting, isn't worth..." She waved a hand.

"Not worth security? Children? Respectability?" I left for another time the whole business of the pawing and panting. Hyperia might well have shared her charms with bumblers, but she spoke as if she'd also explored beyond the reach of the bumblers.

My dear Perry was quite the reconnaissance officer, and for that, I was glad. She knew what she was giving up if she continued to spend time with me. She knew, in some sense, what I mourned.

She was silent for a moment, staring at the middle of my chest. "Why do you keep bringing up children?"

"Because I can't have any? Because I am a duke's son and heir, and my sole redeeming quality at times has supposedly been my ability to sire legitimate sons? Because Arthur, who has never asked a blessed thing of anybody, needs me to fulfill that obligation?"

More confidences given into her keeping.

Of all things, she smiled at me. "You feel like a barren broodmare?"

"Well... yes. I suppose."

She leaned against me. Did not put her arms about me, but gave me her weight. "I am unnatural, Jules. I like children, and I think my heart is as affectionate as anybody's, but a chasm stretches between being affectionate and becoming a mother. Leaping that chasm requires ignoring dangers—to my life, to my health—and giving up privacy, independence, and freedom for the rest of my life."

I wrapped my arms around her and rested my cheek against her temple. "Say the rest of it."

"If I could leap with anybody, it would be with you. But I don't know as I will ever make the attempt, even with you, even for you." She sighed and snuggled closer. "I will miss you sorely, but I cannot allow you to be misled. I am not panting for marriage, much less children. I am not merely content without either, I am happy."

She wasn't waiting for me to recover my powers, in other words. More to the point, she wasn't longing to exercise her maternal instincts.

"We are a crooked pot and a crooked lid, then," I said. "In the eyes of Society, not in my eyes. The dukedom doesn't make Arthur happy. It makes him busy, important, powerful, careful... many things, but not happy. I don't want that title hanging around my neck. Why would I want it burdening my progeny?" I spoke blasphemy to go with Hyperia's treason, but my logic was sound and sincere.

Had Harry died rather than allow the title to imprison him?

Hyperia peered up at me. "Perhaps your progeny would enjoy having the great wealth that goes along with that title? Prestige? Influence? Consequence?"

"Arthur has significant personal wealth, and he'd give up all the rest of it for a chance to live out his days with Banter in peace." Had Arthur admitted that to himself? To Banter?

"So you won't disown me because I have a horror of childbed?"

I stroked her hair. "Your reservations go well beyond childbed. I would not have willingly gone to war, except that England was threatened. You are happy as a civilian, and last I heard, Mayfair is at peace. Why risk your life for anything less than your honor?"

She twined her arms around me. "You understand."

I wasn't sure I did, not entirely, but to be in Hyperia's confidence, to have her trust, meant more to me than reexamining the institutions of primogeniture and coverture.

"I understand that I would miss you to the bottom of my soul if I ever earned your scorn or indifference, Hyperia."

"I am similarly attached to you, Jules, but I owe you honesty. I didn't want you strutting into my parlor someday and announcing that your powers had revived, a special license was in train, and I would have the privilege of making you the happiest of men Tuesday next, pawing and panting to follow."

Would it really be so awful, pawing and panting with me? A moot and wistful question.

"Your Tuesday afternoon is safe." A small, stubborn part of me wanted to add *for the nonce.*

We remained entwined beneath the roses for some time. I considered offering Hyperia the little pink straggler, but instead left the bud to enjoy its turn blooming on the vine. The discussion, about children, pots, lids, and titles, hadn't shifted my circumstances at all, but my heart was more at ease, and I hoped Hyperia's was too.

Hyperia had not disappointed me. She had freed me from expectations I'd never admitted I was carrying. Where we went next was up to us, and as long as we sallied forth with kindness and honesty, I was content.

"Oh, there you are." Lady Ophelia paused at the end of the rose alley. "Canoodling in broad daylight. I vow I am encouraged. Julian, you are remiss. You may tell Arthur I am similarly wroth with him. When will somebody introduce me to my great-godnephew, and what must one do to be offered some potation in the midst of this heat?"

Hyperia slipped from my arms and greeted her caller. Once refreshments had been served, we agreed to accompany Lady Ophelia to Waltham House, there to rectify our oversight.

When we arrived, it was to find the duke pre-occupied by an express he'd received from Banter. While Godmama cooed and fussed over Leander's soldiers—now patrolling the perimeter of a much larger garden—and Hyperia embarked on a cordial discussion with Millicent, Arthur pulled me aside, and passed me a missive written in Banter's hand.

"He's canceling his sitting with Reardon," Arthur said. "Trouble afoot, and I gather the missing hound is the least of it, regardless of the beast's sterling attributes."

I scanned the few lines Banter had penned. "One does get a sense of more being left unsaid. We could all repair to Caldicott Hall."

"I must meet with the solicitors tomorrow, and I think the boy and his mother could use a few days of peace and quiet."

I did not want to go to rubbishing Bloomfield Manor. I wanted to meet Perry for more dawn hacks in Hyde Park, to become the uncle in charge of all outings to Gunter's, to acquaint Leander with Atlas, who wasn't half so stuffy as boring old Beowulf.

Arthur could not go to Bloomfield immediately, and he would sooner sit through all the speeches in Parliament than beg me to investigate in his place.

And yet, I needed a day of rest as well. "Have Banter come fetch me," I said. "If he leaves Bloomfield tomorrow morning, he and I can make the return journey the day after. Perhaps the dog will have turned up by then. I'd rather not tax my eyes by riding the distance on horseback, and Banter has a lovely traveling coach."

I was telling the truth, also presenting Arthur with a plan I knew he'd accept, because it entailed Banter spending a night in Town.

"I'll send a pigeon," he said, jogging up the garden steps. "Once I've finished with the solicitors, I might make a dash for Caldicott Hall myself."

As it turned out, the whole entourage made that dash. Trouble was indeed afoot at Bloomfield, and it took the combined efforts of myself, Godmama, Arthur, Hyperia, and a few noble hounds to bring the situation right, but that, as they say, is a tale for another time!